GREATER LONDON

GREATER LONDON

A NOVEL

JAMES RUSSELL

grand
IOTA

Published by
grand**IOTA**

2 Shoreline, St Margaret's Rd, St Leonards TN37 6FB
&
37 Downsway, North Woodingdean, Brighton BN2 6BD

www.grandiota.co.uk

First edition 2021

Typesetting & book design by Reality Street

A catalogue record for this book is available from the British Library

ISBN: 978-1-874400-82-0

Acknowledgement
I gratefully acknowledge the debt which the Penzance section of the novel
owes to Trevor Burston's brilliant selection of photographs and short
texts: *The Floating World: 36 Views of St Michael's Mount* (published by
The Royal Institution of Cornwall). JR

I knew her but could not be a boy,
for in the billowing air I was fleet and green
riding blackly through the ethereal night
towards men's words which I gracefully understood

and it was given to me
as the soul is given the hands
to hold the ribbon of life!

Frank O'Hara
Poem (for James Schuyler)

For Andy Mayer

Performance 9

The Return 251

Sham Umbrellas 263

PERFORMANCE

1: Steam City

I don't know what to say. I usually do. But now in this present way of being sort-of washed clean I hardly know my own voice; and I need to know that before I can say things. If you think of me, and if I do too, as Archie Rice when he acquires a spot of self-awareness, then we won't go far wrong. Maybe I should, like Olivier playing him, black a gap between my front teeth. Any liquorice bootlaces around? Did I say that? Could be the familiar me? Though I don't feel like doing Archie's soft-shoe shuffle, and I certainly don't want to sing "Why Should I Care?" And *should* I care, given what I've seen and done? Listen, stranger ...

The day had started beautifully. I took my coffee onto the balcony and drank in the Thames turning softly towards where, somewhere between Eel Pie Island and Kingston, the known world ends and the tame things are. The sun silvered the water and I wished I could project myself onto the ait (that's a Thames river island) and drag my fingers in the passing coolness. It was the feeling of a last look at the sea on the last day of a summer holiday; and in a way it was just that. The morning was a hot one. Hot and blue-gold.

It was designed as a big day for me. Francesca Ubley (much more of her later) and I were co-curating an exhibition at the V&A called *Before the Swing*. Fran would be there already, striding about the place in over-the-knee boots, swearing at people from the depth of her leathers. She's pushing seventy; she's pushing it away; and she scares the living day-lights out of folks – including me, if I'm honest. As ever, Fran did all the work, whereas I, by virtue of being a celebrity of sorts, merely add the presence of my very name. But am I being modest? The original idea was Well and Truly All My Own.

I'd long been quietly obsessed with those few years in London after the aftertaste of the war faded and before it became Swinging London, before the carnival of Carnaby Street, and all those varieties of Union Jack nonsense. It was a London in black and white, seeding a style. There were the modernist slight buds long long before parkas and scooters: jazz clubs where a bit of Chicago R&B might be played, where you might see the occasional bell-bottomed trouser. A pair of which was worn by the great Allen Klein in the movie *What a Crazy World*, playing one of Marty Wilde's gang. Lapels narrowed; though please no velvet col-lars (like Liverpool peasants). The era is captured in a novel by Terry Taylor called *Baron's Court, All Change*. It had been touted as a beatnik novel and indeed the beatnik did shade into the mod in this period. Sure, there was a beat ele-ment to the wide trouser-bottom – in *England* only, of course. This is England pure and pure. As English as Turner.

Sure, some of it was borrowed from Paris: the girls in exist-entialist fancy dress, the boys with backcombed crowns and blades of hair before the ears. And it all added up to We're Ready Now So Keep Out. This is the cellar club that you want to visit and hope to join. But you can't come in, so back to your Formica and sandwich paste – to your Double Dia-mond working wonders. Dylan came over towards the end of that time and immediately saw the point of it. As for me,

I could sense it from childhood and craved a pair of bell-bottoms to wear as my visibility cloak. My first pair (mail order) was two sizes too big and smelt of rancid butter; but enough of me, for now.

All I did was make a vague gesture towards all this and Fran went into action; and now that odd corner of the museum that goes in for this kind of thing is vitrined all over with tired Italian schmatta, a harmonica of Cyril Davis' (they say), ancient videos of Alexis Korner being cool about this and that, and warnings about how to tell the difference between a cigarette and a *reefer*. In one vitrine there will be a first edition of George Melly's memoir *Owning Up*, alongside a specially-made chalk-stripe suit based on the cartoon of George on the front cover.

Actually, one minor short trend that interested me was the year or so (1962-3?) in which the front-mods, the "faces", wore Edwardian clothes: chalk-striped waistcoats, and striped shirts with detachable round-cornered plasticky collars that tended to yellow. Top button buttoned but no tie. And this might be worn with bell-bottomed blue jeans and a three-buttoned thin-leather black jacket (*jacket*, not jerkin or blouson), plus Cuban-heel black boots. The idea was to hint at Edwardiana, if that's what it actually was (Georgiana?); though do I recall the occasional pioneer or idiot sporting a bowler too? We represent this as best we can in the exhibition; but Fran and I did have some ding-dongs over it. She won, of course, and so we show an LP cover of those chug-blues merchants, The Downliners Sect, having their dressing-up box spasm. Wrong, wrong and wrong ...

What will the hordes make of it? At least they may catch a glimpse of me on day one with a glass of bubbly chatting or wafting past in one of my better silk scarfs.

There was a problem. My driver Piotr was off sick today. Should it be *is* off sick today or was off sick *that* day. For you it may still be today. Let's just crash on. I could have got Mickey to drive me but he talks too much. And I was damned if I was going to use the car services of externals. So ... something, something democratic in me said: "What's wrong with the Underground?" The District Line lends some dignity. The carriages are wide and unseparated, and this far west they're pretty empty at the start.

Which gave rise to another problem: I am wonderfully recognisable. From the back I look like a twelve-year-old boy in a wig of long immaculate hair, and then I turn round, all leathery twinkle, a groovy gargoyle, a cartoon of myself. *It's him!* So for the tube journey I dug out my plain-glass horn-rimmed pseudo-spectacles, a big baseball cap, and a tracksuit in a kind of depressed taupe. In a holdall I put my jay-blue linen suit, mustard silk crew-neck shirt, white and blue suede brogues, and my longest magenta scarf. A copper gave me a funny look as I left the house, clearly of the view that I'd just robbed the fine gaff of Leo Barber, artist-provocateur, poet, journalist, neuroscientist, scriptwriter. I think that covers it, Mavis.

I remember swallowing two tablets to guard against the pains in my cartilage-free knees, narrowly avoiding popping two Immodiums instead; and then immediately being reminded of something a music-journalist friend of mine who called himself BP Fallon, hip as you like, had said in the mid-'70s. He'd fallen into one hell of a depression and decided to end it all. But he didn't, because instead of gorging on sleeping pills he gorged on laxatives. Reporting this in the *Melody Maker*, he wrote: "It was Squirtsville baby, Steam City."

I tried out the "X-ville baby, Y city" formula in other domains. None of them really worked, especially not the Brexit one. It was what my brother Paul would call "domain-specific" – bog specific, to be specific.

This set a grin upon my face that carried me down the hill to the station. And as I grinned, people smiled back, smiled at this four-eyed short-arse with the magnificent head of fair hair that the cap failed to hide. And as they smiled, my grin smoothed itself into a smile till I felt like Timothy Leary or Al Green sashaying along a busy shopping street glad-handing and joshing in a funny-loving way. I was on a high and no mistake. I remember thinking that if my career (as a bit of this and a bit of that) had any merit in the broader course, it was as one who replaced the barbiturates with the laxatives, replaced dark danger with fatally-embarrassing-funny. It wasn't that at all, of course; but I was drifting away from shore just then.

Down the steps to the waiting train, where I sat behind a copy of the *Daily Express*; for Leo Barber – strictly *Doctor* Leo Barber (those honorary doctorates, doan chew know) – would never read the *Daily Express*.

It would be good to see Fran again, whilst bearing in mind that in seeing Fran these days, indeed in this century, you could be seeing somebody who looked a little like her but without the character. You would be seeing the central tendency of people of that scarily sexy, severely bobbed, gash-mouthed, ice-eyed type. Simply put – why put simple? – she'd had "work done", so the magnificent Frannitude had been drained away leaving an ageless model of her made by a dedicated but talentless student ... Yes I am over-egging it, but I miss the old Fran. I mean the properly old Fran-face would bring back the Fran of old.

It was ages, probably years, since I'd been on the tube and so a fair while since I'd clocked standard Londoners up close. Apart from some prim workers, most of them looked as if they'd been dumped there, loaded for the journey like sacks. Of course, faces were stuck in mobiles. And why not: you give them toys so why be surprised they play with them. It was their slumping that got me. I remember thinking of Fran, against this. She might – not really – march along the carriage with a swagger stick, banging it against the uprights, shouting at them to sit up straight, and to pull their faces away and pay *attention*. I imagined her now-broad beam disappearing down the carriage. Yes – this was my final Fran-thought before The Event – she's a bit of a circus horse now.

We got underway. I'll spare you description, except to say that this time the river was golden with sun as we crossed it. I felt full of joy and full of the joy of ending up like this. I mean, in glorious summer London with something like serenity at a winding-down time of life. The joy was swelling as we rattled on.

Across from me, two guys were performing what looked like man-spreading as an Olympic sport. Silly with this weird joy, I sang inwardly, thinking of the Manfred Mann number ... *Uh-huh, it was the Man-Spreads*. I smiled to myself. Must have. But then, ah then ... as I looked up through my stage-glasses I felt, then saw, somebody smiling back at me. I saw the red rosebud lips of a perfectly beautiful girl. Woman, I mean. She was looking straight at me too, and of course I looked straight back. You could not say, though, that our eyes met. They could not meet across the wide distance of ourselves. I even thought she might be blind. She could, in fact, have been anything – apart from not a perfect woman. But, my God, so strange in dress. Of course, on the tube you see all sorts of fancies, from S&Ms to ironically English roses, because there is no good-style now, it's just a matter of look-at-me. This was different. Her hair was late '40s/early '50s, but not the pompadour mullet or Victory Roll. It was the newly-minted perm that came after that, an elegant first thought that made today's off-the-peg perms look like Gary Glitter's wig. She wore a kind of business suit in navy blue and, yes, with New Look-ish shoulders, and beneath this a white frilly blouse. Court shoes rounded off (I'd bet good money on it) stockinged not tighted legs. She was, give or take, Princess Margaret in her beautiful prime. I felt weak from the sight of her, neither *ready*, nor *steady*, nor wanting to *go* anywhere else.

No, it was not a question of *Baron's Court, All Change*, as the two of us seemed to be trying and failing to lock eyes. Now I don't keep abreast of all the workings of Transport for London, and don't even know what exactly Crossrail is, but I was as sure as shootin' that there is no such station as "East Kensington" after West Kensington, but there it was, and oh ... no, I don't swear ... with a meaningful glance at me, she got up to leave. I was steady enough to know at that point that I had about an hour in hand. We might grab a coffee. I might at least get her number. But all that seemed fanciful: beyond her gorgeousness and obvious interest in me there was the mystery.

You could hardly say the mystery cleared when we – the only alighters – stepped out of the train. This was getting to be too much, because the station, in ways I don't have the patience to describe, fitted around her and not around me. Let's just say that there was an old guy with one chipped Woodbine-like fag behind his ear sweeping the platform with a sensible stiff brush and whistling little arpeggios. He had a short-back-and-sides, but not one of those present-day triumph-of-the-will ones: a standard issue cut, and a low oily quiff above a ratty, blotchy face. I am trying not to sound like George Orwell here.

Anyway, I didn't have time to contemplate the cream-and-chocolate walls, past which other healthier ratty-types scurried, because she was clip-clopping away and up the stairs. A second "anyway" … all this fell away at the hard fact that her stockings were *seamed*. This was the hard fact around which the 1940s stage-set paled – you could see it coming – *into* – I won't disappoint you – *insignificance*. But of course I had to get by on some kind of idea of what was going on. This must be an artist's mock up, and she was my lure. Of course, I, Leo Barber, would be a big fish to catch in this net; and I will leave that statement hanging for now.

Then at the top of the steps and through the station hall and out into the smoking honking street, I knew that whatever the intention was behind all this it was not an aesthetic one. And I stubbornly believed there was an intention lurking somewhere. Yes, this was somewhere I was ending up, and there was no point in thinking about it. Lust dispatched, I simply followed her as she turned left, extracting a packet of Craven A from her handbag. Here I was walking along a London street that would not feel out of place in *Brief Encounter*.

She was a busy sort of bee who managed to keep up a quick pace whilst tapping a cigarette on the pack and, yes, sometimes casting back a glance at me. I saw her disappear into what can only be called an ice-cream *parlour*. Cold from the ices and steam from a "classic" coffee machine, plus the heavenly aroma of sweet cakes and strong coffee. Hellish though, that she seemed to have vanished inside it.

2: But Are You *Mad* on Them?

I was almost reluctant to sit down, in case it had all been conjured up by my brain, so I would end up as an unlovely bundle and a butt for passing hipsters. No, the Rexene-covered benches were solid enough. So was the mirror I glanced at as I sat down, a mirror that gave *no reflection*. At the time I thought this was proof that I was being filmed, and almost relaxed. Almost. This was almost-land.

Across from me sat a mother and son. The mother's style was a three-levels-lower version of my "Princess Margaret's". She was spick and span, but the kind of woman who starts her day emptying all the pos in the house before deciding how much to cut off for the breakfast fried bread. The boy? It was a bit tricky to see him straight, as if I could only catch him out of the corner of my eye. In a sort of lucid fever, he reminded me of the brilliant RSC production of *Nicholas Nickleby* I saw in New York in the early '80s – this shiny-cheeked son of Wackford Squeers. Doughnuts rather than pies, though, must have shined him up. He polished off two jam dough-nuts and seemed to be angling for his mother's as well. Then I saw she'd stubbed her cigarette out in it, half-finished. Both had milky coffees in what looked like tall lager glasses, like lattes from the future.

The boy lifted his coffee unsteadily and Mum said:
— Leo, be careful. That's your best pullover.

OK, I won't muck about. I looked harder at the woman, who was – yes, my mother; and this charming, harmless glutton accompanying her was the young me. In fact, I will call him and all the progressive stages of him "The Me".

The Me said:
— D'you like ring doughnuts too, Mum?
— I certainly do.
— I do. How much do you like them, anyway?
— A lot. I like them a lot.
— But are you *mad* on them?

Silence. Then:
— Can we get the 22 bus home, Mum?
— Not if the 65 comes first. Got to get home to make the tea.
— But if we get the 22 *or* the 65, can we sit upstairs at the front, Mu-u-um?
— We'll have to see if anybody else is sitting there.
— Could we ask them to move?
— Don't be silly.
— Uncle Harold would ask them to move.
— Give it a rest … Please, Leo.

My mother was smiling. The Me wasn't exactly smiling, but his mouth was slightly agape as he seemed to be thinking of all the ways to make something that was perfect more perfect still.

A genre painting it was. Not: *When Did You Last See Your Father?* Instead: *But Are You* Mad *on Them?* Mother and son in soft light, and in the background not rows of severe men but behind the counter, beside the coffee machine, Sam Costa who often played coffee-bar factotums in English films. (Yes, yes: Costa Coffee. Well spotted.) Varnished wood, dark green leatherette, pale green frosted glass panels, and chrome tubing here and there.

The obvious question is: Do I remember these treats? This one could hardly have been a one-off. Obvious answer: Of course I do. We usually went there – a place called Verecchia's (pronounced by most of us Vereesha's) – often after a bit of light shopping; but always after small trials for me like the dentist or the doctor. That it was a two-doughnutter suggested this one was the latter.

We also went there after cinema trips, which were frequent. At these I was the uncomprehending companion, sitting through, while trying to manage the tip-up seats. Anything starring Clark Gable, and later Dirk Bogarde. I have to say there were islands of joy in these for me. In particular there was *Mogambo,* filmed in Africa with Gable and Ava Gardner, which had a scene where a white man was strapped to a sort of giant dartboard while natives amused themselves by throwing spears that got closer and closer to his body – a variety act to the throbbing of drums. More important, this film introduced me to the adult mode of kissing – Gable on Gardner (not making old Frank very happy, I later learned) – in which the two heads engage, to use a fancy term beloved of my brother Paul, *orthogonally*: crossing, rather than lined up as for kissing a child. This I would practise with my maiden aunt Marie (then pretty), jumping into bed with her in the mornings when she stayed over. I won't say this was encouraged, but the cocking of my head on one side to kiss relatives raised laughs in a very satisfying way.

Sorry for all this yacking on. It will happen from time to time. Though I am discursive, I would not say I'm verbose. What is coming up now though is not yacking on.

All at once, there was somebody sitting across from me, as if he'd quietly crept up: a middle-aged man with a grave but twinkly-eyed air about him. Yes, I know, my default is to go for vision, for externals; but here we go again ... Imagine a younger version of General Sir Mike Jackson but with a Ted Hughesian thatch of thick black hair falling in a lick, rather than Jackson's shiny dome. Thank goodness he did not have old Jackson's stage gravitas, but he did have his deep mahogany voice. He wore a good-quality ginger tweed sports jacket with fine green and magenta hatching – ageless – and a blue shirt of the kind policemen used to wear, all spoiled by some sort of regimental tie and awful grey trousers with a first-day-at-secondary-school flavour.

He spoke:
– Mr Barber, it will be.
He offered me his big hand.

I was going to smilingly correct him with, "Well actually it's Doctor Barber", when he added:
– My name is Dr John Fansion. I suppose I could fill you in properly about this rather strange process, but I would only end up talking a lot of guff that's likely to confuse and maybe even bore you. Let's just say that we'll be present, the two of us, at some episodes in your past life, and indeed at one or two that were only adjuncts to it. But let's not, as they say, get "hung up" on the rationale, and certainly not take an *interrogating* stance towards what you might call The Powers that Be. [*here he produced a grin that was not at all heartening and which didn't suit him*]

He then reaching into his breast pocket and brought out what looked like a spectacles case.
– This is my "box of tricks".

You know, I really wish people would *not* use expressions like this. "Box of tricks", "book of words" ... then the long descent to "belt-and-braces operation" and "ready for the off".

Anyway, he opened it, revealing a green featureless screen.
— I scribble on this and then we move on to a new scene or episode within the range of a particular Underground station, broadly construed.
— So, do we stay around here? [*I managed*]
— Oh dear, no. We take trains to different stations when needs be, bearing in mind that this is what one may call [*that grin again, though more generous this time*] *Greater* London.

As The Me and my Mum got up to leave, The Me said:
— Mu-u-um, can I have an ice-cream, Mum? Only a small cone will do this time.
— You've just had two jam doughnuts. [*laughing*]
— But one of them didn't have enough jam in. You said so yourself.

Fansion then took out the object that I refuse to call a box of tricks and will call a "modem" – while not really knowing what a modem is or was – and squiggled on it lightly.

Don't even try to imagine what it's like to feel as if you've been swung round like a cat by your small intestines for a second or so; but that's what it was like. Now he and I were sitting at a dining table covered with a heavy chenille cloth – two unexpected guests. Yes, it was our dining table and we were in our over-furnished, under-lit and generally plush dining room. It felt like early afternoon because the aroma of boiled vegetables hung around. It would be about four hours before the chenille cloth would be replaced by a starched, white one.

We heard the sounds *eeeeeyong, eeeereeech, eeyong, chhh-hsh!* coming from the floor, and I knew without needing to look down that The Me was racing his cars and crashing them on the carpet; Dinky toys having races in which a black cab or a Sherman tank could win against the kind of racer that Stirling Moss – is the pernickety old lizard still going? – used to drive.

Mother's voice from the kitchen:
— What are you doing, Leo? Being good, I hope.
— Just sorting out my cars. Can we play Snap in a bit?
— Not for a while. I'm putting washing in the boiler.

The Me then sprang into action, addressing himself to the long, caramel-coloured sideboard's row of drawers. His placid self had been replaced by one desperately rifling at the backs of the drawers in a race against time. First he drew out a string of plastic orange beads of the kind Woolworths sold then. You could make strings as long as you liked because every bead had a socket and a little ball on a spar for inserting. It was quite satisfying to pop them in and out; and they were horrible. These he chucked on the chenille cloth right by Fansion's big, resting fingers.

Then back to the drawers, recovering a watch missing most of its workings that my uncle had managed to acquire in – surely not *in* – a Japanese prisoner-of-war camp; a brooch of a cat missing its attaching pin; three chopsticks; four brass buttons; a nearly-spent biro; a wall thermometer on a rough wooden base that mother had made at school; three wine gums extracted from a tube in his pocket; an empty cotton reel that The Me had once drawn on in a half-hearted attempt to make a puppet. He hid them all under the table.

— Mu-u-um!
— Yes?
— You gotta bit of paper and a bitta string? I need to do a bitta wrapping?
— Be in in a sec.

While he was waiting, The Me tucked the cars under a Milk Tray box after tearing a hole in the side of it. Do I need all this detail? For you, no. For me, yes.

After mother had handed down a length of sisal and some used parcel paper from a high shelf and left, The Me wrapped up the items in a refugee-style bundle and strangled it with a knot or two. He then hid the parcel under a cushion on the sofa.

Mu-u-um! Can you come and see the garage I made for the cars?

Mum came in with a weary expression and two wet arms and sat down in a fireside chair as The Me whipped away the cushion saying:
— This is a present for you. You gotta open it now.
— Can I do it later, Leo? I'm trying to find the boiler stick. Just hope you've not been using it for a sword again.
— No. Open it now. Come o-o-o-on.

She managed mechanical surprise and joy as each thing was revealed – "Ooo, a handy pen" – till it was all done.
— Guess where I got them!
— Can't guess.

— In those drawers.

— Really!

— You *had* forgotten we had them, didn't you?

— Completely forgotten. What a lovely surprise. But look, are you sure you've not been doing boiler-stick swords?

There was a silence that showed The Me was not at all happy with this reaction. Unconvinced, he peevishly said:

— OK, next time I'll get the things from the shops ... with Auntie Ethel's money.

— Lovely. [*wanting to get back to the kitchen*] You'll kill me with kindness.

The Me's face crumpled with bitter tears.

— NO. NO I WON'T. NO!

— Come here, sweetheart.

3: Don't Have Any More Henry Moore

Just after that it was cat-gut swinging time, onto a new scene and the fast thought, "You've made your point, Doc." I knew what was coming and I was not at all sure I wanted it to come.

Now it was teatime, with Dad there too. We sat on the sofa watching the threesome – "Daddy, Mammy and Leo", as Mum used to call us. Yes, "tea". At that time and in our class (lower-middle), lunch was the square meal, for which Dad came home from work, with the evening meal being high – why "high"? A fry-up. Supper would be a late snack, if it happened. (There will be a test in social history tomorrow. Bring sharpened pencils.)

My Dad? He was OK. No real complaints there. Many years later I heard a Zappa number with the lyrics

> Early in the morning
> Daddy Dinky went to work

He was indeed dinky – dapper, immaculate in dress, elfin almost. If the elves had policemen or football referees, he would be one of them. As a person there really is little to say. "When I think about Adolf" – I read about an early acquaintance of Hitler saying – "*nothing comes to mind.*" It's a bit like that.

He kept his socks up with suspenders and he kept his cuffs back from dangerous gravies and undried inks with silver-coated expanding hoops. He favoured detachable collars of white over richly coloured shirts (though who could be less like Normal St John Steve-Arse, if you remember him). Need I even add the three-piece pin-stripery and the razor creases to his trousers?

As for mother, *too much* comes to mind, so let's imitate myself and do appearance first. She was big. Not over-weight, but big in the frame, statuesque. In fact the statues of which she was "esque" were those of Henry Moore. You might photograph her on the sofa in a dressing gown, get it run up as a maquette, and the Moore job would be more or less done. And she had the stillness which goes with that, and the patience – the enduring gaze, too.

Let me put it this way. I liked playing out in the street with the other kids; loved playing cricket ("French" – or when you chalk a wicket on a wall and play with a tennis ball); liked that flattened-cigarette-packet game where you flick them against a wall and win by covering others kids' cards with your own; loved playing cowboys and indians; never tired of hiking along a shallow stream fishing for tiddlers with a net; but most of all I liked going shopping with my mother or playing Snap or listening to the radio with her. Why? It didn't feel like this at the time, but I suppose ... Oh, I don't suppose anything. At its simplest I got what I wanted, which was her attention. Other kids were rats in a sack. I hated football, by the way – the rattiest game of all.

This was not a typical teatime, being so quiet. "Quiet, yup, too quiet, Ringo." Usually, Dad would be telling Mum about his day, always a day of verbal swordfights in which he was supposed to have delivered the *coup de grâce*. "Anyway, I said to him, I said, then it's up to you to get on the blower to head office. I'm not your blinking nursemaid. And these dockets are not, I repeat not, my responsibility. If some twerp has stapled through the necessaries then well and good or all not well and bad [*pause for appreciation*], but I am otherwise engaged on matters fiscal, thank you very much. You what? I really don't think sarcasm becomes you. You can't ruddy well do it." That's the idea.

But today – the day Fansion and I observed – the two of them asked each other questions and gave answers that looked rehearsed. Or they would question The Me in a phony-matey way, especially Dad: "Did you go up the park today?" "French cricket? Go-o-o-o-d. How'd you get on?" It all ran past The Me like baked bean juice through fork prongs. In fact, for a change, no beans were in evidence. Indeed – and this was the real clue – while they were eating something else they gave The Me his favourite tea, or rather both his favourite teas. His two favourites were sausages, chips and tinned tomatoes, and sausages, chips and fried onions. The Me had been given a plate of sausages, chips, tinned tomatoes *and* fried onions (which I recall annoying me, as tinned tomatoes and fried onions don't go together). Then they told him he would be having his "favourite afters", which was dark choc-ice and sliced banana. Not being stupid, The Me braced himself visibly and tucked seriously in.

We watched this tucking in from the sofa. It involved The Me cutting a trench in each sausage, filling it with tomatoes, then with great attention to detail laying a trail of HP sauce along the tomatoes, pointedly ignoring the onions. As I watched The Me's intense concentration, showing in the way his tongue poked out sideways, I felt sorry for him. Who wouldn't?

Mum speaks:
— Leo?
No answer.
— We've got a bit of news for you. We hope you'll think it's good news. Well it *is* good news ...
— It makes the world go round ... [*Dad speaks, producing a smirk no one could like*]
No answer, so Mum speaks again:
— Well, you're going to be having a little brother or sister. Mummy went to the doctor today and it's definite.
— What's it got to do with the doctor? You ill or summat? [*The Me's reply, very quick and hard*]
— The new baby will grow inside Mummy's tummy so, well, that's a job for the doctors and nurses, isn't it?

All this time The Me was face feeding. Dad speaks:
— Think how nice it will be to have a new playmate.

The Me turned to Dad with deliberation and spat out the contents of his mouth. An impressive lot. A colourful lot. Tomato skins on white collar, brown and phlegmy sauce on the off-pink shirt front, chips on the waistcoat (rain in my heart and you on my mind ... what is that song, if it is a song? Yes, "Tears on My Pillow"). Best of all, a medley of it all (as waiters say: "Shall I bring a medley of green vegetables?") plus a solid sausage lump, right in his shocked-weasel face.

In present or Fansion time I enjoyed this spectacle, putting my memory of the original kerfuffle on the back burner. I mean, I enjoyed it in a sick but arty way. Think of what successful entrepreneur Damian Hirst could make of something like this. In a glass case, two manikins, the male in morning coat and sponge-bag trousers, white tie and shirt, the female in shining Versace, both sprayed with masticated food, faeces, and menstrual blood. The floor of the glass box would be gently writhing with maggoty loins of cod, "tiled" with them. The title ... ooh, let's say: *Do you like pina colada, getting caught in the rain?* I guess the successful entrepreneur would mumble something about its anti-capitalist message or, if that didn't seem to play, its Dadaist "sensibility". People would ruin their days off to struggle against the wind over the Millennium Bridge to that horrible Kultur-mountain to see "the installation", looking forward to telling all about it at coffee the next day.

— Don't WANT a playmate ... Bloody buggers!!!

Mother cried, Dad looked like he would like to, and Fansion whipped out his modem.

This time the cat-gut weirdness was less intense. I assume because we had less distance to travel – in time, that is.

In the next scene – in fact, old Fansion did rather over-egg it by making us sit through scene after scene on this here theme — we had moved to the kitchen, where I was pretending to measure things with a tape measure I'd found somewhere, and Mum and Dad were doing the washing up.

— Guess what? I learned a poem at school today.
— Let's hear it then, darling. [*Mum*]
— *Put a penny in the slot*
  See what Marilyn Monroe's got
— Leo! [*Dad*]

— Two fat tits and a hairy cock
That's what Marilyn Monroe's got

Dad forced on a calm, telling me that I would have no sweets and no puddings for two weeks and that all my toys would be confiscated for two weeks.
— What am I going to do then?
— Hold your tongue and be grateful I don't wash your mouth out with soapy water.

In fact I didn't know what tits were, but I had a pretty good idea they were "dirty", so it was a fair cop. Very fair, in fact, as I had a fair idea what a cock was. My mother and certain aunts would refer to my *cockalorum*, which must be the genitive plural of *cockus* (I paid attention in Latin): "of the cocks". My mental script for *Carry on Declining* forces me to say "genital plural", sorry.

But, fair cop or not, I was bent on a revenge event, presented to me by Fansion in what we sometimes called "the lounge" or "front room" – never the sitting room. When we eventually got a telly it was the television room. (Sorry, being boring ...)

We were again on the sofa and Daddy Dinky was indeed off to work. A word about Daddy Dinky's hair ... He had a good head of dark hair but it was only recognisable *as* hair after he'd been swimming in the sea. Otherwise it imitated the action of a patent-leather skullcap. To get this effect, he applied not working-class unguents like Brylcreem (I hear they're now branching into beard oil, by the way), but stuff from a tin labelled brilliantine, sometimes adding a bottled delicacy called hair oil. But mostly he brushed it, brushed and brushed with a battalion of brushes ranged along the mantelpiece – *this* mantelpiece, the one in the front room. For some reason or other he splayed his legs for this performance, despite the fact, or because of the fact, that it lowered him so much that only the patent-leather skullcap was visible.

EEEEyyyyyong, kirrrrssh, eeeeeyyyyyong, etc etc. The Me was racing his cars at the feet of the Dadda.
— Why not play in the dining room, Leo?
— I need a special carpet for this race, Dad.

It was difficult for Fansion to see, but easy for me to know, that as well as little cars, The Me had in his hand Mum's nail scissors. The race seemed to be circling one of the Dadda's shoes.
— Careful, son … OW!!!

He looked down to see that The Me had managed neatly to cut open, from the back, the trouser leg nearly to the knee. The scissor point had nicked his skin. This time Dad was not shocked: he was an army-scrapper again. It impressed me to see it now – the lightning pivot and the all-body-behind-the-blow WHACK – and it hurt like hell, as I recall. The Me ended up halfway across the room …

One thing stopped this from being a scene from *The Simpsons*: my right hand was pumping blood into the pink and navy-blue Axminster, because the scissors had gone a good way through my palm, so that now, in addition to my love, heart, life, and brain lines, I have a short trench of a line that I can't decide whether to call the hairline or the Leonine-line. Both are too *Carry On*. Of course, my guttural screams brought mother in, and thus began a couple of weeks of Indian summer. I, this creature with suspected

brain damage and a swelling paw, had her exclusive attention and was breakfasted on milky cocoa plus either a
Punch Bar (fudge) or Golden Syrup and thick butter on the
heel of the bread. My father's guilty goodwill soured my
bliss at mother hauling her huge self upstairs to tend to me.

After a mini gut-yank, we witnessed a breakfast scene
between Mum and Dad. Mum:
— You've got to make allowances, Frank. He's been pushed
off his little throne into a sort of ... desert.
— Don't talk wet, Ade.
— He's a very angry little boy.
— Well I was a very angry li—, angry man.
The Me from above:
— Mu-u-um! Did you remember to get another can of
Golden Syrup? Mu-u-um?

4: I Can Cure Your Fluency

My God, that was one gut-yank of the swinging cat, so we must have travelled some way in time. Not in space, though, as Fansion and I were together again on the sitting room sofa. The room had changed, being both neater and more disarranged. For one thing, there was an abandoned vacuum cleaner and a wooden heirloom of a bassinet in the middle of the floor, meaning that Dad had been trying his hand at domestic science and proactive childcare. We were waiting for them, as if the modem had had a precision-lapse. But it seemed the pause was for Fansion to sound me out. Or was it just that I, while getting fed up, was looking fed up.

— Is all well, Mr Barber? We don't like this to be too stressful an experience.
— It's not stress. It's more that I have never seen my life as episodes of *Eastenders* ...
— I'm sorry. East ...?
— I mean that these bits of sentimental violence, these psychodramas, are corny. The point of them is signalled too well.
— Let me put it this way: our procedure is punctate indeed, but it is up to you to connect the dots.
— By straight lines? What drawing do you get when the dots are linked? The crazying of a mixed-up kid? An Easter bunny? The substance is in the lines.
— Please be patient.

— I'll try, but surely you know that human life is not a series of red alerts. There's more truth in the little changes of gear. Like what started *not to happen* when I came in from school after the baby announcement ...
— Just wait.

Out comes the modem, and he applies scribbles more subtle and says:
— This is BEFORE ...

We sit in an empty dining room and, as the front door is flung open, we hear:
— Mu-u-um. Guess what a boy said to me today? He said my mouth watered. It doesn't water, does it, Mum? And I saw Miss Harding's brassiere safto [*this afternoon*] when she read to us.

All this was said before The Me had even seen Mother.

I then said to Fansion:
— OK, that's enough. No need to do the "after". I don't want to see myself slinking in in silence like the coalman, then opening the *Radio Times* to look at the pictures in silence.
— Fair enough. Let's get back to where we were, shall we?

Then we were again – after a modem squiggle – regarding the abandoned vacuum cleaner and the bassinet, hearing a key in the lock. In they came, first the cat, then Mum with her bundle.
— Frank! Push that bloody cat out of the road, will you. We'll have to think of getting rid of her. And what the hell is a Hoover doing in the middle of the room?
— Steady on, Ade.
The Me followed Dad into the room wearing a red blazer

with gold buttons, pressed short trousers, white shirt with clip-on royal-blue bow tie. Oh, and dark green shin-covering socks. If you'd given me a baton, I could have been one of Liberace's dancers. But as you can well imagine, I lacked these dancers' maniacal grins.

I stood up and sidled next to The Me as he peered into the bassinet. As before, I could not look straight at The Me, only out of the corner of my eye. What I could see clearly, and The Me could only just see, was the baby – my brother, Paul. In fact it was the maquette of Mum I mentioned earlier. Having seen a few babbas in my time, I could see this was a *big* baby, probably weighing about as much as a family turkey. The face was mother's, with the addition of a "strong" chin, a *menton volontaire* as I would later mock it.

As Mum and Dad were about to leave the room, The Me spoke:
— Can I stay with Pauly for a bit?
— Paul. His name is Paul. [*Dad*]
— Of course you can, darling. Isn't that nice, Frank? He wants to get to know his little brother.

The Me waited, knowing that the cat would soon slink back into the best room, dying to get its claws into some fresh moquette. The Me of course would prefer these claws to be sunk in the fresh *maquette* ... there goes my *Carry On* instinct again.
— Come on Tibs ... puss [*makes a squeaking noise like a sucked-in raspberry*]

The Me tiptoed up to the cat, a very large Persian job, and did his best to lift it, succeeding only in grabbing it by the shoulders as the rest of her dragged along.

— Tibs ... I'll just swing your bum round and you can sit on its head. Hup!

Dad came in, having been driven back by instinct.
— I was just showing Tibs to Pauly. Look at her, Pauly. Isn't she a good cat, then?

Now if I'd reported "*showin'* Tibs to Pauly", you might have thought all this was a William Brown clip. Nope. *William the Baby-Smotherer* doesn't make it.

It was all getting a bit much for old Frank. He looked like one of these little seaside postcard chaps being dragged out shopping by his all-fat-and-wide wife.
— Leave the cat and come away. NOW!

I watched as Fansion applied himself to his modem with more focus and for longer than usual; so I braced myself for a mammoth gut-wrench, which came. Actually, I see little point in describing what happened inside me as we lurched from scene to scene, so you can take them as read ... usually ... sometimes. Let's see ...

We were back in the dining room with an older Me at the table, minus the cloth and plus layers of newspaper as he was painting a watercolour. The radio was playing *Children's Favourites* (presenter: Uncle Mac), so it must have been a Saturday morning. Paul was toddling about heavily carrying wooden bricks from one site to another, till he spotted a brick he needed on the table out of his reach.
— W-wanna b-b-bick, Lee. Wannit.
Like a lot of kids of that age he had a stuttery way of speaking, especially when he was excited.
— You wanna brick, do you, Heap? A Bu-Bu-Bu-rick. Shut up.

The radio played "I'm a Pink Tooth Brush" as The Me decided to have a bit of fun. He put his face up against Paul's and sang:

— You're a p-p-p-p-ink Big Heap, you're a b-b-b-lue Big Heap. You're as big as a bloody Hou-Hou-Hou-House.

— N-no [*facial contortion as he forced out the first person singular, eventually putting his hands over his ears*] ... I n-n-not.

Paul cried, Mum came in, and The Me claimed that Paul wanted his paints. Now ... there's plenty more where that came from. I would volunteer to "mind" him so I could go in for just this mode of torture. Fansion made us revisit a trip to the shops: The Me, Mum and Paul, with Paul rocking madly forward, hands over ears in his pushchair, eventually producing "I". The Me, of course, said to Mum, "Poor little Paul. Can we help him, Mummy?"

Yes, yes, The Me is *unlikeable*, now ain't he just. It's incredibly unlikely, according to my extensive lack of research, that I *caused* his stutter. After all, he was born with a big chin, and chin formations like this tend to be found in stutterers. (Yeah, you say, like Mussolini and Trump; and Tommy Trinder.) Oh, can we worry less about cause – for now and for ever?

The lazy option right now is to use the term "fast forward" or "cut to" ... old Chris Logue got away with murder using that in his Portobello Road *Iliad*.

But Fansion is a completist, a thorough plodder, not an imaginative man; though I have to say I developed a soft spot for the guy. He took me through a grim long stretch of The Me's Paul-torturings; and one sticks in the mind. We were watching a kids' programme on TV. I was doing a bit of my famous "minding". Paul was a very rational, big animal, and I was about twelve.

— *Now, we know a song about sheep, don't we children? A song about a black sheep. Can you remember what it is?*
Paul seemed delighted that he could – puffed up, in fact.
The Me turned to Paul – The Me in Elvis hair, a pullover with semiquavers on it, and horrible turned-up jeans – singing:
— *Barber, big heap, have you ...*
The Me grabbed his own throat as if about to choke on a whole potato and not just a glottal stop, flung himself onto the sofa and eventually, through a red face, sang:
— *any wool. Yes sir, yes sir, three ...* Cheeks as if they would crack over the "b". Then he collapsed onto the floor like a dead fly.

You get the idea.

At this point it's tempting to imitate the action of Martin Amis and tee you up, dear listener/reader, with "You may think this is as bad as it can get. No, we're nowhere near the asymptote of bad; there are deeper trenches of cruelty to be waded through, much sharper inversions of peaks to which we must scale down." No, that hardly works as a parody, now does it? Sounds more like me when I'm putting on the agony. Well, actually, you will hear about my re-experiencings of The Me's horridity re the stutter; but you will also soon hear, by way of my drawing of lines between these famous dots – some fleshings out of those lines – that I was certainly not all bad. First, a couple of predictable scenes after Fansion's modem scribbles.

First, Fansion and I are trailing The Me on his way to school. He approaches a group of younger kids, one of whom is Paul, now bigger than The Me. The Me sashays past in a sort of straight-backed, short-striding Mod walk (his version), and as he passes he calls back over his shoulder to Paul:

— Here, Floppy. Mum says you forgot to do your floppies this morning, so do two lots tonight. Ciao!

The little'uns think I'm cool (*avant la lettre*), so they ask what floppies are.

— Oh, it's just Floppy's relaxation exercises. Ciao!

From that point on his "peers" — yes, peers — called him Floppy. This only stopped when he became a pretty devastating prop-forward that gave him the confidence to thump his "peers" when they got uppity.

To explain, or if you like, "flesh out the line" (ever tried that?) ... Mum was exploring ways of treating Paul's stammer, and one of them was an NHS route that involved after-school trips to a Miss Gable in the back room of some crummy civic hall. Her theory was that stuttering can be overcome by relaxation, and that relaxation is efficiently achieved by sitting in a straight-backed chair and saying in a slow, deliberate manner "Flop ... pee, Flop ... pee" for twenty minutes. The poor devil had to do this, and it made not one gnat's kneecaps worth of difference.

The other route Mum explored was private treatment. She found a certain Mr Murray in Highgate to whom mother and son bus-rode every Wednesday after school. *His* theory was that what the poor devil needed was to lengthen the breath after troublesome consonants, so as to soften the consonant or glottal hurdles into smooth gradations. Paul lay on his bed, either before or after or during the season of the floppy, and intoned Baaaaa, Caaaa, Daaaa. (D's were a devil.) And uppermost was to BREATHE THROUGH THE DIIIIIIIIIIAPHRAGM. It made not one gnat's ...

I imaged this Mr Murray as Stephen Murray, an actor who would keep popping up on TV at the time. For some reason or other, Dad had made Murray into a kind of family butt. ("Ooo, good. It's got Stephen Murray in it.") Once there was a trailer for a Saturday play starring Murray in which he was wearing an unconvincing grey wig, causing the family Noel Coward to go round saying "Stephen Murray's in a wig tonight. We shall have to be getting excited." In fact, to give Dad his due, all this was done to lighten the atmosphere, the heavy atmosphere of maternal anxiety, a cold aggressive-despairing kind about Paul's stutter. As for me, I tried to make light of the business in a different way that old Fansion made me relive.

Mother had reported that Murray and Paul had made a major breakthrough. Paul could now say "Eamonn Andrews in Crackerjack". No mean feat, said Mum. So Fansion and I watched as Paul produced "Eaeaeaeaeamonn Aaaaandrews in Craaaackerjack" at tea. The room seemed to breathe a sigh of relief, until I said:
— I went to see a film today. It was Aaaaaaaaaaaaaaaaaaaa-aaaaaaaaaadam Faiaiaiaiaiaiaiaiaiaiaith in [*here I broke into the title song from the film*] "IIIIIIIIIIIIIII've Gotta Horse".

I got up and did a little Adam Faith-style dance as recently seen on *Thank Your Lucky Stars*. Even Paul laughed. Mum, too. (Actually, The Me had made most of this up. It was a Billy Fury film; but I needed glottals for the name and I could do a fine little Adam Faith impersonation.)

But to darken things back, Mum was in the grip of her own theory, the origin of the theory being unknown to science; but I bet good money that Murray, the looming presence in the imagined grey wig or thunderhead, had a hand in it. Looking back, being forced to look back, this here theory was in about as good a shape as the Nazis' World Ice Theory that was supposed to replace Einstein's "Jewish Science". For Mum, what lay at the heart of Paul's problem was ... threadworms. The idea was that these worms – don't most kids have them? – irritated the gut, when they were not actually causing the dreaded "itchy bum", resulting in nervousness, and thence with beautiful simplicity the causal chain led to an inability to name the Irish broadcaster and his teatime TV show for kids.

Every night, Mum could put a trouserless Paul across her knees just before bed "when the worms come out to lay their eggs". Having dug out a worm or two, wearing a hanky on a finger, she would apply cream, I think a kind of poison that the little devils would ingest for their supper. This did not help the ingestion of my own supper (toasted cheese and cocoa, pre-diet). "Happy hunting," Dad would say. Dad and I were like two standard-issue humans watching the initiation ceremony of giants.

Sugar was "worm food" so no sugar for Paul. I recall her saying to us in a conspiratorial way – a well-didn't-I-just-say way – that Murray had asked whether the biscuits Paul used to be given with his cocoa had sugar on them. She claimed she could tell when Paul had been eating sweet things because it gave him dark rings under his eyes ... "You're only feeding the worms." So it was around this time that I began to feel seriously sorry for him. I would slip him the occasional Mars Bar and this was NOT – listen, Fansion, you with your judgemental old gravitas – because I'd started dieting in my early teens. Who *wouldn't* feel sorry for him? To give Fansion his due, this time he picked out a particularly grisly scene at Sunday lunch.

What Paul used to do was to set himself speech challenges. If he succeeded he would be full of joy; and if he failed he would descend into hell. Here was a hell-step, bearing in mind that the hard G was the highest brick wall of all for him.

We are eating roast beef and listening to "Sydney Mincing" being feebly funny on *Ray's a Laugh*.

Paul [*starting fluently but with that glassy look in his eyes that meant disaster would be coming soon*]:
— I noticed yesterday that Magg's chip shop is now a dry cleaners called the ... called the ... called the ... called the [*he seems to be trying to cough up his voice box*] ... of-course-the ... yes-the ...
— The Golden Guinea. I noticed that too, son. Good.
— Let the boy speak, Frank.

We were supposed never to finish his sentences for him, according to Mum. We were supposed to sustain a look of relaxed-benign *curiosity* as he tried to bring his guts up over a word.

Mother's face, as I saw it then – by "then" I mean today, on my little trip – was of bleakest contempt over which she'd managed to spread something like indifference of a weirdly furious kind. I can't paint the picture. I could go on; I could apportion blame, or rather divvy up the blame between me and her for the hell that Paul lived in. Maybe, I say maybe,

I set him on the road to impairment, but she stamped in the destination. She didn't mean to – not quoting Larkin – but she did. She wanted the best for him and mucked it up. An idiot could tell you it was a psychological problem, not one with saying words. Case in point: he simply could not say Murray's name, but would ask me if I could spare a Murray Mint as good as gold (another word he could say when reporting his gold stars at school).

Christ, at that point I just wanted out of there.

5: But *Are* the Kids Alright?

I've no idea if Fansion had sensed this, or whether it was already on the cards, but we did leave at roughly that point; out the front door, along some privetty avenues, to the main road with its walking smokers, Austins of England and Standard Tens. Here was the "East Kensington" Underground again. I wondered idly when the oldness – isn't this like Trump's "bigly"? – of the station would morph into the modernity; but it maintained its period stamp. Only the trains were in the modern world. At the top of the escalator there was a notice:

DOGS MUST BE CARRIED.

— D'you think they'll let us on if we don't have dogs to carry?

That was my little joke to Fansion, perhaps having relearned the habit of lightening the atmosphere; and got no reply, just a hint of a smile. His style suited me.

A tube pulled up and on we stepped to find ourselves back in the world of beer-can-carrying Polish builders, narcissists, and Scruffy Herberts. In the streets I'd just been walking through only the poor were scruffy. Standing next to these modern people I was a million miles away from them and heading west. Out at Hammersmith then on to the Piccadilly Line, again westward ho.

Boringly enough, the Piccadilly Line is just about my least favourite line. The cars are too narrow, the seats are down at seat, and the trains sit too low beside the platform. I do like its blues though.

Past Acton Town, towards Ealing. I used to have a mate at the Ealing Art School ... maybe there would be some scenes there. Nope. Just past Northfields I got that o-o-o-o-old feeling: the catgut-swing-wrench but with a bit of added lung this time. I was braced, and indeed we stopped somewhere called "Boston Fields" (a very clever blend of Northfields and Boston Manor) and all I could think was: what-the-who-the? The train pulled into a kind of hangar, and when we got out there was a station name, lots of featureless brick, a Way Out sign, and no people at all. The Way Out sign made me think of my many attempts to read Kafka: quickly narrowing into cement steps and a dark-blue handrail leading up to a double door. But before we went through it, I heard screaming and a low rumble of talk. Sort of joyous screaming. Manly-hysteria screaming.

We were in a spartan hallway or vestibule with hard benches and lots of scrubbed pine, the old kind, before bare pine became fashionable; and a reception desk with *"Wellcome Stranger!"* misspelt in giant italics. Some kind of unpalatable food had just been boiled. When I looked out of the window onto the lush green, I had an inkling of where we were, and when I looked into the room next to reception's interior, I knew. There was Nick in his lankiness; there was The Me looking like his bored mascot; there was the Youth Hostel manager punctuating sentences with a hyena laugh; and there were the other members of the West London CTC (Cyclist Touring Club). No, we hadn't cycled all the way there; we'd travelled in the goods wagon from Paddington to Bath Spa.

Fansion to me as I looked at him:
— I did say this is *Greater* London, Mr Barber.

Before I get down to some serious context-setting, I must say a word about the Youth Hostel guy. I wonder if it's possible to call somebody a "screamer" without being homophobic? In this case, yes. He was literally a screamer and he was literally gay, as well as being gay. He screamed with laughter and dapped about the place like a joyful sprite.
— Well don't start me on the local pub. [*he started*] The bitter is like the juice of the gnat. [*a laugh that only certain dogs could hear*] My advice is to stick to the bottles. Mackeson ... I go for Mackeson ... I go for it in a big way. Happy to show you the ropes, chaps.

He was as short as me but only had eyes for Nick. "What's the weather like up there?" "Scattered showers," said Nick.

Now you may dislike my reducing elements to clobber, but, as I say, in this case you really could. He was wearing tiny and very tight and very red needle-cord shorts (our CTC colleagues called him Bunny Bum), white socks to the knee, and big hiking boots. His top was a kind of *Sound of Music* halter. Milk stout is the only drink for such a one.

He had a blonde (of course) fringe that put me in mind of Brian Jones, who himself was not unimmune from dress volume. In passing – there will be a lot of in-passing – I find that suit he was wearing in the early scenes of the Godard dog's breakfast *One Plus One* heartbreaking: deep blue with pink stripes that must have been at least half an inch wide and a least three inches apart, and above it a face drug-puffed to doom. (There will be many more Stones flavours to come.)

I guess the whole point of the scene is that Nick and I didn't go to the pub that night (though we used to haunt London boozers at weekends). We wanted to, but Jack Cash, the peddle-pushing bossman, knew we were only sixteen, and as he was what he called "in local parentis" he said we should stay back. This was fine by me as I never did like beer, and to quote Jagger this time (I warned you), "I don't know how people can drink a pint of anything." Also, we were both knackered from what was then called "fit-racing" up and down the Mendips.

Fansion and I sat on a bottom bunk and waited for Nick and The Me to get back from the ablutions bunker.

More background: *Not Only ... But Also* was unmissable TV in those days, and Nick and I would often go into a Pete-and-Dud act in the 6th-form room. Nick was quiet and in the upper bunk.
— Dud? [*Nick speaks as Pete*]
— Yes, Pete ...
— Why are you such a cunt?

Now I hate this word and I apologise for it, but better that word than evasion. I saw a TV play once where some miserable old foulmouth called his slapper daughter a "custard". If you can't see why this is *worse* than cunt, then I ... well, I must say, with John Major, "I don't know why I bother." Back to the dialogue ... Derek and Clive *avant la* whatsit:

— I'm not a cunt, Pete. I may look a bit like one an' that but cunt I am not.

— Weighing one thing against another, Dud, and taking a broad general view, you are a total cunt.

— How'd you reckon that then, Pete?

— You're a cunt to your brother, Dud.

— I ... [*struggling to stay in character*] ... maybe I used to be, but I'm OK to him now, I'd say.

— No. You don't make fun of his speech no more, Dud, granted; but you ignore him when he's around us and don't stick up for him when some cunt takes the piss out of him when he's not around. Certainly cuntish, or cuntine as folks more learned than me would say. Ergo, you are definitely a cunt. The whole idea is that you should look out for your little brother and give him something to look up to – though physically impossible this last disideratit.

— Don't you mean a disidersatat, Pete?

— Shut up, Dud. Look, when I was born I was a right little cunt to our Trev, who was seven years older than me. Pretended he'd been hitting me to get sympathy ... that kind of thing. But he put up with it and we're mates now. He always looked out for me.

— Well ... Paul ...

— Added to which, people *like* Paul even if you don't. He's a nice guy and a very clever chap. Five years younger than me and doing stuff in maths I only got to last year.

Pause as The Me tries to shift terrain.

— OK ... but maybe you're a cunt an' all, Pete. Are you not ever one of them cunts.

— May wee, Dudley. I can *come* the cunt. I can deliver nasty behaviours if needs must and the Devil dives, but I am not a cunt *per se*.

— My name is not Percy, you cunt.

This went on for a bit, then they stopped and talked about fellow CTCers, then fell asleep till woken by a scream. (Fansion had done a sort of fast forward.)

Nick was my best friend. Strictly, he was my *better* friend as I only had two proper friends, the other one being a fellow Mod called Malc. The problems with Malc were that he used to copy me, that he wasn't all that bright, and that he was too big to be the Mod he wanted to be. Now, on to Nick ... I know you're supposed to show and not tell, but I'm too impatient for showing so let me tell you this: Nick was laconic, ironic, and not remotely Teutonic. He had a kind of decency that's rare in adolescent boys and his interests were wide enough to include mine, despite his belonging to the Sciences as much as I was Arts all the way down. Sure, he could be what my Mum would call "a funny ossity", but that was OK. For one thing, he never let out a proper head-back laugh, nor even cracked an innocent wide smile. Rather, he had a range of smirks that could express anything from ecstasy to disgust to "tell me more". Malc fancied himself a poet, writing poems about the other kids, one of which included the lines about Nick:

> The Beatles and the football pitch
> Would make him smirk with joy.

(Good, for Malc.)

After this, it was a quick scribble on the modem and we were walking behind Nick and The Me along a High Street. I knew what was coming and knew too that this was Taunton and that we had just stopped for afternoon tea. (It could have been renamed The Cyclists' Tea-and-Scones Club.) It was just the two of us.

At this time (1960s), the Teddy Boy species was more or less extinct in London, but here in Somerset they existed like Japanese soldiers in the jungle still fighting the last war. (Not sure that tipping my hat to this cliché was really worth it.) Anyway, two of them sat on a bench spitting through their teeth and watching us pass. What must be borne in mind here was that I chose to dress as if I were on the Tour de France. This meant that you could hear me coming from the clack-clack of my cycling shoes, that I was wearing track shorts (showing, to my mother's disgust, what she called the wearer's "shape"... an enhanced shape, in fact), and that I shone out in a tight bright-yellow top advertising Firestone tyres. The bigger of the two Teds had a flat cord cap, striped maroon and cream (very narrow stripes; Teds went in for these), that was set behind a Vince Eager quiff that topped off the enhanced shoulders of his drape. He spoke, as Homer might have put it, with winged words:
— Yer! Why don't thee piss off 'ome to Queer Town.

Now, I'm not brave but I have dangerous (dangerous for me) verbal reflexes.
— I'm not a queer, as you call it, but *you* are certainly a thick yob.

His mate tried to hold him back, but sure enough he was going into action, though in a pretty deliberate way. Deliberate enough for Nick to step in coolly, insert his middle finger behind the knot of the Ted's bootlace tie, twist it stranglingly, trip him over and continue with the strangling circuit on the ground, like a workman unwinding a manhole cover. "You'll fuckin' kill 'im!" his mate advised. Nick could have killed him *sine dubitate*, as we were told to say in Latin.

— Where the hell did you learn to do that, Nick?

— From our Trev.

Thank goodness this was not true, as it would just be too neat. But indeed, when I got home my warming towards Paul warmed further and quicker. In fact, we became allies.

Time to get expositional ...

Why cycling? Because it's Mod. Why is it? Because both are *Romance* – French and Italian certainly, Spanish too (Miguel Induráin, my best example).

Stop! Don't let Bradley Wiggins touch your mind at this point. Wiggins the "Mod" cyclist, with his Steptoe sideburns and his waisted, vented, *double-breasted* jacket as worn by your average clown. And that *stance* – one hand clutching a wide lapel, head-back proud stare into the middle distance. All targets missed, old son; neither holy nor Roman nor an empire.

But you want more ... Because both have "beautiful" (a word tainted, post-Trump?) clean lines. Somebody defined Mod as "clean living in difficult circumstances". Well this may do for working-class Mods; but I was never working class. For me, it was a matter of drawing clean lines whatever the circumstances. Which reminds me: I also shaved my legs, and this may have helped to set off the Taunton Ted. (I couldn't see my legs so well from where Fansion and I were standing.) Racing cyclists say they shave their legs to cut down wind resistance. *Laugh!* They do it for *aesthetics*.

The word "racing" could hardly be applied to me. I did join

The Fulham Flyers (a racing club) but was humiliated when it came to road racing. Too wedded to my Disque Bleu, and too busy working to train. Every spare hour when I should have been doing my French and English A-levels, I was working to pay for clothes. It was not cheap to have suits made, even if it was only in Lambs Conduit Street. These shirts from Jermyn Street that look like they have been made from pyjama material don't buy themselves, you know. I would not wear Hush Puppies; only shoes from the best places that looked like them. I worked in a photography processors in Neasden, a BRS (British Road Services) bay in Brentford, in a Fine Fare supermarket, in a bread factory burning my hands on new loaves.

Because I was not a working-class Mod, I was not a *group* Mod. I knew plenty of them via Malc, but they were the kind of kids who, if they got their girlfriend pregnant, would boot her in the stomach. Even Teds didn't do that. In fact, the correct term for me was *stylist*. Indeed, one with his own look. I was not unfriendly to the polo shirt, even to the hound's-tooth jacket. Indeed, my hair was not the corny-as-hell-backcomb-and-side-blades job but a style inspired by the most relaxed man in show business, Perry Como. Thoughts of Perry. People seemed to like his being relaxed more than they liked his singing.

By the way – I did warn you – one incident that Fansion missed (perhaps because it was pre-Paul) was Perry-related. In all innocence The Me decided to delight his parents with another playground poem, after "Catch a Falling Star" (and put it in your pocket):

> Catch a Perry Como
> Wash his balls in Omo

(I thought a "ballsinomo" was an object.)

Yes, his relaxation. If they liked performers being relaxed so much, why not cut out the middle man and just have the relaxation: a stage show where a star of something-or-other comes home, hangs up his coat, brings a cuppa and a biscuit over to the large radiogram on which is playing *The Organist Entertains*. He settles down, shuts his eyes, lifts himself gently to break wind into the Parker-Knoll recliner ...

I never went in for relaxation then, and don't go in for it now. I also had a Saturday job in the Woolwich Building Society, often starting work at 9.00AM after about three hours sleep and so, needless to say, I popped pills to keep going. This meant that for every note I dispensed, I produced about five chews of my gum. I was very efficient, sharply chewing like a smoking beagle, and not well liked.

All this brings me, though not very neatly, to music. Yes, I liked Mod music, and not just because it's great to dance to. (I'm still a brilliant dancer – after a fistful of painkillers.) But apart from that, it was jazz and the Rolling Stones. Jazz ... You might think, from my dressing choices, I would have gone for West Coast "cool" jazz, especially given Art Pepper's penchant for the boxy hound's-tooth jacket. No. Neither *Birth of the Cool* nor even Miles figured much. For tenors, it was Lester Young and John Coltrane; for trumpeters, the Clifford Brown/Freddie Hubbard axis. The point is that I loved and love the classic popular song – "It Never Entered My Mind", "Stardust" – and the building up from them and the taking apart of them that jazzers do. While my mates were grooving away to Hendrix, I lay on my bed listening to Coltrane excavating "Nature Boy". (The only time I have written a letter to a magazine was to *Downbeat* when that racist nutjob LeRoi Jones wrote about how Coltrane shows us the way to "murder" the popular song.) His tone is *clean lines* itself, the definition of it. As for his later stuff, *Ascension* was a boiling cauldron of faeces, and *A Love Supreme* was po-faced.

Are you taking notes? An Upper Second is only an attendance certificate these days ...

Need I even add – though in adding it you can probably guess where my tongue is located – Young's and Coltrane's dress sense was spot on. Lester with his famous mauve suit and porkpie hat (the slogan *Great big eyes for Pres*); Coltrane in a seersucker jacket and blue-and-white pumps. No accident then, in my philosophy, that Ornette Coleman's clothing options could be crass. In '66, with a quietly protesting Nick, I saw Ornette playing in a powder-blue linen suit with a silly Mao jacket, topped off with little dark glasses that just covered his eyeballs (bought from Portobello Road, like a good American tourist). They were showbiz clothes. "This is my act," they said; "this is how somebody looks whose voice is that of a lost soul striving and failing to pull alongside the human ship." How like the home life of our own dear selves.

Of course, I only thought a *version* of this. But I admit it was the kind of rubbish that attracted itself to me.

Next slide, please ...

The Rolling Stones – Eel Pie Island. What a coming together! Here is the symmetrical opposite of *The Black and White Minstrel Show* and The Rex cinema. I saw them playing in Ealing and Richmond, but Eel Pie Island was the favourite.

It was certainly a dump, stinking of BO and with an acrid smell too that I only smelt again when I opened one of the early packets of salt-and-vinegar crisps some years later. The floor was rotting and threatening to give way under heavy dancing, and the toilets were revolting. But it was heaven too. In those days Keith was the musical leader and the girls went for Brian; but since 1965 or so the Stones have equated to Mick ... and that's fine by me, whilst admitting to a soft spot for Charlie and Bill.

Let me do this by quotes ...

NME questionnaire circa 1963: Dislikes?
Mick: Indolent people.

Interviewer, 1983: Can you tell us who you will vote for?
Mick: My heart says Michael Foot, my head says the SDP, but my wallet says Conservatives, so that's what I'm gonna do. (Said with a wide grin, so impossible to know if sincere; which was the point.)

Interviewer, 1984: Can you tell us a little about the new tour?
Mick: It's the biggest tour we've ever done.

Now two suit-related ones:

Charlie Watts, 2014: Muscles? I don't like muscles. They spoil the fit of your suit. (Another illustration of the close relationship between Truth and Beauty.)

Bill Wyman, early '90s (Now this is horrible, as well as showing Bill's superhuman indifference and his touch of evil; and where would the Stones be without those two ...?):

Michael Caine: [*meeting Bill at a party with a* very young *young lady*] Christ, Bill, how old is she?
Bill: About as old as your suit.

I apologise if this is all too familiar; but what's wrong with familiarity? I wouldn't apologise for reading "Sonnet 18".

Now, before this becomes too colour-supplementy, let me say that Fansion and I were heading back on the overcrowded Piccadilly Line when I underwent a cat-gut torsion in reverse.

After changing to my beloved District Line, we managed to sit together. This at least gave me the chance to engage the chap in conversation. But I could think of nothing much to say. I tried:
— Where next?
— "Oxdour Circus", Mr Barber.
— What an awkward blend ... Oxford ... and *dour*?
— It's an awkward business, sir. [*tired smile*]

At Victoria we changed onto the Victoria Line, getting off at "Oxdour Circus". I should have guessed. Yes, we were walking towards War*dour* Street and, yes, to the Marquee Club. Blessèd Fansion! Here would be a pool of happiness after this bead-string of mental, verbal and physical violence.

The fashions of the people we walked behind through Soho were lateish '60s – brighter colours, better cuts, a younger central tendency. And rather little in the way of Brylcreem.

We stood behind The Me and his girlfriend Jenny (pure blonde Mary Quantish hair, that suede coat the colour of baby crap, a full-fine-petite body) as they joined the queue and heard, with them, girls assessing boys in terms of how good a dancer they were. The Me was seventeen and today was Jenny's sixteenth birthday. A celebration building! I never, or hardly ever, by the way, talk about sex, and certainly not about my own sex life; but we were certainly looking forward to the party – I mean the party her parents were going to attend the following night that would leave us alone in the house for three hours. Fansion whipped out his modem to speed things up and we were inside.

At this point the audience was in a full spate of laughter as Tom Jones – yes – was leaving the stage to ironic cheers. To explain: we had come to see the new arrival into The Yardbirds – Jeff Beck – but the venue had been borrowed for a recording of the Radio Luxembourg programme *Ready Steady Radio* (with Keith Fordyce). Acts would be interviewed with the pretence being that they would perform their latest single, which of course they *generally* did not. The gorgeous Adrienne Posta did an interview and then cleared off as her single played to an impatient audience. Not so Tom Jones. After his interview he hip-swivelled, lip-synched, and crotch-thrusted along to "It's Not Unusual", using his arms to propel his hod-carrier's body to greater and greater depths. And he did this in yob-jeans with turnups and a sort of cardigan, as the audience collectively wet itself.

Now, to give the Welsh Ted his due (a clause I will never use again), he had *something* – something between chutzpah and bovine ambition.

The Yardbirds came onto the stage, Beck as a cat emerges from under a sofa. After the interview with Keith Relf, "For Your Love" played and Jeff waltzed Fordyce round the stage, still wearing his guitar.

The sight of the future Sir Tom had temporarily turned Jenny off, but I fancied I was in love with her and did not need to fancy that right at that moment I was perfectly happy. My goodness, The Me looked it.

Then it was live. Beck laid down the riff:

Da, da, da-da-da, da-da
*Da, da, da-da-da **DA DA***

I'm not talkin' [Relf]

CHORD

That's what I gotta say ...

6: A Threat from Simon Dee

After a cat-gut wrench hardly worth writing home about, we travelled from "Oxdour Circus" up to Euston on the Victoria again, and then onto the Edgware branch of the Northern Line. Really, whoever was organising this Magical Mostly-Misery Tour was verbally challenged, because we got off at "Chalk Form" just after Chalk Farm, a very clever reference to the fact that we were going to my school on Haverstock Hill. There was the Falafel House across the road, a favourite lunch venue.

We drifted into the school and drifted further into the art room. Here we found The Me drawing some sprigs of horse chestnut, blemished and curling brown, in fine pencil – a bit of peace after the snapping elastic and electric music. The Me was at a kind of peace, between preying and praying. We watched for about fifteen minutes before the art master came in.
— Still at it, Leo? We need to vacate the premises soon, on pain of death.
— Just trying to get this right, sir. It's defeating me.
— [*looks at drawing*] No it isn't. Some good work there. Very good.

The Me was in standard school uniform. This sentence is not as boring as it may seem because you would have thought that he, like other Mod-types, would have *mod*ified it, putting a school badge on a Moody Blues jacket, for example. No, that was not The Me's way. The uniform was OK: three-buttoned black woollen jacket, white shirt, grey trousers, with a green, black, and white tie and badge. If it had been one of those Greyfriars efforts of the kind poor little Toby Young might have designed, then The Me would have toned it down or sought expulsion; but it was already toned down. He did not, though, buy the trousers from the school suppliers as C&A had a nice line then in grey trousers – parallels.

The kind of poncy "rebels" who modified their uniforms were the kind of people who self-righteously sat through the National Anthem because they "weren't monarchists"; the kind of people who excreted little *Bon courages!* little *Plus tards!* and little *Quelle surprises!* into their chat. They might well have swayed to "We Shall Overcome" and would certainly have decided that the electric Dylan was an assault on the Goddess of Pure Prig.

The art master – his name was Sidney Tranter – seemed to be building up to say something significant before breaking off from the big jump and saying:
— Tell me. I overheard some of the 5th formers referring to me as "Nuck" or "Neck" the other day. Having drawn a blank, I was wondering if you could enlighten me.
— It should be spelt with a K. K-n-u-c-k. Short for Knuckler Sid, sir.
— [*laughter*] I *have* been trying to give it up; but it's so *effective*.

Knuckler Sid was very tall and very thin and he used his height to control scallywags milling around his door with intent, or in a free-range manner in the playground, to restore order. He knuckled them hard on what Paul would call the "frontoparietal region".

He was not a soft touch, then; but the kids liked him a lot. Hard to nail down why. He was an anarchist at heart who only really took art seriously; but he had a tongue-in-cheek authority about him that you were allowed to recognise was not the real thing. (No, I don't like psycho-social babble either.)

The previous Christmas he'd invited all the final-year 6th to a party at his flat in Kentish Town. It was like a capsule of the near future with bare pine, white walls, the only colour from paintings and throws, plus his wife's Giacometti-ish sculptures. You wanted to be part of his world, or at least line up with him.

— Actually Leo, there was something I wanted to talk to you about ... before the cleaning ladies come in and start chucking tea leaves on the floor, or whatever they do. A confession, in a way. I just don't get you. You have a dedication to pencil drawing and exactness, *water*-colours, and to some-would-say outmoded ideas of beauty that one associates with conformist girls not with guys like you ...

Yes, I know. This was not exactly how he put it. It's a blending of the actual words I saw The Me hear, with exposition that ends up like the stilted stuff of a teaching dialogue. I will, though, try to give my own exact words, marbling in some undermining comments. Goddit?

— I would have thought you would have gone for Picasso, surrealism, abstract expressionism, Bacon, Hockney. Stuff [*he broke into American*] of that nature.

— I suppose it's like this [*actually it was not*]: I think a real visual artist is sort of in love with how the natural world looks. If you are in love with something or somebody, you want to possess it, and drawing or painting these impressions is a kind of possession for me. To get to the truth of the impression, which is of course *of* something real, you produce the beauty you desire. You know, John Keats on the truthfulness of beauty and vice versa and all that. Though of course we do tend to idealise the loved one. Idealisation can be the name of the game.

I would not say that this was phony, exactly; but it was a sales pitch for the course The Me was carving out. He was trying to cut a course, to stand out and make a splash, though in a subtle way and against the bombastic grain. Also, The Me *was* good at plant drawing and reproducing the classic forms, and it's a good idea to do a lot of what you are good at if you want to go forward. He was in search of a constrained, intriguing splash.

And by the way, this was essentially the script he had rehearsed for an upcoming art college interview.

— But you like some modern artists. Matisse, I think you said.
— Oh yes, he was a passionate lover. Picasso, though, is a bully who wants to bend the world to his will. Surrealism is adolescent – all that Freud baloney. Abstract impressionism is curtain patterns. Hockney is good when he's like Ron Kitaj; and yes I do like Bacon. His impressions are just very extreme ...

I'm bored with this now. It's like one of these Open University dialogues. No getting round it.

I mentioned Art School. Why? The Me had a good brain. In English, again, The Me was a kind of conservative. He loved Shakespeare and despised the modern novel; loved poetry and thought most modern prose was anybody-can-do-that. He would study *The Winter's Tale* endlessly, almost never opening *Howard's End*. If it had contained just one sentence like

> My life stands in the level of your dreams

then it would be worth looking at. This The Me "would have thought" (as biographers say).

Who cares – The Me cared not – about Leonard Bast's bloody umbrella?

When Jenny was about to chuck him after yet another indiscretion, he wrote to her:

> For I cannot be
> Mine own nor anything to any if
> I be not thine.

It worked.

Much the same in French. The Me found syntax, out-of-the-way vocabulary, and tables of irregular verbs banal and simply did not bother. He would, though, learn Mallarmé poems by heart, not understanding a word, when he needed to woo new girls after Jenny had finally had enough.

Well, it was clear that Knuckler Sid was unconvinced, though in a kind of tolerant way. Sid did not follow it up and suggested they walk out together. On the way out, as we shadowed them, Sid told The Me about his being thrown out of the pub across the road for sketching a holding-of-court by Simon Dee, then in his pomp (the word fits, in this case). Dee was drinking Red Barrel with whisky chasers, surrounded by hangers-on only there for the free booze. Dee saw what Sid was doing and got him thrown out, saying that if he did not destroy the sketch he would sue him "for all you've got".

— He's a difficult man to admire. (This was one of the Knuckler's catchphrases.)

Pupil and teacher parted, as Sid would go down to Camden Town for the High Barnet branch; and we went back to "Chalk Form", also travelling north. North-west, not the due north of the other branch. Bored with this yet?

I had a fair idea where we were going. The Northern Line is a rattling line, as Lonnie Donegan did not sing; and within the rattling I braced myself for a mighty bungee leap of cat-gut grab, which came just after Golders Green. This time there was no silly punning, but instead of Edgware it said Shudehill. There were no other riders in the car; and we stepped into a brick-arched railway tunnel whose sides were moss-green ceramic, looking well worn despite the complete absence of other people. There was only one narrow exit with concrete stairs that quickly became dark, bashed-up wood and a door leading to ... the back room of a tobacconist's.

Fansion led the way, and to my surprise the guy behind the counter said to him:
— All well, Doc?
— Absolutely fine, thanks.

And yes, it *was* "absolutely fine" to be back in Manchester, to Shudehill and its bustling media-rich life, where once there had been market life:

Heaps of oranges and apples,
Piles of "tates" and curly greens,
Bananas, sprouts, and artichokes,
Late peas and early beans,
Inside a great glass market
Is what Shudehill really means.

There was the pub that served chilli con carne with crusty bread, there was the *Manchester Evening News*, there was that particular rickety easygoing air, and there, just up the road, was another pub where I was sure we were headed – The Lower Turk's Head, whose façade was tiled HP Sauce brown and coffee cream.

We were in the smoky innards of the Turk, a pub for old men whose souls HP Sauce and Camp Coffee with condensed milk had entered just below a tank of best bitter. ("Awk" as my English teacher would have put in the margin.) And taking my ponce's hat off, I can say it was a perfect little pub of a kind that's much missed. Any more angles to cover? I watched as Fansion went straight to the door into the stairs, at the top of which we would find The Me.

I had better tell you how I came to be there.

My choice of Art Colleges was eccentric, by which I mean I wanted to get out of London towards some sea air, and not even Brighton would fit the bill. I did my "pre-diploma year", as it was then, in Penzance.

To own up, if I'd gone to one of the London colleges the pressure would have been on to live at home, and I wasn't, as I learned to say in Manchester, *having any of that.* Paul and I were getting on OK, and we were often in league against Mum and Dad; but he was becoming a prodigy, a science star. He didn't have to try; indeed, I spent more hours studying than he did. He was as at home in the world of science as he was estranged from the world of casual chit-chat. His great, lumbering, shyly smiling self was aimed at Oxbridge. The stutter almost seemed to be part of the package: the flaw in the perfect vase of his brilliance. And yes, Mum and Dad made him the centrepiece, with me as the hedonistic satellite, a compact, often poker-faced self destined for a rude awakening.

But it wasn't just that. London was full of guys like me; and I would have bet good money that Cornwall was not. A small splash could be made. To which I can add with some embarrassment that there was a romantic element too. I'd been undergoing a passion for John Cowper Powys' novels, especially *Wolf Solent,* and somehow thought that if you travelled west from Dorset the Dorsetisity would somehow grow more intense. God help us, I even wrote a long Powysesque rhyming poem about St Michael's Mount.

Well, Penzance. Everything changed there, but not so much that it couldn't be changed back again. I was as likely to do fine pencil drawing there as to darn socks. There was a loosening and a colouring up. Lots of "girlie action" (almost more than I could handle), but lots of beery action too; and I'd never been a drinker. We would stand around outside pubs holding tepid pints. When I hear the word Penzance I get the treacly taste that comes after one too many pints – or swallows, in my case – o' the brown stuff.

There's no point in dwelling on why the loosening happened – a combination of the open air, the company of the raucous, the absence from home, and maximum art-life: that'll do. As for the form it took, it was a matter of thicker brushes, not mixing the paint on the pallet – why am I so addicted to what Paul calls "iteration"? I must call a halt – and having a central idea within which I could be free.

Triplets figure a lot, too, don't they? This central idea arose from seeing the woodblock prints of Hokusai called *Thirty-Six Views of Mount Fuji*, which had the kind of delicacy and clarity to which I was still addicted and which it would be impossible for me to emulate. It also arose – hello, Auntie Iteration – from seeing some of Emil Nolde's paintings in Paris, in particular those he did quickly in the open air, sketching in vivid paint, all first thoughts and all the colours in the book; and the exact opposite of Hokusai. My Fuji was – no surprises here – St Michael's Mount.

I painted forty-six (not thirty-six) viewpoints around Mount Bay, from east of Marazion to Penzance (mostly there), through Newlyn, and west to Mousehole, working quickly and in good weather. The original idea was to add texts, perhaps poem snippets, to each, like Kitaj; but this required some clarity in the image – lacking completely. A painting of a guy in Mousehole hose-washing his car with the Mount in the background could equally well have been of an ancient peasant pulling a giant tapeworm out of a hayrick. Also, given the splashiness of the paintings, how would the texts be shown: Art School italic? – terrible. Surely not Letraset.

I impressed myself immensely, but not my tutors, who muttered "Derain" or, more often, "Munch". "This art lark", as some mates back home called it, was proving more of a

challenge (a new-millennium word this) than I'd anticipated ... and that basically is my Penzance story. Back to London? The good schools would not have me because my
tutors had not enthused, so I went for Manchester, simply
because Knuckler Sid had gone there. Also, Knuck had written a thesis of some kind on the Manchester painter Annie
Swynnerton, whose work – derided by many as "decorative"
– I adored. (Maybe she was not as good as G.F. Watts, but
some of her paintings were like Wattses that had been
grown outdoors.)

So there I was in Manchester, a place that suited me despite
it being difficult to confuse with me, being well-earthed,
low-key, *thinly* witty (hello again, Auntie Iteration). It's better by quotes, as before; albeit non-historical ones.

Mark E. Smith: "They've got some nice things in Primark."

Morrissey (when asked about James Dean): "James Dean?
Whatever he wore he always looked good."

So, back to the present of the journey, with us climbing the
dark stairs and with the smell of dope getting stronger and
the guitar doodling louder. Five people dangled about the
room passing a joint, some of them making elaborate fist
shapes round the limp effort like you do when imitating an
owl hoot and then sucking for dear life. Grim, for sure; the
music too. I used to imagine the opposite ritual of "getting
straight" where you started stoned and then drank lemon
juice and strong coffee till you were discussing plot lines in
The Archers and listening to Elgar.

Be that as it wasn't, there was a single female among the five
who was – I don't believe in cranking up the tension –

Francesca Ubley, the Fran who you were introduced to a couple of hundred words in. We'll get back to her and think about The Me for a second. His hair was longer now but nobody could mistake him for a hippie. For one thing, The Me was wearing maroon Doc Martens polished like conkers below immaculate blue Levis. Above the waist there was something Peter Blakeish going on with the jacket – three-buttoned, Oxford, blue cotton, nicely crumped, and an unimaginatively Blakean badge, too, of a no-entry sign. Unlike the other three males, I looked alert, as did Fran who sat in a dining chair as if posing for a *Vogue* shoot. She didn't touch the joint as it staggered round but was smoking what they liked to call a "straight", held at a Noel Coward angle (brandished away from the body to one side as if showing it off, cigarette level with the lips, palm displayed). Yes, she could easily have been on a *Vogue* cover. To say she was striking was not enough, unless it included the idea that if you made an insipid remark or bored on for a second too long she would strike you. Disdain was there, and exciting angles, from the blonde bob to the ... why not recycle? ... "gash-mouthed, ice-eyed type", as I said before. You can recycle the account with Fran because she was a kind of cliché, not just in the way I present her, but in herself. A "cartoon" is probably a better phrase. When I'm waiting, sitting around in an airport lounge or somewhere like that, I look at people and tot up the number of cartoon faces: about one in forty. So if you think my treatment of Fran is cartoonish then we're home and dry.

What was a hard-nosed belle like that doin' in a dump like this? Fran was doing a PhD in Philosophy at the University (after an MA at Oxford) and her topic was aesthetics. I really had little of a clue here, but this included what she called an "empirical" element, meaning that she would interview artists from the distinguished to the grubby underlings about what she called their "intuitions", about things like good form, authenticity ... another iteration looms. It had been very formally arranged that she would meet up with us. I like to think she came back to the flat because she liked the look of me.

The record finished and Matt, my roommate, got up from the floor to change it. Now the way he did this, in fact the way people like Matt did anything when being watched by fellow "heads", must be noted. The guiding idea was "Look man, I really don't want to disturb the air around us. Let me just slide through it, like this and this. It looks dopey man, right? But it's cool."

The main thing to mark was that the head bobbed forward with each step pigeon-style, not a simple thrust forward, more like an upward yearn. And timed with this was a pushing forward of the hands, palms down, as if doing the first phase of the doggy paddle, together with bent knees and a kind of soft-shoe shuffle. I'm aware that this description is less than the sum of its parts. Better to say that it was the performance of "Don't mind me as I go with the flow." If it was like anything else it was like the vaguely Egyptian dance performances of Wilson, Kepple, and Betty who I saw in pantomime with Mum and Dad. Wilson and Kepple – Betty was a *delight* – spread sand onto a mat and shuffled in a way I was striving to capture, especially the hand pokings, as in-the-souk music played.

The Me couldn't help smiling. It was closer to stifling a laugh. Likewise with Fran. Their eyes met and smiles widened. Mildly stoned as The Me was, he had to break the horrible fog barrier of these smoke-ins and did so with this nonsense that I hope he hoped would be taken in the spirit intended:

— Would you ... care ... to see ... uh ... my etchings?

— Love to!

She grabbed The Me by the upper arm and in a couple of shakes they were in the room I shared with Matt. Of course, Fansion and I followed them.

Instead of asking The Me which bed was his, and without a further word, she carefully sniffed both of them from top to tail.

— Good grief! We'll use that one. Definitely that one.

— That's mine.

— Good old you. [*she examines the door*] There's no lock on this stupid door. Jam your bed against it.

The Me did as he was told, and when he moved the bed he uncovered his portfolios on the floor.

— Nowhere else to put these things.

— Hang on. Let's have a quick look.

Quick look it was not. I was getting undressed and wondering about her doing the same as she glared at my work. First the St Michael's Mount ones and then some Manchester stuff. ("Stuff" – dread word. "Dread word" – dread phrase.)

I must tell you what I'd been doing. There was always a general idea with me, and this time it was to photograph everyday Manchester scenes – a chip shop, a bus queue – and sketch onto Bristol board the basic contours with faces, etc., filled out in grey with the occasional blush of pink on a cheek or a dog's tongue. There was always a space left for a full figure or head or body top half, and this I filled with my renditions (oils on hardboard) of some of Annie Swynnerton's work. My original idea was to render works by the old masters, but I soon realised that this would be nothing more than the kind of ho-ho you see in *Private Eye* ... bathers at Brighton and Botticelli's *Venus* on her shell amongst the chip wrappers – that kind of thing.

For example, standing in the queue for the number 72 would be my version of Swynnerton's lovely *Glow Worm* in her yellow gown; a scene in a betting shop with guys checking their betting slips; and to one side *The Letter* (a large-headed, swollen-featured, flush-cheeked girl in a white dress reading a letter in profile). Emerging from behind a hedge, as two skallies eyed up a posh car, was my version of Swynnerton's magnificent *The Sense of Light*.

— You're a funny chap.
— Really? [*The Me resisting the turn-off idea of folding his jeans*]
— No, I just mean that you have got yourself completely wrong. You think you are a dutiful fine artist who just happens to like frameworks to work within; but really you are a conceptual artist.
— No!
— Through and through ... Undo my back, will you.
— There! [*and here The Me's frustration bubbled up*] ... But conceptual art's dogshit.

This was exactly what The Me thought then, and despite it all – the "it all" is to come, of course – is what I think now. I find John Lennon a person – my favourite Knuckism – "difficult to admire", but he could hit the nail bang-on. When asked in *Rolling Stone* or somewhere what conceptual art was to him, he simply said: *Leave out the "... ceptual"*. I couldn't help but argue back, despite the current state of play:

— Yoko Ono?
— Sure, she's a phony; but Gilbert and George?

She touched my weak spot here. There was something perfect about them; perfectly droll. My favourite was their
doing a rigid twist in their tweed suits, leaning into each
other, back and forth, as a transistor radio played Dave Dee,
Dozy, Beaky, Mick, and Titch's "Bend It".

— You're a performer ... what's your name?
— Leo.
— Leopold ... just like they are.
— I'm not going to argue ... err ...
— Fran. Pleased to meet you. Now ...

At this point she told me exactly what I was expected to do
and in what order; and as she reached the end (pun half-in-
tended) of the list ... someone, surely Matt, was trying the
door.

— Hey man, there's a problem with the door, man. You in
there, man?
— Piss off, stinky! [*Fran, who else?*] Come back no sooner
than, um, [*looks at me*] forty minutes.

7: Hermann Hesse, for Fun and Profit

Before things got physical, Fansion squiggled and we found ourselves in a shining loft. I knew it was near the canal and that it was the penthouse suite of some dull offices and that it was Fran's place. And you are about to know that Fran and I began living together shortly after that evening. ("You'd be a good lover if you'd only shut up," she said.) There are many ways of being in love – *Ah, Monsieur ees a pheelosopherr* – and the way whereby the loved one is the star and you are the orbiting planet is definitely not mine now. But it was then, for that short time. I swallowed all she said, transfused into myself what she believed – and this was one opinionated woman – into my already eccentric cache of beliefs; and I set about thinking about a *performance* for my final-degree show. The Swynnertons alone would not be enough.

I kept drawing blanks, with pressure building. For Fran it was logically impossible – "false in every possible world" as she would say – that she could be wrong, so if I failed to come up with some brilliant conceptualisation of to-be-performed nonsense then this would be down to my being a weak-minded noodle and backslider. And that would be the end of us. So the thought of there being an end-of-us focused me smartly.

It was Sunday lunchtime and we were cooking for a couple

of guests, Fran making a pasta sauce and The Me preparing a salad to her instructions. I was surprised by how different The Me looked. Somebody had confiscated his arrogance at the door and much of his humour and in its place put an eagerness to please. Maybe it was different on the inside, but that was how it looked. He wore a loose white linen collarless shirt, and black jeans, and, weirdly, Fran wore much the same. To Fansion and me, squatting on a sofa as big as a stretch limousine, we looked excellent.

— You won't find these people at all interesting, but I told Joanne I'd entertain them and entertain them I will. *We* will.
— I don't have much dentistry chat.

I said this because they were a couple of dentists from South Africa, holidaying in the UK, with the woman being the child of a friend of Fran's aunt Joanne: Lansley and Jessica Blum. We stayed for a lot of this. Maybe Fansion was tired. I was too.

In they came, Lansley a small intense man and Jessica a big, muscular Yiddisher mamma. Lansley really should have been a scout master; born to wear shorts; with khaki-coloured hair. More interesting than them was Fran in social mode, speaking with Field Marshall Montgomery clipped diction, over-focused on the just so. "You find us at sixes and sevens," she said, surveying a space as clean and ordered as an operating theatre. I had no idea what to say when I was left with them for a couple of minutes.
— I have always associated dentistry with South Africa.
— Maybe it's a psychological quirk of yours, Leopold. [*Jessica*]
— I mean, that often dentists do indeed ... hail from there.

— Tell me, Leopold, [*Lansley*] what do you think IQ tests measure?

— Intelligence?

— The ability to do IQ tests, is my position.

— Lansley is *such* a controversialist. [*Jessica*] He was stirring up our dinner companions just last night in Liverpool ... Now what an interesting spot that is, compared to Manchester.

The Me's expression was Gawd-'Elp-Us; and the conversation continued in much this way. Jessica gushed and dispensed views on the state of England while Lansley strove to have some kind of bookish-philosophical debate. Fran has a short fuse, but she only smiled weakly when Jessica said, "Oh, I do hope Lansley doesn't once more denounce philosophy as 'intellectual masturbation'. What would Francesca say? I warned him."

— [*Jessica*] It's actually quite a good thing that there's such a *dearth* of bookshops in Manchester. If Lansley sees a bookshop he's in there like a rat up a drainpipe. Don't deny it, darling. And he's such a *re*-reader too. Quite recently Hermann Hesse's *Steppenwolf* it's been. A book I adore, by the way.

— [*Fran*] I've not read it.

— Oh you *should*. A deeply religious book.

— *Steppenwolf* is not a religious book, Jessica. [*Lansley*]

— Ever the controversialist, Lansley. *Steppenwolf* IS a religious book.

— As I say, Jessica, *Steppenwolf* is NOT a religious book, Jessica.

— You are simply wrong, Lansley. It IS a religious book.

— The wrongness is with you, Jessica. *Steppenwolf* is DEFINITELY NOT a religious book.

Such delight fell on The Me's face at this moment. He seemed to be revelling in the ecstatic light thrown from the lightbulb above his head. Fansion squiggled.

We were in a large hall, milling with people. It was the degree show of Manchester School of Art. We wandered around, with me knowing that we would not see The Me as one of the millers-around. Some of the work was good, some was phony (say, "found" objects dolled up to Dixie), and many advertised the gap between what-I-want-to-do and what-I've-ended-up-bloody-doing. None of them betrayed the absolute determination to make a splash that lay in the breast of The Me.

Here we are ... A sign on a table easel.

CANTEEN MEDALS
A performance by
Leo Barber
11.00 am
2 pm
6.00 pm
11 pm
The Claremont Rooms

It was just coming up to 2.00PM and here were The Claremont Rooms, just off the main hall, and here too was a slightly beery haze hovering over an impatient audience. We took our seats a little off to the side, right at the front.

The Me emerged, walking and looking and dressed like a funeral mute. I could see Matt behind a curtain manipulating a tape recorder. The Me pointed to where Matt was and music burst out. The theme from a TV show called *Criss Cross Quiz*:

Criss – Cross – QUIZ
DADALADDLE LADDLE
LADDLE LADDLE
UM PUM PUM.

The Me made a kind of *oy veh* gesture to the audience at the first couple of plays, but on the third he went into a scarily manic twist to the
DADALADDLE LADDLE
LADDLE LADDLE
UM PUM PUM.

This was done at least ten times. The shock of seeing him dance wore off, but the tension mounted.

The Me then said, slowly:

Canteen Medals all over my best halter.
What is one to do?

Matt then handed him a large cardboard paddle with a painted head on each side in profile, one side a grotesque cartoon of Lansley, the other a grotesque cartoon of Jessica. Standing side-on to the audience, he displayed the Jessica head in one hand and held a loudhailer in the other. When he spoke, his accent was a grotesque cartoon of the South African dialect; and indeed, it must be admitted, with Jewish tones too. In falsetto, for Jessica:

Stippenwolf uz a rrreligious buk, Lansley.
change profile sides
No no no, Jissica, *Stippenwolf* uz NUT a rrreeeligious buk.
change profile sides

How can you say that, Lansley? *Stippenwolf* UZ a deeply rrrreeligioius buk.

change profile sides

If innything is NUT a rrreeligious buk, it uz thus buk, Jissica.

change profile sides

Werr is your sinse of bilance and sinse, Lansley? Werr uz yurr sinceibulity. I im all it sea with regard to thus, my dear. Why do you say what you say, Lansley?

change profile sides

I say it, Jissica, on the grounds that thus buk uz totally licking in rrrrreligious CONTINT. It uz NUT, I rrrepeat NUT, a rrrreligious buk. To be a rrreligious buk, Jissica, there must be rrreligious CONTINT ind it licks this.

change profile sides

I am getting worried I shall say something I will regrut, Lansley, so I shall play with a straight bit ind repeat *Stippenwolf* UZ a deeply and profoundly rrrreligious buk!

It was clear to most people, and it was the case, that after a certain point The Me began improvising. It was clear to some too that he was often on the point of corpsing. It went on and got weirder.

I hiv to insust with ivery fiaybir uf my being, Lansley, that *Stippenwolf* UZ a rrreligious buk in exikly the sinse in which *The Holy Bible* UZ a rrreligious book. Would you deny the *Bible* uz a rrreligious book? You hiv to, to be consustint, Lansley.

change profile sides

Jissica, Jissica, Jissica mine. To me, rrrreligious intails and implies the clear prisence of rrrreligious CONTINT, licking here. Do my trowsiz hiv rrrreligious contint? Does my food processor or the bogies un my nose hiv rrrreligious contint?

Inswer me, Jissica! Do the teachings of Jesus hiv it? Can you till the difference? I rist my case.

Fran paid for some of the performances to be filmed on 16-mm and I presented the best one to the examiners.

After the next squiggle there was a morning scene with Fran sipping coffee as she dressed. Addressing a knackered-looking Leo, she said:
— You're a hit, as I knew you would be. Aren't you getting up?
— I'm a hit with dogshit, Fran.
— It's not dogshit, Leopold.
— I insust it uz, Frin. The CONTINT is dogshut!
— Not funny.
— Not funny either that they won't let me graduate. "Simply a comic routine with more than a hint of anti-Semitism. Final degree: Failed."
— Sue them. I can help you sort that. Ciao!

We watched as The Me waited for the front door to slam, then fumbled in the bedside table for a packet of Senior Service and his matches. The Me knew that Fran could indeed "sort it". It wasn't just that she had oodles of family money and many contacts in the legal profession. Disputation was her hobby. Dissatisfied with the outcome of a small-claims dispute against her builders, she was taking it further and enjoying every second. In fact, it seemed that philosophy was only a preparation for the legal career she would later have in London. The law is written down in multiply hedged sentences and so is modern philosophy. No, I didn't put it this way – she did.

Fansion squiggled, and we were at a table in what I knew to

be The Chop House pub in Cross street, right next to The Me and a young female reporter from the *Manchester Evening News*.

— Thank you for agreeing to see me at short notice, Mr Barber.

— Leo, please.

— Well, Leo, you've created quite a stir locally with your court case against the Art School. And may I say, you've captured the imagination of many of us. Are you confident of victory?

— I did not embark upon this dreary process in the hope of a *victory*. Let them withhold the formal degree from me. It won't stop me being an artist.

— But you must think you have a case?

— It is not a question of *my having* a case. It's a question of *there being* a case out there, whatever I think. [*this irritating mode came naturally to me in those days*] I embarked on all this to raise questions about the nature of art and to disturb the dogmatic slumbers [*this phrase straight from Fran*] of a complacent establishment. My performance, *Canteen Medals*, was surely a work on art in so far as it had sensory [*thanks, Fran*] elements of sight and sound; it was original [*would the reporter have heard of Dada?*] and it had an aboutness [*thanks again, Fran*] with regard to the art-independent world.

— "Aboutness"?

— It refers to something beyond itself, just as Van Gogh's painting of his bed is about that bed. In this case, it highlights impediments to human communication and human thought that often skulk in the darkness. [*my own over-egged contribution*] As the dispute between Jessica and Lansley continues, it is clear that this is not simply an absurd dialogue of the deaf: it is a performed manifestation of two subjectivities with no common ground. Is this not all around us today – in politics, in inter-class communications, in dialogue between the younger and older generations?

—Why call it *Canteen Medals*?

— It captures the tawdry nature of the medal – the feather in the cap, the pat on the back that is a prize or indeed a *qualification*. [*smiles*] (The real reason was that it was a phrase of my mother's that I liked, perhaps from her days in the ATS, to describe the stains left on Paul's jackets by his sloppy eating – by eating and trying to speak.)

— I see. [*she could clearly see that this smelt fishy, whilst being secretly amused by it*] But can you give us a rather more, err, *punchy* message for our readers?

— "This is a shot across the bows of the conservative art establishment and the old men who squat below decks. It forces them to question the CONTENT ... or *CONTINT* [*winks*] ... of what they teach."

— Great!

— Fancy another drink? In fact, how about a spot of lunch?

The point about all this is not that I won the case and graduated from the Art School. It's that I didn't just feel comfortable with being in the public eye: I adored it. It was as alcoholics describe having their first drink – the body saying *Welcome Home* or *Now You're Talking*. My mind said *Welcome Home* AND *Now You're Talking*.

I carried on drawing – I still draw every day – and carried on while knowing I was riding on the back of dogshit. I loved the kind of publicity the dogwork gave me but it did not stop me wishing I was even the lowest grade of Matisse-esque, with art pouring out of me, uncontroversial art popular with high- and low-brow because it was beautiful. But this was the goddamned course I was set on.

In the spirit of testing the solidity of the "goddamned course", and again with the help of Fran's money, I did some more performances and "concepts". One performance was done in the persona of a West Country idiot. I mostly won't do the accent … Something like this:

> I was over in Paris a few weeks ago, havin' a bit of a holiday like. Nice place mind, plenty of things to see and that. Bit nippy though still in March. But what struck I was the scarves that them Paris coffee-bar cowboys and cowgirls haves round them throats – really high scarves like bandits on the telly. They sometimes chews the tops of 'em, 'specially the grils. So I asks this chappay, right, who worked behind the desk in the sort of brothel place I was stayin' in what it was all about loik. He spoke lovely English mind, lovely clear English. Anyway, he told I this, see. To put no finer point on it, the wind whistles round them outdoors bistros *like nobody's business*. You wanna catch pneumonial? **Do–you–want–to–catch–pneumonial?** Well that's the way to go about it – by not wearin' a good-sized scarf. A mate of this bloke's, right, went out one day without 'is scarf. Doid in agonay … No word of a loi.

It then continued for ten minutes till I started to improvise.

Not very good, is it? I used to do this kind of thing at poetry readings to keep my hand in. I only improvised when I was in the mood.

As for the so-called concepts, these were no more than *Goon Show* formulae. The one that springs to mind was a series of adverts on the buses and streets for Rialo-fome, "the foam for the home". This was a multi-purpose foam generated by something that looked like a vacuum cleaner.

The foam could be used to fill up a spare room, thereby cutting down on heating bills; secreted in "dangerous corners" of the home to soften falls; it could be left to harden and be sculpted if an extra chair or sofa was needed ... and I grew a silly beard and grew my hair to a silly length to be in-keeping. I occasionally appeared on Granada's local news.

Good job Fansion didn't make me revisit this period, which was like staying too long at a party when all there was left to drink was eggnog.

He did, though, make me re-experience a visit from Nick. By this time Nick had got his degree in Engineering from Imperial and was well into a PhD. He hadn't changed a bit, as I knew from seeing him back home. The change in my appearance and my career in dogshit did not phase him at all, but the relationship with Fran did. He'd met her once very briefly at a party, but it didn't come from that: it came from my telling him about our life together. He started calling her Sven – after Svengali.

When I raised the possibility of his coming to stay for a couple of days, Fran was not keen. "You mean that lugubrious beanstalk?" "What will he actually *do* here? We're both too busy to entertain him." "An engineeeeer? What could I possibly have in common with *him*. And what do *you*, now?" "Is he interested in anything apart from ... engines?"

8: Calais-Bound in Silence

I think we can take most of the cat-gut yanking as read now. Only worth mentioning at the violent extremes. Any road up (as I've never heard anybody actually say), Fansion and I were now sitting on the enormous sofa watching Fran smoke a cigarette and drink whisky as something bubbled on the stove. Laughter could be heard coming up the stairs, for Nick and I had managed to fit in a couple of pints on the way back from Piccadilly station.

When The Me and Nick rolled in there was no sign of Fran's public-Monty style. She was cool and quiet, letting it be known that her smile was forced, before going to the kitchen. She plonked the food on the table, pouring herself a glass of wine, then pushing the bottle to the menfolk. With a dangerously-amused smile, I watched her say to Nick:
— You look like you've recently fallen over.
— Thank you very much, Mein Kapitän.
Nick was addicted to put-on voices and comedy names; the last two words were said in a Bluebottle voice. Then, to The Me, he said:
— You look like you've recently been lying down.
— Thank you very much, Mein Kapitän.

A too-long silence

— I was watching a wildlife programme on the telly this

week [*Nick*] and learned something interesting about the hyena. You should never look them in the eyes because if you do you're in their power and they can rip your throat out whenever.

Yes indeed, describing Fran's eyes right now as those of a killer canine would be "just the ticket" or indeed any Woosterish equivalent of that phrase. The reference was obvious to Fran who took pride in her ability to instil fear.

Another too-long silence

— So [*Fran*] how is life in the world of engineering, Nick?
— Struggling to find the right supervisor for my thesis right now. Not that many bridge-men around.
— Aren't there bridge-women? [*then, rapidly* ...] But engineering ... isn't one over-reliant on tried and tested notions? Don't you feel the need intellectually to question the concepts and formulae handed down to you?

Yes, this does sound grotesque; I can't recall her being that bad. Spurs the reminder that these scenes were versions, *not recordings. But, I mean, who cares at this distance!*

— I like bridges to stay up in a tried-and-tested way. And you need an intellect to understand the maths and physics of it all.
— Couldn't a computer be trained to design the things you design ... make.
— Programmed by engineers.

A shorter silence

— This lunar beauty has no history. It is complete and early.

[The Me quoting Auden – desperately, and merely to cre-
ate a diversion]
— Can you put some Bach on, Leopold?
— Yes [*Nick*], chop-chop. Can I call you Pold? So, Fran, I
understand you're a philosopher. Nothing's tried-and-
tested there, is it? Bet you yearn for a bit of the old tried-
and-tested.
— I simply yearn to think critically, examining and ques-
tioning the concepts we use.
— Engineers do that. We have a course at Imperial called
The Conceptual Foundations of Welding, taught with some
philosophers at UCL.
— *Really?* [*Fran*]
— Oh yes.
— *Nick!!* [*The Me*]
— Yes, conceptual issues arise in relation to whether two
welded pieces are now a single piece, because, as you know,
there is no joining medium, as there is in soldering, but
simply high heat uniting the two.
— That's interesting, actually. [*Fran, in earnest*]
— Of course, it's an issue that applies in other domains. Or,
if you like, there can be metaphorical extension. In human
relationships, for example, some marriages are soldered,
but only a few are welded.
— And indeed the fusing of concepts.

The Me looked at Fran now as she spoke with near pity:
— Let me think ... "playground" and "self-service" are welding, while ... "exit-strategy" is soldering.

The Me stared a hole in his risotto till his patience snapped;
snapped humanely. He took her hand, saying:
— He's joking, Fran. Typical ... I should have warned you
about this bugger.

Fran did not explode but froze and changed up to a gear he'd never seen before.

— So what are you boys up to tomorrow?

— We'll go and see United play. [*The Me*]

— But you hate football. Ever heard of standing up for yourself? Anyway, I have an early start tomorrow so I'm off to bed. Nick! I didn't get a chance to make the bed up in the spare room. Bedding's in the airing cupboard. Leopold will show you. [*this was a new and nastier kind of Monty*]

— Jawohl, Mein Kapitän! [*Nick, standing up*]

— Good night, you two. You might want to sleep on the sofa, Leopold. I don't want to be disturbed.

— Gute Nacht, Mein Kapitän! [*Nick, of course*]

It was a disaster. Like the man that Dad used to refer to as "Old Hitler", Fran could *not* be made fun of. If I gently ribbed her, there would be a water cannon of fury. While Nick could not be bullied. A bullying manner was enough to set him off; and he had been primed about her ("Sven", recall). But I don't need to tell you this, do I?

Nor do I need to tell you that Nick and I steadily finished the risotto, not even bothering with formulaic jokes like "So that went well." We were starving, as we'd been putting away too much of the devil's buttermilk. We shared the joint Nick had brought up from London and talked low-key about women. Nick tried to get a Pete-and-Dud routine off the ground on the theme of "Women – can't live with them, can't live without them", extending it to things like toilet paper and Liquorice Allsorts, but I had no will for it. "Having no will for X" was a Fran formula, by the way. I – leaving this ambiguous between The Me and I-now – was thinking about the soldering of our relationship, while Fansion squiggled and we were back in the tobacconist's in the early morning waiting for a crowd of people to thin and let us through to the back room and the Northern Line. I was fed up and spent my time reading ads on a noticeboard, some clearly from what we now call sex workers. I was thinking of pointing this out to Fansion and making a joke about Fags, Mags, and Shags ... but this only showed how much the badness of this time was seeping into me.

I wanted to ask Fansion the where-next question, but if ever a door was closed his was; though we did chit-chat about the crowdedness of the carriage, silly ringtones, and so forth. I anticipated stops either at Hampstead or at Camden Town – maybe called "Calm Down Town", "Cam-Shafted Town", or both. Hampstead it was; because when we moved down to London so Fran could pursue (the correct term) a legal career and earn even more money to keep with her other money, we lived in Flask Walk, in one of her father's smaller houses. Camden Town was to witness the gentlest humiliation of "Mr Barber" imaginable. The fact is, we never stopped at either, but went on down to Embankment to join the eastbound District. But I owe you an explanation – sorry for the mess – of what I've just said about Hampstead and Camden. Camden first.

This bit of the early 1970s saw the fag end of the Arts Lab trend. This was a hippyish idea that you can easily google ... so there. These labs were all over the place. Some contained serious, left-field, hard-up artists, and many contained bandwagon-loving layabouts. The one in Camden Town had a good reputation, so I thought I might go there to find like-minded people. *Like-minded!* Eh? You mean people with a mind to become famous by pedalling dogshit but who were also eaten out with mainstream-fine-art frustration and love. "Can I have both, please?" thought the poor Me.

I called in at the Camden lab (actually more Mornington Crescent ... thoughts of Frank Auerbach) one day. A dreamy-looking girl told me I should meet up with Zak who "should be around after lunch". No Zak. I left my phone number and asked her to pass it on to Zak. No call received. I went in again and met a more alert guy and said I wanted to show the film of my Lansley-and-Jessica performance to them, hoping for some "hook-ups". Then Zak walked in, by chance, and listened to me, saying "beautiful" at random points. Zak said he would convene a group of drippy-trippy ones (well spotted: not his words) to watch it. About two months later it was done, after much mucking about with booking a projector and screen. Three people, minus Zak, watched it with me. When I saw Glenda Jackson sitting on a platform some years later as a kind of drama school statue, it reminded me of them. I felt I should check their breathing. One left halfway through; then Zak turned up with a kazoo. (That sentence could be the start of the doggerel version.) The two who were left chatted to Zak about "Anissa's costume" and then about what the coppers had been doing locally, then left. Zak said to me: "So, is everything cool? Good to see you again, man. Be lucky!" [*laughing*]

In fact, while I continued to scribble ideas for performances and installations, I was allowing the "conceptual artist" project to auto-destruct; and about this Fran seemed not to give a damn. This was a good, calm period for us. I liked painting her nude, though this was tricky because she could not keep still, always bubbling with things that had to be done immediately. Or more often the idea of being naked gave her good ideas (phnarr, phnarr, phnarr). The law suited her better than philosophy. "Philosophy is a contact sport; the law is more like chess," she said, not meaning it.

Some of the changes in her were obvious. Hair, for example. The severe bob was gone and her hair was allowed to grow and her face was allowed to make her into the Joni Mitchell lookalike she was always destined to be. She didn't keep her contact lenses in all the time now and sometimes wore Lennonish National Health glasses that made her look ridiculously wholesome. I gave her the nickname Moira when she wore them – which she liked. (Why not add "which was nice", you smug noodle! Yes, point taken; it's just to give you the general idea and prime you for the cracking to come.) I started to cook for us and spent a lot of time reading poetry, some novels, never modern ones except for (Exchange-and-) Mart Amis' two. Can you stand any more of this? And … living in chic/dainty/aged Flask Walk was like living in a Dickens novel, with me as the gently wayward artist, she as a mysterious benefactor-cum-muse, and the little French restaurant the place where we entertained our friends when Fran rebelled against my greasy cooking.

As I said, we rattled past Camden Town, down to Embankment … and then back to the District Line (like touching base) eastward bound. And bound for a long time as I sat there clueless while Fansion hummed something that could well have been Brahms. After Elm Park there was "Hornchurch-le-Mont" and I knew what was up; yes, this certainly was a greater London. The station was large, like a baronial hall, tiled dark blue and white. I noticed an advertisement for Dubonnet and for a Johnny Hallyday concert. The current me was wanting to get this over with as quickly as possible. How much would I be made to see?

The exit quickly became wrought iron, like a fire escape, and soon we could smell hot bread and other delicious, sweeter smells. I knew we were in the back room of the *boulangerie*

I used to visit most mornings for our baguette, though I did not recognise the middle-aged woman behind the counter. She was the same type as the one who usually served me, being Frenchly prim and crisp, but she was different.

Docteur Fansion!
Enchanté, Madame. [the old charmer kissed her hand]
Très content de vous revoir ...

And a bit more of this sort of thing.

It's explanation time again. In her late teens, Fran had been given a sum of money and had bought with it a very dilapidated ex-presbytery in Picardy, in a village called Bracy-le-Mont, which is where we were. In her telling, the effort of getting the place into the lovely shape it was in in 1975 could only be topped by the efforts of Peter the Great in building St Petersburg on a swamp; though it seems she had recruited a series of boyfriends based on their building and interior decorating prowess.

Being there was heaven to me. The ex-presbytery stood at the top of a long valley, wooded on the far side, where the horns of stag hunters could be heard, and on which, in the early morning, mist sat as if scene-setting a fairytale. She would fling open the shutters onto this view. The sunlight on the white duvet had a bluish tinge; and I am getting carried away now.

Fansion and I followed the narrow street from the *boulangerie* to the *presbytère*, and let ourselves in through the kitchen door, where the silence was a pressure that pushed against me. Then through to the sitting room, shuttered and cool, where The Me was sleeping soundly on a sofa. Around the sofa – indeed, all over the room – were small shards of wood and black plastic covering the richly patterned carpets on the flagstones. (I think that will do.)

This was the day after Fran's birthday, and we had been spending a long weekend in Bracy. It didn't feel to me as if there was anything in the air particularly, but things were not quite right. Fran employed her social-Monty style a lot on those rare occasions she had anything to say. As for me, Bracy seemed to bring out exactly what was wrong with the low-soft-swing of Flask Walk. I mooched about and played a lot of guitar; or rather I thrashed away at a semi-acoustic with a plastic back that was plugged into my amp, a huge old Vox that, when warmed up, sounded as rough and 1963 as you could possibly wish. I sang, or rather I mimicked Dylan and Jagger like a drunk busker. Indeed, drunk was not far from the mark, as my performances were helped along by chain-drinking Leffes. This was done in my study (*study!*) in a far corner of the house, but was well audible to Fran ... well audible to the deer in the forest too.

I need to point out two dangers here. Yes, it's lecture mode again ... Booze and Dylan. We all know booze has to be treated with respect, but some people, like me, should touch it hardly at all. Fran was a drinker. I learned to join in but in doing so turned my flickering but distinctive personality – should people *ever* say "my personality"? – into an ugly unfocus. As for Dylan, somewhere in the world right now there is some poor swine being made to do the washing up by a girlfriend who is singing Dylan snippets to dramatize the situation. These may include ...

> Can you cook and sew
> Make flowers grow?
> Do you understand my pain?

"Do you understand my pain?" says it all. This is a late line but there's a lot of it about, even in my beloved *Blonde on Blonde*, among the accurate surrealism and other glories ... you know this already. In short, whatever Dylan himself is like, his lyrics fuel a special state – of hero-victim, artist-child (there, I've stopped short of my usual triplet). But what's important in all this is that it's a real turn-off to women. The yommered lyrics to "Positively Fourth Street" have a similar effect on women to fiddling with a shoe tree while passion beckons from the duvet or going into an Eccles-Bluebottle routine after an exploratory kiss.

At the tail end of supper the night before, during which Fran had been monologuing about the true nature of this and that in an unnatural way, I got up from the table and nipped into my study (*study!*) for some reason. More likely than not I'd been thinking of something while she was going on and wanted to jot it down, or check a chord in my chord book. When I got back to the kitchen she had cleared the table and was strenuously washing up. I poured myself another glass of wine and went to the sitting room, settling down with a book of Robert Crumb's strip cartoons. Fran came in.

— Leopold?

— Yes?

— I think we're finished now. Surely you know there's something missing. While you were cooking supper I packed your things away in your drawers.

— You *what!*

— I washed all your bits and pieces yesterday and put them away in your drawers so you can pack them for tomorrow. We leave tomorrow, early.

I went straight to the bedroom and pulled out the top right-hand drawer of the *commode* – as she insisted on calling it.

(I had the right hand, she the left.) There was the birthday present I'd given her the day before. I'd bought it in Oxford on a trip to see Paul (yes, he got in easily). He was thriving there, marked out in his Junior Common Room, so far as I could tell, as a sweet-natured-though-odd (the speech) boffin and excellent rugger player who liked a drink. I had seen it in the window of a ridiculously overpriced art shop in The High – a dusky pink dish or plaque with a design on it in white, after Chagall's lovers, with flourishes of blue here and there. I thought it was gorgeous; though some would have put it down as "pretty" and others as "pretty-pretty". It had cost a fortune (to me, because I really had no money of my own, only access to Fran's goods-and-services).

— Why did you put this in here?
— Don't like it. Clearly you do, so you can have it. Junky stuff.

I took the thing and smashed it hard on the stone floor. Why? Haven't got a baldy surr. Maybe two things were going on. My life was collapsing, falling in from above, so I felt the least I could do was to join in and do some collapsing of my own ... oh, just to show I had a drop of *agency* here. Oh, and I had to show just how much she had hurt me. I did not have to look hard for ways to strengthen the point. I rushed into my study (*study!*), got my guitar and turned the sitting room into a threshing floor. My God, this was thorough guitar destruction, making Pete Townsend's efforts look like minor adjustments to the machine heads.

She went straight to bed. I went straight for the whisky and drank deeply before keeling over on the sofa. And now Fansion and I were watching The Me from the other sofa, until

Fran bustled in. She told The Me to wake up and get up if they were to catch their booked ferry. She sat on the edge of the sofa.

— Come on, Leo. [*Leo?*] Get up!
— Sorry about the mess.
— I'll clear up some and leave the rest for Monsieur Dupont.
— Look. I don't know how to say this. You may not have much confidence left in you and me, but I've got enough for both of us. Did you really mean what you said last night?
— Yes. [*tenderly, and she took his hand*] I don't love you any more. [*this soft voice was new to The Me*]
— But [*he seemed to take this as good news*] you've never said you loved me in the first place. So at least you *did*.
— Of course I did. How else could I have put up with you. [*kindly but patronising smile*]
— Wassproblemthen?
— Living with you is like living alone. You aren't really there when you are there, so being with you has become worse than being alone. You don't *engage*. You talk, you make jokes and plans and narrate things, but I could be anybody or I could be a hologram of me. You know what a solipsist is?
— Of course.
— You are that weird thing – a total solipsist who is also a gifted actor who's learned over the years – why, I've no idea – to *act* engagement with others when really the only reality for you is here. [*she taps his head*] Now come on. I'll make coffee and you can get some bread.

I recall the *Bonne journée!* of the real boulangerie lady that morning.

Fansion did something that was more of a tap than a

squiggle, and we were in the back of Fran's big Mercedes sitting either side of the Vox amp – roadies from the future.

They started in silence and continued in silence. There was total silence in the car till Fran turned on the radio and translated (that kindly patronising again) that the bulletin was about Britain's forthcoming referendum on whether it should leave the Common Market (EEC). Now, obviously there is projection aplenty here, but I fancied I could almost *see* The Me thinking, from behind.

After about half an hour ...
— Fran?
— Yes?
— I have an idea for a killer performance. It'll be political and countrywide.
— You're the least political person I know.

Then The Me stiffened and in strangulated stage-cockney said:
— And so is Jimmy Paxton hun-political. He would like to be hun-political, Ma'am, but how can he stand idly by an' see the country wot he loves being a slave to those Europeans in their big shiny offices. We never got independent from the Romans and from Charley Mane only to enslave ourselves all over again, Ma'am. Albion Unchained, I call my group. They'm small right now, right enough, but we'm growin' like a bloody virus. Pardon my French.
— I'm behind you.
— You'll support this?
— Sure will. We'll talk in a couple of days. Of course, you can't stay at Flask Walk so I'll let you off at a phone box when we get back to town and you can call Nick. I'm sure he'll let you crash at his.

Pete: So you reckon this was when the iron entered your soul, Dud?

Dud: Yeah ... Could of been that. Or it could of been me chalfonts givin' me jip.

9: Leo is No Saveen

As I'd had one foot on the platform of "East Kensington" earlier today, and one foot on the train at the start of this journey of mine, the country had one foot in and one foot out of the European Union. Look, there is nothing I can say about the 2016 referendum that's not already cliché-mud as soon as it's said. But that doesn't stop me saying this. In his novel *Success*, written three years after the 1975 Europe referendum, Exchange-and has his main character say "the yobs are winning". I don't know when the yobs started winning, when the sad heavies began to get their sad way, but sure as hell they're winning now. They won the 2016 referendum, after all, though they were rather little in evidence in 1975.

To put it in a completely different way, the 1975 referendum was called, as now, merely to keep the ruling party together. "I waded through shit so that others could indulge their consciences," said Harold Wilson. But public opinion in those days was firmly on the side of staying in, and the issue of sovereignty had rather little to do with it. Neither did the issue of immigration.

— You, boy! Second row from the back ... Why was that?

— Because there was no single market, sir, in 1975, sir, and so no "freedom of movement", sir.

— Good. Now fetch me some tea. Moustache-cup, remember!

Enoch Powell and Tony Benn were banging on about loss of sovereignty, but Powell was off the map in Northern Ireland and many on the left thought Benn was a flaky poseur. "Posturing ninny" is a nice phrase I am borrowing from Auberon Waugh, who used it about Michael Foot, but it could be pretty freely spread over many of the left-leavers ... *maybe*. And ... and this is the main point: there were no popular figures on the right or centre spouting about our sovereignty, "our" laws, "our" money ... Who remembers the renegade Liberal MP Oliver Smedley and his Keep Britain Out group? I've forgotten him already. Now, of course, The Me wasn't thinking thoughts like this on the motorway to Calais. He was not following any line of reasoning: he had spotted a loophole and was planning a way to climb into it and then kick the ladder away.

When Fran parked the Mercedes in the ferry queue, Fansion and I got out and headed for a tacky bar inland a bit. *Ça Va, Jean!* said the barman, blowing fag ash on the glasses he was polishing; which Fansion acknowledged with a wave. Same old drill: into the back of the shop, down fire-escape-style stairs, then out to a tiled box of a tube – not Metro – station. It was called "Ubley", which later reflection told me was a tired hint towards the station between Becontree and Barking – Upney. Ha! I say. Ha-Ha!

We got off at Monument and on to the eastbound Central Line at Bank, after a cartilage-challenging trek through a tunnel, and then off at White City after a cat-gut yank that nearly left me on the floor. It was a good bet that we would then have to get to the BBC Television Centre and to the recording of the show that introduced the country to Jimmy Paxton. Needless to say, Fansion knew his way both from tube to the Centre and from within it to the right studio. I was dying to sit down but the place was packed so we leaned against the studio wall like a couple of invisible groupies. (Ever tried being an invisible groupie?)

There was The Me at the end of the row, having transformed himself into a spruce, upstanding, [*keep going*] wholesome, dull, [*stop!*] oddity. I can tell you, it was a hell of a job finding a barber who would give you a "short back and sides" in those day, especially one as severe as mine had to be. His hair had a sharp, high parting and a little quiff with a strand falling down from it, as if he'd just been doing a spot of cobbling. But the masterstroke was the shirt. This was a very bold red-black-yellow check, like a boy's cowboy shirt or a garish tartan, and with the collar turned up and the tips winged out, as favoured by the early Rockers. Tommy Steele was brought to mind. There were brown braces holding up sensible charcoal trousers, which The Me's character would have pronounced "trahziz".

This was the live broadcast of a programme called something like *Decision Time* or *In or Out?*, with an *Any Questions* format: questions from the audience that each panel member had to answer, after which it was back to the questioner to say what he thought of the answers. There were two leavers (not called that then) and two remainers (not … etc.). The leavers were Denzil Davies (Labour, nice, emotional) and Edward du Cann (Tory, "soppy-stern"); the remainers were Nigel Lawson (Tory, a Europhile then; funny old world) and Denis Healey (Labour, funny, difficult to control. I remember before the broadcast started Healey's mic picking up "Oh fuck *orf*, Nigel"). The Me knew that his question would be towards the end and he knew this because Fran's father had friends in the BBC who owed him a favour.

Robin Day was in the chair. He said in his usual impatient way:

— And the next question comes from Mister Jimmy Paxton from Leytonstone.

— Here, sir.

— Go ahead then!

— Would the panel agree with me ... [*by now The Me had perfected the high, constricted way of speaking working-class London, and it was ultra-clear, like someone calling for a toast in tin mugs of hot tea at a boy scout jamboree ... that'll do*]

— Not so fast ... I'm old and ugly enough to know [*general laughter*] that's a prelude to a speech, not a question. Please ask the panel a *direct* question.

— My apologies, Mister Day. I just want to know why we have 'erd so little tonight, and in the whole weeks up to now, about Bri'ish culture. How can we hang on to our precious way of life that has kept us goin' through wars and all kinds of freats from outside if we are watered dahn by European-ness. I am English first, Bri'ish second, and not in the littlest bit European. That's alien to blokes like me, sorry.

— I'm still not sure that *was* a question from our "bloke". But, Edward du Cann ...

— [*harrumph harrumph*] The economic case ... [*harrumph harrumph*]

— Nigel Lawson!

— *De haut en bas* simper *De haut en bas* simper not only not a question but fails to make any substantive point at all *De haut en bas* simper – Does Mr Paxton read the newspapers? *De haut en bas* simper ...

— Denzil Davies!

— [*Welshly soothing Welshly soothing*] The young man speaks with great passion [*Welshly soothing*]; one can sympathise with his feelings, but ... [*Welshly soothing*]

— Denis!

— Anybody listening to this young man will have heard the best case articulated, though in an extremely bizarre way, for remaining a member of the EEC. Frankly, no one *cares* about what you *feel* you are; and you are in a tiny minority in any event. The fact is, we *are* Europeans – by history, geography, and blood. I know that, like all friends, we fight amongst ourselves; and this Europe-wide alliance is putting a stop to that. Does this young man not like peace? He presents himself [*I had the feeling at this point hearing it again, but did not have it at the time, that Healey thought something was fishy about our Jim*] as a patriot. Patriots want what's best for their country. Would he like us to be isolated and poorer ... and weak? I ask, like Lady Bracknell, merely for information. [*laughter*]

— Satisfied, Mister Paxton?

The Me had been stung by Healey, and some of the anger was genuine here:

— I fink the panel succeeded really well in trying to make me look small. Succeeded in tryin' but not in doing it. [*silly, clever-clever, bad start*] I'm pretty sure in finkin' that all of you on the panel have got good educations at Oxford, or if not, Cambridge. I don't have one of them and speak from me 'eart. And what's so blinkin' funny about being a bloke? There are plenty of blokes and girls [*pron. gewls*] out there who fink like me. I'll take you in turn. Mister Doo-cunn, we're on the same side, but you try to impress people like me wiv talk about economics and arguments on money lines an' that. It's not so hard really. Me and my old Mum knows all there is to know about economics: you lives wivin your means. Same applies to a country. [*was Margaret Thatcher watching this? I wonder*] Just do that and let

Europe do what it wants. It's about the British soul, not abaht money!

— Please hurry up! [*Day*]
But this was "good television" so they kept Paxton on.

— And Mister Lawson, what's the point of readin' the newspapers when they all feed me propaganda about how good it is to be in the Common Market? Eh? [*some audience shouts of "hear hear"*] Mr Davies ... again, I'm not quite sure if I got the right word here, but I fink it's patron-onising. Fanks anyway. Finally, Mister Healey. It's not what you are that counts, it's how you *feel*. And people like me can't ever feel like Europeans or citizens of the world [*pron. wewd*]. We can't afford foreign holidiz or foreign food. We stay at home and proud to be here. Yes, you talks about being isolated and poor ... well [*wewl*] I'd rahver be isolated and poor and FREE than a sociable, well-orf SLAVE. And if you agree wiv me, folks, [*looks into camera*] join our little party called ALBION UNCHAINED. Write to PO Box 114, London, or phone 01 8654331. PO Box 114. Fanks.

By this time Robin Day was laughing his head off. (After an emergency phone call to the producer, I think.)

This did the job. The PO box letters (poured in) and the phone number (ever-ringing) led to a flat between the Euston Road and Bloomsbury – one of those solid, stolid joints where quite elderly people kept themselves to themselves. Here I lived, planned, worked, and had my pretend-being going in and out in a Beatle wig and shades. Fran and Fran's family rented flats all over London, so not only did they provide this one but a just-plausible address for Jimmy Paxton, which was in the sub-suburban no-man's-land between

High Road Leyton and the Leytonstone Underground Station. Here the population was fairly respectable but sometimes transient and often Indian or Jamaican. Almost no pubs or corner shops. So it was just about possible that a "young bloke" and his "old Mum" could have recently rented a basement (hard to spot comings and goings) flat there. The idea was that Jimmy was an unskilled labourer and his Mum a cleaner who moved from pillar to post in London wherever the work was. His Dad had died ten years earlier.

Two precautions. There had to be an "old Mum". She was an actress called Eileen who tottered in and out of the flat in Hainault Road looking sweet and dopey, sometimes carrying shopping, and sometimes accompanied by Jimmy at times when there were people about. Actually, it was real shopping: vodka, orange juice, crisps, Cadbury's Fruit and Nut, and more vodka. The Me wrote little scripts for her. Also, The Me had to tell Mum and Dad, and Nick too, to deny as best they could that Jimmy Paxton was Leo, saying the guy just looked like him; and they only had to keep this up until the vote. Dad said down the phone, in Dad-sardonic:
— Yes, of course, it's an artwork. It's a work of art right enough. What else could it be, Leo?

Nowadays this backstory would have been exploded in a day. But apart from some sniffing around by *Private Eye*, nothing was done. Two factors here. The main one was Fran's Dad, a businessman who owned majority chunks of lots of things, enough to exert influence when he needed to. Threats to withdraw advertising from the main papers added up to a case for their sitting on their hands. He helped Fran (and therefore The Me) out of guilt, having left her mother when she was three. Also, the press and other media did not go in for heavy-duty investigation in those days. Too expensive. Yes, there was the Insight team at the *Sunday Times*, but they went after medical issues or political scandals, not dodgy loners. And Jimmy only became relevant in the run-up to the vote, so he was ignorable.

The TV appearance was a kick-start that we – Fran headed the "we", and it's boring to go into the whole operation, personnel, and so forth – followed this up with newspaper ads and fliers in the streets. But we needed a rocket of publicity to get us to true celebrity. Fran again; and yes, you may ask why she did this. She just liked *doing*. She threw a birthday party for Pappy that touched him so much he coughed up for a series of TV ads for Albion Unchained.

They started with a back view of Jimmy whitewashing a wall (in vest and dungarees), with intermittent shots of his happy singing mush, singing this (The Me had heard the song in an episode of *Dixon of Dock Green*):

> Slap-dab slap-dab up and down the brick work
> Slap-dab slap-dab all day long
> In and out the corners
> Round the Johnny Horners
> We're a pair of fair clean goners
> Slap-dab slap-dab with the whitewash brush

He puts down his brush, wipes his hands, and says to the camera:

Hello there!
Now, we've all got to earn a crust, and this is how I earn mine when I'm not on the campaygn trail. Hard work for a decent screw, and I knows who me boss is. I see him every Friday wiv me waygies.

The guys and gals in this country used to know who their bosses was. Used to, till we joined the Common Market. What do they call it now? The E–E–C, innit? Now our bosses sit in shiny offices on the continong passing laws that we got to obey or else. Parly-ment used to be our boss, but it ain't no more.
Wanna do something abaht this?
Join us in Albion Unchained.

A beshadowed suited man screen-left hands him an envelope.

Hello, Charlie ... Friday today, almost forgot. [winks at camera] *Fanks a bunch.*

This too did the trick. Most things did, and we were soon rolling in money and celebrity endorsements, so much so we were able to pay back Fran's Dad a fair chunk ...

But to return to the tour ... Fansion and I went back to the Central Line and headed west, with a sizable cat-gut yank around Marble Arch that told me we would be shooting well ahead in time. Off at Holborn, round the corner to Red Lion Square, and into the Conway Hall.

We came in while Jimmy was winding up (in both senses). But more interesting than his ultra-predictable act was the audience. These were not the dregs, apart from some sad heavies in platforms (to be sung to the tune of "Bengali in Platforms") and skinheads trapped in last year's look. There were a lot of families with children enjoying a night out, and a solid block of old ladies who no doubt wanted to mother Jimmy. Through his teeth he lied away, accidentally predicting what was to come.

An' let me tell you, the *Daily Mirror, Express, Mail* and all the rest don't want you to know this, but there's a document going around that proves there's plans on the continong not only to make it easier for Europeans to come over here to work but plans to have one currency for all of the EEC. After all, the second E is for *economic*, am I right? Well, let me tell the establishment that hides the troof from us these two fings:

One – Haynds off Bri'ish jobs! Unemployment's high now. Just fink how much higher it's gonna get.

Two – 'Ere's a question for yuh ... What's the strongest country in the EEC? [*some shouts of "France"*] Nah, Germany, that's who. Do you fink my old Dad – God rest his soul – and his mates fought a war only to lose it to the German Mark? Do you wanna say goodbye to Her Majesty on a pahnd note? Wanna buy your pork pies wiv Deutschmarks? I know I don't.

Haynds off our jobs and haynds off our pahnd! [*huge cheers*]

Now, I'm going to give you a bit of a musical treat. [*shocked silence*]

At this point I'll tell you that during the height of my jazz years I had taken trumpet lessons, getting good enough to play a couple of bebop numbers, the intention being to become a kind of bluesy Don Cherry, knowing that Freddie Hubbard was beyond me.

Jimmy took out The Me's old trumpet and with maximum head-shaking vibrato played "St James Infirmary Blues" straight into the mic. He played it a few times, stopped and said, "Feel free to sing along, ladies and gents." He played it a few more times – a perfect choice of a tune because it suggests a kind of noble self-pity, which so many of the audience carried before them like a banner. (Yes, this is oversaid, but never mind, eh?)

As the audience was singing the simple line, Jimmy hushed them with his hands and said:

— Now I got anuvver treat for you all. I'm gonna innerduce you to my new gewl. Come out, Days!

A pretty blonde with bubbly curls dressed like a librarian walked out from the wings and into Jimmy's arms.

— Now listen, my gewl's real name is Jacqui Bailey, but I call her Daisy May. Anybody know who Daisy May is? [*some shouts of "Saveen and Daisy May"*] That's it, Saveen and Daisy May. Used to love that when I was a nipper. Anyway, when Days – as I call her – first said hello to me I was reminded of the way little Daisy used to speak ... Say hello to the people, darlin'.

— Heeeellooo. [*I'm sure some of the audience thought Jimmy was ventriloquizing a four-year-old's voice*]

— Anyway, my gewl and I reckon tonight's gone really well. Who agrees? [*hoorays, of course*] – so we're goin' on up to Walfamstowe tonight to get a fish 'n' chip supper to celebrate. What? You what? [*to the skins, mainly*] "Saveen" sounds foreign? The geezer's real name is Albert Langford. Now go out and enjoy this lovely May evening and VOTE NO to save your country!

I was shocked by this, shocked by the conviction, the transformation. Actually, in the moment of saying it, if I recall, The Me believed every word, not giving a damn that the larger project was a dogshit project. A word about Jacqui. I'll call her this rather than Days. Jimmy looked too wholesome to encourage groupies; but Jacqui had kept presenting herself night after night in the front row, following him backstage. She was besotted. Also pretty – very pretty, in fact. Also, Jimmy, or rather The Me, was lonely. He did not go in for one-nighters, but always had a girl on the go. Added to which, in Fran's words, without a partner Jimmy could come over as a sexless Mummy's boy. Of course, the downside was that he had to keep up the act all the time with Jacqui, even in bed.

By this time, Jimmy and Jacqui had a couple of minders, who whisked them off, followed by us after a tap of the modem, to a dimly-lit curry house in Fitzrovia. We sat on the table next to theirs, with the minders filling their faces a little way away. What struck an observer was the way Jacqui would not take her eyes off him, following every forkful of lamb rogan josh to his mouth, hardly eating herself. Secluded as this spot was, Jimmy still needed a disguise, and as on most days he wore a pork pie hat and large plain-glass granny glasses tinted yellow. Not a bad look, in fact.

— I been thinking, Jim.
— Go on.
— About our future, after the vote like.
— We'll just lead a quieter life, go on the same way, doll, that's all. Don't fret, doll. [*Christ, this was hard work some-times*]
— Are you the marrying kind, Jim? [*yes, I know this tends towards Ron-and-Eff – but Eff would have said "beloved"*]
— I could be.

Actually, The Me was not just stringing her along. I love adoration and there was something ador*able* about her. She hardly had a word to say for herself, had no education to speak of (worked as a school secretary), but being with her was like opening a fairytale that you knew would turn out well. Actually, it wasn't like that, but you get the idea. I'm not the protective type, but I wanted – adopting a favourite phrase of hers – to "cuddle her up" against the world as it nastily is.

— Mum and Dad were asking if your intentions were honourable. [*a smile that betrayed a total lack of innocence*]

— 'Course they ain't, Days!

She lived with her Mum and Dad in Acton, where I'd been for Sunday lunch, acting up a storm. In the afternoon we watched some sporting event on TV while Jacqui watched me watching.

— Call me old-fashioned but I think that if a man and a woman are in love, then the best thing to do is to get wed. Soon as poss. You are in love with me, aren't you, Jim?

— It's like you'm askin' me if two and two makes four. I loves you, Days, heart and soul. [*The Me meant every word*]

At this point, a point that brought a tear to my eye and a shrug to the shoulders of Fansion, we left for the Warren Street tube, the Victoria Line, a change onto the Central at Oxford Circus, and another westerly transit.

Around this time, the polls were not looking so good for Wilson. When the referendum was called, a Yes vote was a racing certainty, but as time went on there'd been a narrowing, a narrowing that – let's face facts, brothers and sisters – I had more than a minor hand in. Articles in the *New Statesman* would refer to "Paxton Nationalism" and "Paxton's shameless, faux-naïve harvesting of right-wing isolationism". Given this, I felt – OK, Fran and I did – that I had to submit myself to a properly probing TV interview. My routine turning down of requests was beginning to look fishy. I turned them down not because I feared political exposure, because at this time in my life I feared nothing; I did it because a TV close-up would make me easy to recognise by, say, old college or schoolfriends who had found me "difficult to admire". ("Day would be on the blower to da press in two shakes," as Jimmy would say.) I got round this by wearing contact lenses that darkened my light-blue eyes to a dark between blue and green, and by wearing in my mouth a patented transparent device (common now) that dentists give to people who grind their teeth at night. This "filled out me old chops a treat". I had guessed that we were on the way back to the Television Centre where this would be put to the test on a late-night news programme called *Twenty-Four Hours*. Only a modest cat-gut yank, more like mild indigestion, happened this time.

I had guessed right. Off at White City then swiftly in to the studios. I'd refused to wear makeup because the makers-up would soon spot my enhanced chops and because I wanted to look pale, intense, hungry [*another triplet, note*]. I wore a plain white shirt and a narrow black tie – looked a bit Hitler Youth when I saw it again. Fansion and I sat next to Jacqui, just off camera. She was visibly willing him on. An angel.

I recall that my interviewer, Robert McKenzie (also a Professor at the LSE), was charm itself before the live broadcast, chatting to me about anything but politics; but things changed when the red light came on. The early bit of the interview was easy, with The Me being allowed to do his act. But later ...

— You say you don't read the newspapers "on principle", but

if you did you would see that the latest polls put the Yes campaign only two points ahead of No, which is well within the margin of error ... And please don't say I'm blinding you with science. So there's a real danger ...

— Danger!

— If I could just finish my question: *danger* that in two weeks time we could vote to leave the Common Market, something that the overwhelming majority of people who are thoughtful and knowledgeable [*camera cuts to Jimmy pretending to stifle a yawn*] about these matters believe would be a disaster for this country. Do you not think it is, to put it mildly, irresponsible of you to be encouraging a No vote by stimulating what Nye Bevan called "an emotional spasm". After all, you have no arguments – only emotional appeals to an idea of Britishness and a frank aversion of for-eigners.

At this moment, The Me was toying with the idea of "doing a Hailsham" on McKenzie. (The old fraud had pretended to explode with righteous anger at Bob McKenzie during the Profumo scandal.) But this would not suit Jimmy. Instead, he smiled an unwise smile (the anti-grinders) and said:

— To be honest wiv you, Mister McKenzie, I takes no notices of what Aneurin Bevan said about anyfink. During the last war, when our backs was against the wall, he spent all his time sniping at the National Gov'ment and going on abaht nationalisin' coal and that. Underminin' ol' Clem is what he did.

— The National Health Service? [*amused*]

— Oh yeah, Clem put him in charge of that 'cus he was a bulldozer. If he hadn't done it somebody else would of.

— You seem to know a lot about politics; that is, for some-body who says he's completely ignorant of it.

— My old Dad used to tell me a lot, before he passed away.

— What job did your father do, if I may ask? Your biography is strangely thin.

— 'E was a cobbler. Then towards the end of his life a night watchman. The fumes of the brazier did for 'im.

— That's sad.

— Yes, he was a cobbler, going from aahs to aahs.

— From what to what? From house to house?

— Yes [*mock posh*] from hows to hows. As you're Canadian, you may struggle wiv [*not a very Jimmy expression*] me London accent.

— I understand you very well, so well indeed that I can't help thinking, along with a number of commentators, that there is something counterfeit about what one may call your working-class persona. Are you not, as you would no doubt put it, [*an excruciating Cockney*] "just 'avin a larf"?

— [*Jimmy puts his head in his hands: to give The Me time to think, and to wind himself up for an Oscar-winning performance*] This 'as been a very hard time for me, Bob. I am not a natural leader of men at all. I'm shy and keeps meself to meself when I can. I suppose it was a kind of "emotional spasm" that made me stand up and be cahnted. But every day is a battle wiv stress an' tension an' that, so much that the docs says I'm near to crackin' up; which I just pray I don't do before June the fifth. Tell you what: me stress levels is so high I can't 'elp but keep grindin' me teef. Look! [*Jimmy whips out his tooth guard*] I go'a wear dis otherwise I'll be wearin' me enamel away and producing dangerous enzymes.

— I'm sorry.

— That's OK, Bob. [*quickly puts guard back in*] I don't mind going frew a bit of pain of the mind if it helps me country come to 'er senses. Frow off the chains sounds a bit rich, dunnit; but that's what it's all abaht.

Bob McKenzie said "thank you", and shortly after, "shit!"

The next broadcast on behalf of Albion Unchained showed Days and her Jim wandering along the beach at Southend, eating fish and chips and drinking Vimto. Voiceover? No, I can't be bothered. Use your imagination.

On the phone to Nick the night after, they improvised an alternative voiceover: "Vimto. The perfect drink for washing away fish-and-chip residue from your tooth guard. Like fish and chips but hate grinding your teeth? Drink Vimto!

With about a week to go to the vote, Yes and No were neck and neck.

As for me and Fansion, it was ... back to the Central, east to Oxford Circus, south to Victoria on my beloved District, then east to South Kensington where I had been headed at the start of this day of days. Not the V&A this time – the Albert Hall. We passed the V&A in the tunnel from tube to Emperor's Gate, and it seemed to shout "Water under bridge, or what!" Up the road and into a box on the second tier.

The place was packed and accents were heard from all over the UK, and many Jimmy lookalikes were to be seen. Ten trumpeters walked on to the stage and started to play "St James Infirmary Blues" repeatedly as The Me's words to the tune were projected onto a huge screen. A recorded Jimmy on a tannoy encouraged us to join in ...

> *Jimmy Paxton is the man who speaks for us*
> *Jimmy Paxton is the one we trust*
> *It's as simple as the Clapham omnibus:*
> *We'll leave Europe 'cus we know we must*

Then the man himself strolled on, dressed in a white suit, emphatic red boots, black shirt, and white-and-blue tie. "Altogever nah," he said. Then:

— OK, folks, settle down. Fanks, fanks a bunch. Right.

Nah, ladies and gents, boys and gewls, victory is in our sights. [*huge cheer*] And because it is, we have to fink about what's going to 'appen to the

Country we love when we're aht of the EEC. What

We gonna do wiv our hard-won freedom?

But to help us fink abaht this I need to quote the words uv Will Shakespeare, oo said:

Meanwhile we must expose our darker purpose.

Right?

Darker purpose? I mean I gotta speak frank abaht Europeans

So we can fink aah much we wanna be doing with them after the fifth of June.

The French? Researchers at the University of Oxbridge has shown

That 67% of French women is prostitutes, yeah!

Talk about supporting the economy by oo-la-la, right!

The Germans! Ooo likes a frankfurter, a nice smooth sausage? Know why they're so smoove?

What is the secret ingredient?

Aborted human babies is the answer.

Anovver fing. Professor Damien Trench of Oxbridge University has documiniry evidence, right, that Helmut Schmidt is the love child of some Swiss tart an' Adolf blinkin' 'itler, that's ooo.

First shocked silence in the hall, then chatter and some scuffles and some people leaving.

The Dutch? Know why them tulips grows so well? I'll tell yuh:

They fertilizes the soil with old folks oo's just kicked the bucket.

The Belgians? Cowards.

Spaniards? Their women, right ... their women is so hairy that 75% of 'em shayve their chins every blinkin' day.

I wanna turn nah to fish. We all like a bit of chish and fipps, don't we, Missus, eh?

Well, here's the news. Our quo'as is shrinking fanks to EEC law.

We will have to protect our fish, and to do this,

I, James Raleigh Paxton,

Call for the erection of a floating barrier between us

And the continong.

Tell you what too, the fish near their coast tastes of garlic.

Mixed shouts were going up, many in support, much laughter from the journalists down the front. Mostly people were looking puzzled and depressed.

Turnin' to our shores, I tell you our darker purpose has got to be

To punish those who leak aaht foreign sympathies, right?

I mean these stuckup tarts and ponces oo say:

Ontray noo, vees ah vee, on passon

Velt-an showung. That kinda thing.

Any oo drink French wine rather than good British beer.

Tell you what, Missus ... put em in the stocks and empty the pos over 'em.

No ... no, listen ...

I could see the Frankie Howerd echo was nearly making The Me corpse.

... 'angin's too good for 'em!

The Me stopped and smiled on the mess in front of him and said in my own low, reedy, implicit voice ...

OK, just relax people. Jimmy Paxton doesn't exist. He's a work of art constructed by me; and my name is Leo Barber, who studied art in Penzance and Manchester. You might call me a performance artist or conceptual artist.

Art? Where's the art? you might say. Well, I'll quote Shakespeare in earnest now: *Art holds a mirror up to Nature ...*

A very long pause as two big minders got ready to carry him offstage, à la Dylan thence in 1966.

... just as a chimpanzee [*he got this from Paul*] will use a mirror to look at his own ARSE.

Off went The Me to a waiting car and on to the stage came Jacqui, like a bird fallen out of its cage.

We did not linger. Back to South Ken then north on the Piccadilly to Russell Square. The lift to the hall was crowded and I was squashed against people. This had happened on tubes but this time the oddness of my physical presence was brought home. We were substantial and visible, people avoided walking into us, made room for us, and I could feel them. But we were ignored, not attended to. Analogy? None, absolutely none come to mind, guv.

At the Exit side of the lift there was Jacqui, so I knew what was afoot.

We followed her up Marchmont Street towards The Me's flat. She had an uncharacteristically brisk walk and was much better dressed than usual – properly high-heeled, a chic pink dress and dark tights, handbag clutched to her side as if it contained all her worldly goods. When The Me opened the door and let her in, we nipped in behind her.

The shock on The Me's face, if I recall, was not due to seeing her again. I'd been expecting Fran, who'd promised to educate me in how I could syphon off money from what we'd raised in a nice and barely legal way. In fact, I'd given Jacqui very little thought, my consciousness ragged from the threats of extreme violence from one No-quarter and another.

She was smiling but looking hard at him as she said:
— I thought I'd take the bull by the horns, er, *Leo*. That was a bit of a smart exit.
— I'm so sorry. I could hardly let you in on it, so …
— Apology accepted. In fact, to tell you the truth I'm relieved. I was beginning to think you were a bit thick, and actually quite nasty deep down.
— I'm not perfect …
— And I was going to vote Yes actually.

Silence from both.

— And it's much nicer the way you speak – your real way, Leo.
— My colleague Fran is going to be here in a bit.
— I'll be quick then. I don't love you any the less Mister *Whatsisname*. I'm back for you. I'm all yours.

The Me looked tempted. I *was* tempted. As I say, not just an angel but a pretty angel.

— It can't work, Days … I mean Jacqui. It was all fiction.
— Our love was real, as real as me. Look, I know I'm not as educated as you are, and I don't know much about art, but I

can go to evening classes. I can take an Open University course on the history of art. I've got English GCE too.

— But ...

— Yes, I know I'm a bit dull compared to other girls you've been out with. Anyway, the thing is, Leo, we're having a baby.

— *You're* having a baby, you mean. [*having hardened his face*]

— It was meant to be.

— No it wasn't, love.

The way he said "love" was as a sexist interviewer would say it to a pretty actress who was getting the better of him. He scribbles on a piece of record card.

— This is the number of Francesca Ubley. She'll help you sort out the financial and, uh, medical side of things.

The Me obviously saw her tears as she tore up the card, but did not attend to them. Now, *there's* your analogy to mine and Fansion's physical presence.

Pete:
Tell you what, Dud, if I was a bit of iron I wouldn't be seen dead in your soul.

Dud:
If the fault is with the soul, the sovereigns
Of the soul must likewise be at fault, and first.
If the fault is with the souvenirs, yet these
Are the soul itself.

Pete:
You've come down with bloody
Wallace Stevens again, Dud. Try deep breaths.

Dud:
Better than that bloody Spinoza, Pete.

10: Too Early for "Rostle"

So I got *it,* and that was how. "It" was not just celebrity. Guys who play *football* for a living are celebrities. It was not notoriety. That comes to crooks. It was that special thing I'd always wanted: to be a shadowy, ambiguous self behind a somebody that was as recognisable as the Queen Mum and as safe as a concealed cliff edge. And it was near-universal attention. Before that time I could struggle to the surface for a gulp of public attention, but now I could swim along the surface. In fact, if I ever publish an autobiography, I'll call it *Swimming on the Surface.* No I won't: I'll call it *Performance* ... with a nice Stones hint. Actually, it's beginning to occur to me that *this* is my autobiography, complete with lashin's of what I've learned to call *l'esprit de l'escalier,* but in fact is not that. I'm telling it as it happened. Trying to.

Enough of this. As I mentioned before, I'd made a lot of people very angry and so I needed police protection. Death threats were sent to the papers – why there? – and to the Albion Unchained addresses. I could not eat in restaurants for a month or so after the Albert Hall event unless there was a plainclothes guy in the shadows with his lager and a sarnie. This did not stop papers like the *Mirror* from taking photographs of "brave Leo" eating out "defiantly", especially if the girl with me had an agent who was owed a favour by the editor. But more to the point, before Jimmy came on the scene, support for a Yes vote was falling, while the Yes sympathisers also seemed the ones less likely to vote. It was not neck and neck but it was far from healthy. Straight after the Albert Hall, polls showed the Yeses riding high, and in the end the Yes vote was about twice as high as the No.

I wasn't dumb enough, when asked, even to agree publicly that I had a hand in this, and yet neither was I dumb enough to say I was apolitical. I stuck to my mirror-up-to-nature line. I stuck to my less snappy if-the-aesthetic-motive-is-pure-it-will-reveal-the-truth-and-the-vote-should-be-based-on-truth-not-on-the-rantings-of-a-charismatic-idiot line. I didn't have time to vote, myself.

Otherwise, to those happy on the morning of June 6th – D-Day, by the way – I was the saviour of the nation; important, brave, yet refreshingly comic, as if an overlap could be found between Churchill and Cheerful Charlie Chester. The phrase "national treasure" didn't exist in those days, but that's what I was, for part of the nation.

This may seem all well and good; but it was not. For the obvious reason that to call what I'd done an art-performance or a piece of conceptual art was a lying, dogshit move; and those grumpy columnists who said what I did was nothing more than a prank that had damn-all to do with art were correct. This returns me to my watery metaphor. I had bounced myself up to the surface by stepping on something nasty, the back of a sea monster maybe, a water trampoline that was a giant shark's tongue. Do sharks have tongues? I was swimming now but would I need to call on the monster's support again? Could I keep swimming? Would my arms tire, just as I'm tiring of this metaphor?

This is not helpful, but these were the thoughts I had in mid-June of '75; and they were the thoughts that repeated on me as I walked up to Euston Square with Fansion. There were thoughts, too, of a Tony Hancock film called *The Rebel* in which he plays a talent-free modernist fantasist – enough already! – who becomes famous because the work of his talented flatmate is mistaken for his own. The poor sod keeps trying to show his own work instead of the good stuff, hoping for acceptance on the back of the counterfeit. It didn't work for the Hancock character and it wouldn't work for me. It didn't work for him because his own work was modernist dogshit compared to the well-executed, representational canvases of his flatmate; and it did not work for me because people only wanted to know about the dogshit. I made soundings by showing the *Guardian* art critic, who had been to interview me, some of the Annie Swynnerton stuff, and also some pastels I'd done in Bracy-le-Mont that took their cue from Moreau, showing Fran in various Goddess poses. He reported on my "directionless" path pre-Jimmy. I continued to draw every day and indeed did copies of some of my favourite Moreaus.

But I had to keep bloody swimming. The stroke I chose was the installation stroke. No snag that installations are hard work and expensive. The hard work was done by youths with rich mummies and daddies who slaved for nothing because I was Leo Barber, and the money in question poured in from sponsorships. Lloyds Bank would pay for the hire of the gallery, as would Colmans of mustard fame. Materials electrical, materials wooden, materials plastic; it was immaterial. American Express would foot the bill in return for a stamped-in mention. Workshop time and space fell into the lap of Leo.

As to ideas for installations, there was something in me that was past caring. There were a number of them. Some so corny and lumpen that they were even bad as dogshit – turds yellowing in the sun. One of the yellow ones involved a fashion show of metal clothes in a laundrette.

The only one I had any fun with was called *Radial Art Self*, and was inspired by something Paul told me about the learning experiments done with laboratory rats. More about Paul later, but for now I'll just say that he'd finished his brilliant degree at Oxford and was starting his PhD, shuttling between computer science and physiology.

For reasons I can't be bothered to go into, the rats have got to learn whether they have already visited the arm of a maze at the end of which there's food. Have they already finished the food there? They start out in a central, circular area off which a number of maze arms radiate. (Think of those horrible clocks with radiating prongs, like cartoon suns.) One may end near the door, another near the window. No matter; the main thing is that visitors to the installation walk to the end of an arm to see a slide of an artwork, most of them famous ones. Before they do so, they have their photograph taken and they type their date of birth into a clever-looking machine. They are supposed to be assigned to an arm of the maze based on their physiognomy and date of birth, but actually it's random, and the artwork they see is also randomly generated, though they are told that the *Radial Art Self* program is designed to work out which artwork best represents their "hidden self".

You may think of yourself as a shell-shocked tomato grower from Surbiton, but really you are one of Goya's "black" paintings. You may think of yourself as a lout whose soul floats on beer, but really you are as sensitive and measured as a Gwen John.

It's addictive for all the reasons that astrology and personality questionnaires are addictive. It's top-shelf, top-notch dogshit; and it was a hit for me.

Rather closer to art itself, to sculpture, were things I called "melds". All I had to do here was sketch a blending of, say, a leather glove and a leather jacket, an electric iron and a kettle, a skeleton and a birdcage, a sprinter made of felt and balsa wood shooting forward from the starting block of a two-seater sofa. I could then select between the talents of Jocelyn Wright-Hawksmoor recently graduated from the Slade, Pippa Lorry-Lode recently graduated from St Martins, and various others, and it would be done. In fairness to myself I did advise and chivvy along and even shape the thing sometimes; but it was a piece of cake.

Meanwhile, back at the Underground, we were travelling west on the Metropolitan Line from Euston Square. At the time I hadn't the foggiest where we were going, because it was around this time I'd started to employ drivers. My cars were modest affairs, and so were my drivers.

We got out at Wembley Park and headed for an unpleasant modern building called Fountain Studios; and when I saw the logo for London Weekend Television I knew what was afoot. This was the recording of my interview for *Aquarius,* a frothy arts programme that ITV put out in the seventies. I chose it because I was unlikely to be duffed up there by intellectuals – 'cus I ain't one, innit – and a sharp showbiz interviewer could skewer me with laughs (a Jonathan Ross could have pinned me to the wall). The interviewer was Russell Harty. He would, I thought, be easy meat.

As for Harty, I'm tempted to say "Google him, stranger." The question was why and how this camp chancer with Lego hair and a face that was too successful in catching the light ever came to prominence. In fact, lots of people, my Dad for instance, would "refuse to have him in my house" (i.e. turned off the TV if he was on) and decided it was all a matter of "pull" and "who you know". To put it simply, he was irritating.

But people seemed to *like* me, found me endearing, found me a chancer too but one that could be indulged so they could see how I would turn out. And in contrast to our Russell, the machinery of my coming to prominence had all been laid bare; indeed, the machinery was the message.

As I saw things, his self-confidence was fragile, held together by surface tension. What I would do was tease him in the first-pass exchanges, lobbing back answers that were broad-castable but with little burrs that would scratch at this surface. Why? Because word had got to me that he was planning to give me a hard time, that he had sharpened some questions in pursuit of a bit of intellectual "bottom". (Oooo, missus!) He had a third-class degree ... and as I add this you may wonder what on earth they found "endearing" about me.

The recording was not a relaxed affair; though when Fansion and I saw him smoking contentedly on the sofa, The Me seemed perfectly together. I remember Russell being alright when I turned up, like a naughty schoolboy wanting to share a joke, but once on the set he was more like a stern headmistress who'd been at the sherry. They were to show most of the Albert Hall address, some clips of Lansley and Jessica, and vox pops of people emerging from *Radial Art Self*; plus footage of me walking down Haverstock Hill and into a coffee bar. The voiceover was a would-be portentous Harty ... "But is it art? We have every right to ask that ..."

and so forth. We settled down near The Me as a voice said: "Studio. Recording 5-4-3-2-1. Russ!"

— You are, are you not, an artist, Mister Barber?
— I am not *not* an artist, yes, Mister Hah-*té* [*pronounced thus*]. That's what it says on my passport.
— But one could also, quite reasonably, refer to you as a prankster, could one not?
— One could, yes, one could *not* not do that [*broad smile*], but Mister Hah-*té* the question is what I actually *am*. Do you think that that's *all* Jimmy Paxton was ... err ... Russ [*pronounced to rhyme with puss*].

Russell did not like this one bit – the questioning of him and the name-play.

— Will you stop that! [*knowing this could be cut*]
— Stop what, Russ? [*rhymes puss*]
— OK Kevin, cut. Let's go again. [*his eyes referred to me as a "little shit"*]
— I thought your name was pronounced Hah-*té*. No idea how it's spelt. I'm dyslexic you see, like many ARTISTS.

They took at least "five" and started again. Actually, The Me didn't look very happy either. He had been expecting the name-play to upset Mister Hah-*té*; but also that he would plough on, weakened. What a pity, I thought, as I watched The Me, and am thinking freshly now, that Julian Barnes only became the *New Statesman*'s TV critic a few years after my interview. He used to call him – Harty – "Rostle". Which is *perfect*. It captures his posh-Yorkshire but absolutely nails his prissy faux-fastidiousness and prickliness (thistle). Imagine a Dickens character called Mr Rostle Harty. He, like Russell, would *also* be likely to say to a shy, tongue-tied girl (a beauty queen contestant, in this case), "Are you ever oother than monosyllabic?"

"Rostle" is genius, so I'll call him that from now on. Rostle began again ...

— In the clip we've just seen, you say that Jimmy Paxton is an artistic constrooction in so far as you hold a mirror up to nature. But does not the *true* artist, if I may say, hold up the mirror as an *end in itself*, not in the service of a political wind-up? A very dangerous one too. [*The Me looked surprised, and it seemed Rostle had been wound up in quite the wrong way*] Training your torch into some dark corners is hardly art, is it not?
— Don't you mean "is it?" – you don't need a "not" this time, Russ [*puss rhyme*]. Look, I'm ambitious. I wanted a big canvas, and the referendum was a big canvas. And a little bit of danger is no bad thing; ratchets up the tension.
— But my point, if I may press you a little harder, is about the word "art". Why call it this and not a prank – a prank on a big scale; never mind about canvases.
— Because Jimmy was an invention, the performance of an idea, of a concept.
— But concepts are one thing and – heavens to Betsy – doing and making are quite oother.
— There are two faces of art, Mister Hah-*té*: ideas and skills. I have some skills, but I want to be judged on my ideas, on the concepts that start up in me. Jimmy was one. He came to mind. What is creation other than having things come to mind? The artist is just somebody lucky enough to have interesting or attractive or *provocative* things come to mind – happening to him ... or her.

Everybody in the studio, including The Me and Rostle, obviously felt this was all wrong – the tone, the striving faces. The Me then said in broad Scouse:

— *It's hard werrk this, in't it?*

— My job is to put you on the spot.

— Why haven't you asked me about beauty? [*Rostle hated being questioned, and his upper lip was catching the studio lights a treat*]

— What about it?

— Art generally seeks beauty; and Jimmy was an ugly little toerag. I thought you'd get your teeth into that, Roos.

Rostle was rattled.

— Well you certainly made a beautiful career for yourself, if one may say. You have a beautiful house, apparently.

— I gave people what they liked and what they needed even if they didn't know they needed it; and I was rewarded for it. I *did* something, and it took imagination and guts. You've had a good career, too, Mister Hah-*té*. What exactly is it that you do again?

The cameras were still running. They kept this in and kept in Rostle's sudden backing off before the spotlight fell on himself.

— Like you, Leo, [*a forced smile*] I'm a kind of provocateur, without all the fuss [*rhyme with puss*] and pretention.

Then The Me, in a pantomime of Jimmy's voice:

— GAWD 'ELP US.

They cut after this, and The Me and Rostle recorded some anodyne stuff about The Me's biography, for which Fansion and I did not stay.

So The Me had not wiped the board with Rostle. When the interview was aired, critics tended to say they were "two peas in a pod", each of them mixing the earnest with the bitchy. If it did me any good at all, it showed there was a bit more to me than people thought. But what really had happened was that the serious and the ironic had killed each other off, leaving a flavourless residue.

The lesson for me was not to mix it: try to be taken seriously while dipping in to the frivolous now and then; all the while ignoring the dogshit foundations whilst building on them.

My seriousness project tended towards journalism, the kind where you don't go out the front door but wave some opinions about from your desk. This had to be in the broadsheet press, and so, through some people I met while pretending to be a drinker, I was able to persuade the *Guardian* to let me try a series of columns in the Saturday edition, called "The Neglected". Each was only 200 words and had been whittled down by subs from my 500-600. Each one was about an artist or musician I thought, or pretended to think, had been undervalued. Not a bad list:

• Gustave Moreau
• Earl Bostic
• Jimmy Powell and the Five Dimensions (A weird sort of R&B group whose small-of-stature lead did scat-singing of a desperate kind. A young Rod Stewart used to play harmonica and sing in the intervals when Jimmy went off to refresh his scat-chops.)
• George Frederic Watts
• Grace Slick and The Great Society
• John Tchicai (free jazz alto saxophonist)
But this was not *personal* enough. These could have been writ-

ten by anybody, especially as my prose was flat even after some rucking up by the subs and sharp prods from Fran. What I really wanted was to write about my doings or invented doings in the way that Jack Trevor Story did in the same edition of the same paper. The last eight words give the reason why they would not let me. But the Saturday *Times* did. The persona I presented there was as much an invention as Jimmy Paxton. I don't particularly like clubbing or art exhibitions, but I knew people who did, so I stole from them. Mostly it was a ratcheting up and a prettifying of my love life, with appropriate pseudonyms for the woman who shared time with me – Jolly Wilmot, Peggy O'Weed, Mable Black, The Faun – making sure that the tone was always one of self-deprecation and wonderment at the ways of those "girls". I hear Kingsley Amis liked it. Despite my determination not to mix seriousness and fun, I did hand down some rather sour judgements on fashion, music, and the theatre ... Kingsley again. But to suppress the Kingsley element, I also did some low-key performances, that I called my Personas, at poetry readings and literary festivals and other places beyond the Rostle-sphere.

I was all over the shop.

Be that as it was, we were back on the Metropolitan again, heading east to change at King's Cross, then north on the Northern Line, Edgware branch. I assume we were heading for the "beautiful house" Rostle had mentioned; and I was right. Off at Hampstead, then up and across to Frognal.

You may have thought my story really started with the Albert Hall scene. The public story, yes, but the story of the person who was the thread between the various Mes begins around here.

11: Psyche

It was a dark early evening in – I know this – November. We let ourselves into The Me's quietly splendid house and found him checking a casserole, turning over roast potatoes and up the music ... a barely conscious zeugma there. The Me had not seen Nick for ages and wanted to show him and his fiancée a good evening and that he was the same old Leo ... zeugma? Some excellent reds on the table and whites in the fridge, and a magnificent brandy waiting in the wings; for Nick was as much a boozer as The Me was not. Who knows about this "fiancée". Nick had given little away beyond that she was an engineer, an undergraduate when he had been a postgrad.

Fansion and I sat in separate chairs, of which there were many in the public-spirited sitting room, and heard the doorbell ring. Among the voices in the hall I thought I could hear the name "Lois" and I could certainly hear a failed change of gear, a hesitancy. "After you, Madame" we heard Nick say with a false brightness, and Lois walked in. This was difficult for me – to see her again. It was very difficult indeed; but you don't need to hear about that.

To help you out, you might think of a young Beryl Bainbridge or, in a more generic way, Juliette Gréco: dark clothes, long black hair, and a glowing paleness. Let me expand on the Bainbridge. It wasn't just that her face was a triangle and that the large eyes were linered all round: her eyes, with the support of a small, slightly smiling mouth, seemed perpetually to be asking a cheeky question to which she knew the answer. (Whew!) The clothes were all dark, as I said, but not corny all-black: deep chocolate and deep green with lighter green "witches'" boots. You have, of course, not heard the last of me on her.

"Give us a twirl!" said Nick in a silly nod to Bruce Forsyth.

She spoke:
— What a lovely room! [*her voice is low, accentless, unhurried and careful, like laying tiles*]

Everything in the room was white (memories of Knuckler Sid) bar the chairs (deep blue); and most of what was on the wall (mainly limited edition prints) was reddish. All of which led Nick to say:
— A most patriotic room, Mr Barber.
— We were just saying on the way over [*Lois*]: wouldn't it be funny if you turned out to be a patriotic headbanger after all.
— No, hardly. [*this was The Me, a new Me with no comeback at all*]

What made this so strange to watch was that neither man could take his eyes off her. Nick from overwhelmed pride and The Me – here I go – from a kind of sad hunger.

The conversation did its best before giving up, so The Me left the room to fetch drinks.

— He's not at all what I expected. So nervy and wanting to please. And sweet.

— Leo *sweet?* I don't think so. It hardly matters. We're the couple around here and he can be our satellite tonight.
— Don't be silly, Nick. The food smells delicious. He's gone to all this trouble. Shh.

We followed them into a room that was a dining room, with a distant kitchen just round a corner. Around the large pine table things began to settle down a bit, as Leo asked:
— Have you named the day yet?
— We called it Nadine McWhirter. [*Nick*] Leave all of Spring open in your diary.
— Well [*Lois*] there are all these moves afoot. Nick – or as I now call him, Herr Doctor Morris – has just landed a fabulous job in Newcastle, and I need to wind up my job here and look for one up there.

Something happened within the Me, and I know what. He recalled at that instant a bit of podium posturing by Ted Kennedy, stood up and said very loudly in American:

— **THIS MUST NAHT STAND**!

Then to their shocked faces said:
— Sorry, folks. One G&T and I'm nobody's. Oh … somebody had been asking me for an American persona for a show they're doing. Mine are so English.
— What about [*Lois*] the legendary Lansley and Jissica? South Ifricin, are they nut?

The Me was in seventh heaven.

— I'm amazed you know about that.
— You can't [*Nick, in a funny voice*] rest on past glories, Leopold.

— Is that Fran?

— Your mother.

They then talked about family and local things as Lois ate patiently. No change on the Mum-Dad front, but Paul was going from strength to strength. He had stayed on at Oxford with a research fellowship at Wadham. Nick seemed to know more about him than The Me did. Certainly Nick knew more about his work, which still lay somewhere between computer science and physiological psychology, with a sprinkling of philosophy. The Me spoke:

— Is he still wearing flares? Must be the last person in England doing so?

— Superficial as ever, Leo.

Paul, as you must know, was a big, burly chap with legs like the bridge supports that Nick was so interested in. When wearing flares he looked like a shire horse, as well as eating like one. This spurs another Ava Gardner memory – on Gary Cooper: "Gary could not only ride a horse, he was hung like one." That really was not worth it; but like The Me at that point I am growing excited.

Around that point, The Me decided that Nick's glass would never be empty. The Me had decided to smudge Nick's outlines with drink. Lois did not drink much and The Me didn't drink at all, so in the intervals when Nick was not bumbling forward Lois would say to The Me things like, and with a cheeky edge:

— I admit I find the whole idea of conceptual art a bit obscure. But then I'm a scientist through and through.

— Whaddabout all the politicking? [*Nick, ignored*]

— Well, *I* must admit that given the choice I would take painting over that kind of stuff. I still paint, and draw, and

do pastel work most days.
— I'm so pleased.
— Do you like paintings?
— I love Monet.
— Tick.
— Van Gogh
— Tick.
— Turner
— Double tick.
— Tock. [*Nick*]

Fansion tapped his modem to fast forward through pudding, then we followed them into the sitting room where The Me poured Nick a huge brandy, a tiny one for Lois, and a medium one for himself – this is not The Three Bears – so he could sniff it whilst pretending to sip.

Nick almost dragged Lois to the largest sofa, and The Me sat on a chair between them, the brandy bottle at his side for topping up Nick, who said:
— Could we havva bitta music?
— Any thoughts on what music [*The Me*] ... Lois?
— Have you got any of that punk? I'd like to give it a go.

I would have loved a bit of The Damned at that point, but The Me said:
— Would Dylan do ... or Debussy?
— The latter, please.

Lois was clearly not overjoyed when Nick put his arm round her, oafishly; but things were going well for The Me.

— You two lovebirds look great there. Do you mind if I sketch you?

— Fine by me, squire! [*Nick*]
— Well ... [*Lois*]

This was odd. Fansion got up to look over The Me's shoulder. I followed him, knowing that he was pasteling a version of Swynnerton's *Cupid and Psyche*, a painting I loved and which could be bent to my purposes beautifully. In the painting, a naked Cupid has large blue wings and is kissing a naked Psyche as his left wing covers his genitals (hers are a blur). To me, it looks like he's being pushy and she demure/withdrawn, but that's not really the message. Her eyes are closed but only because she must not look on his face. Her right arm reaches to his neck, and this could be to restrain him or in tenderness. It's sexy – her slight pout; and she is more naked than nude. The face seems to be in motion and so unlike the china perfection you see in so many Victorian paintings of girls' faces, almost a modern face, the kind you'd see in any wine bar; all of which led one silly sod of a critic to call her face "coarse and blubbered". Another contemporary critic, who said Swynnerton's flesh painting "has a certain quivering reality", was nearer the mark. In my version it is the best shot I could do of Lois ghosting avoidance of a slightly amused kind – shall I shut up now? – while Nick looks like a dumbo intruder. Lois was surprised and embarrassed, saying:

—Why have you given Nick those blue wings? Do you know something about him I don't?

— He knows [*Nick*] I'm an angel at heart.

The Me began to explain, and went to fetch his copy of Knuckler Sid's thesis, which had a print of *Cupid and Psyche* in it. I fancied I caught Lois glance at The Me as if she recognised his drawing had distorted the original to make her reluctant and Nick pushy. Anyway, The Me thought he'd better lighten things:

— Next time, Nick, I'll do you as Superman rather than an angel, after all you're with a *Lois.*

— A mere Hapgood, though, not a Lane – foot soldier at BCM Associates W1, not the Daily Planet, no higher degrees, unlike Superman here.

Nick was actually swaying by this time.

Wide smile from The Me at this invaluable bio; and I could almost see the machinery behind his eyes whirr into motion at these gold nuggets. I knew that first thing next morning The Me would be telephoning round to get recommendations for a good private eye. It was easy enough to know that BMC Associates had its head office in Charlotte Street and that it was a contractor for minor engineering projects; but when did Miss Hapgood go to lunch, did she go alone, and where did she go, and for how long? The PI firm he decided on wanted a detailed description of her, so The Me sent them a drawing.

Nick put the Judas-Me in a bearhug as they left the house, and the Judas-Me helped himself to a peck on the Lois cheek. Off they went into the dark.

Lois. OK, what was going on here? Two things. The romantic one was that – running slap-bang into the cliché – I did not meet her, I recognised her. I felt like saying, "Ah, there you are at last." The unromantic but aesthetic one involves me saying that there's no big secret to the physical beauty of humans. The essence is symmetry. Her face and figure had a symmetry that was out of this world. It wasn't just that there were no thick ankles or taxi-door ears in the ointment: it was *impossible to imagine* them being there. And by "physical" I mean speech too – see above for that – plus a sly, feline humour that felt like an intimacy.

Fansion and I left just after the couple did, dawdling to make sure they caught a tube well before ours. For us, it was a simple matter of catching the southbound to Kennington, and my failing to enjoy a cat-gut wrench that acknowledged the fortnight or so between the dinner and the beginning of my brief career as a stalker. Off we got at Goodge Street tube and up Goodge Street we trickled, to borrow a Wodehouse-ism. Soon we had sight of The Me doing some trickling on his own account. I recall his cover story and a rather tacky feeling and the thought, "What if Nick is meeting her for lunch?" The private eye (or can I call you a dick?) never mentioned that happening. The Me stationed himself on the terrace of a café in front of a large cappuccino, across the road from the offices whose door served many other companies.

Eventually, Lois shot out – no trickling here – deep in conversation with a woman of about her own age who immediately hailed a taxi, which, after it departed, left Lois hesitating on the pavement. Seizing his moment, The Me shouted out:
— Lois! Is it?

Fansion and I took the table immediately behind and watched things unfold. An unruffled Lois crossed the road to a rather ruffled Me, saying:
— So can I add "stalking" to your other accomplishments?

Now this looked terrible, but later I learned that in her eyes it was sweet: The Me blushed deeply.

— No, I tried stalking evening classes, but it wasn't for me. No, what's happened is that I've been stood up. I was supposed to be having lunch down the road in Pescatori with a guy from Faber who is pretending to be interested in a book idea of mine, but the dirty dog cancelled at the last minute ... Look, this is incredibly cheeky, but it would be a pity to waste the Pescatori reservation. I don't suppose you fancy joining me for a spot of lunch. If you like seafood, that is.

— Love it. Come on then.

She was already on her feet. Was she always this brisk, or needing to be back early? From our rear view of the couple as they walked down Charlotte Street, the briskness was part of something cold. Lois and The Me were the same height, and they walked in step, but The Me was clearly struggling to make contact. His head often turned to her in inquiry or whatnot, but she kept on looking straight ahead.

We ducked into the restaurant and squatted across the gangway from this awkward couple. I recall wondering what would happen if I tried to order a bowl of pasta and a carafe, and whether creatures like Fansion could eat or even wanted to. As ever, I could not look straight at The Me, which strengthened the general impression of him as an element of Eurotrash, with his light-brown linen suit, dark T-shirt, tie-thin silk scarf, and loafers worn over sockless feet.

With a tone that was as wrong as it could be, The Me began:
— Would a working girl like you be able to manage a glass of wine?
— Wine! I could manage it but would really rather not today, especially as wine was just what I wanted to take issue with you about ... Look, I only agreed to join you for lunch because I have something to say.
— Go on. [*looking as if he'd been slapped*]
— Why did you get Nick drunk the other night and do it as

part of what looked like a plan to drive a wedge between him and me?

— He got himself drunk.

— Hardly! You kept on filling up his glass before it was empty, and usually when he wasn't even looking. Then you gave him enough brandy to fill a bucket.

— I always try to keep the guests well-lubricated. It's up to them to resist. He *is* a drinker, after all.

— By which you mean it's a weakness of his. One you were happy to exploit for your own ends.

— Bloody hell. And what kind of ends do you think these were?

— You tell me.

Around this point I remember thinking this was a stupid project. Yes, it had felt like I'd fallen instantly in love with her, but this was before I knew what she was actually like beyond the glow of being a pampered guest, beyond the jolly-dinner bubble. She was a Little Madam, a Missy High Horse. I had been seriously thinking of walking out; but these thoughts only made me look desperately shifty, as opposed to Eurotrash-shifty. I decided to say the following, not in the spirit of hope but in the spirit of throwing a grenade into a crowded lift:

— I felt then and feel now that it would be the best thing in the world if you were *my* fiancée, not Nick's. The moment I saw you and heard you and got some kind of measure of you – "measure" is wrong, sorry – I fell for you. Fell in love with you. And of course, meeting you today was no accident. It was easy to find out when you went to lunch. There!

Lois all this time had her eyes trained on the menu, and was now shaking her head slowly, as if she could not believe the prices. But there was a little smile too.

— You are a seriously strange man. Really. Let's order, then we can sort this out.

When she ordered lobster thermidor, The Me (relieved and weirdly happy) told her that the lobster portions were small here, to which she replied that she would fill up on pudding. He ordered a bottle of Pino Gris, without thinking. A little later she spoke, for he was obviously not trusting himself to do so:

— It was clear to me that something like that had happened. Even Nick, pissed as he was, thought something was fishy. "Leo wasn't himself," he said. But it never occurred to me that you were just a womaniser. You aren't sufficiently in control of yourself. It was clearly not a matter of "Let's see if I can get her." [*she was joining him with the wine now*]

— No. Thanks. Fact is, I was smitten.

She laughed at this.

— And you use such old-fashioned terms – "smitten", "chap". You're really a conservative, romantic kind of ... twerp ... aren't you?

Passing up the chance to continue in this light vein, he played the straight bat:

—Well, yes. I am.

—Here's what I think we should do. *My* problem is that I find there's something sweet and lost and, um, *empty* about you. You really interest me, and I would like to get to know you in some way, to find out where the darkness or the wound is. There's got be something of that somewhere.

As I watched, I thought, "This is terrible. Has she rehearsed it? Nobody talks like this." No, not rehearsed – a lie, surely, to make plausible – eh? – her decision to see The Me again.

— You can get to know me as a dark, wounded twerp.

— No, be serious. We can meet for lunches ... and talk. Nothing will come of it, I'm certain.

The ice broke over surprisingly warm water. They chatted, filling up on background. She was from Chester, so they reminisced about the North-West. The conversation was quite dull from then on, so Fansion and I left.

— We'll leave this where it is for the time being and take a bit of a break. [*Fansion speaking on Tottenham Court Road, how odd*] Westward Ho! [*even odder*]

Back along Goodge Street, right down Tottenham Court Road to the Tottenham Court tube and down to the Central. As we got on, Fansion said:
— I warn you to brace yourself, Mr Barber. [*why the new communicative, Fansion?*]
— Because of time or distance?
— Distance. Try breathing deeply.

And yes, between Notting Hill Gate and Holland Park it happened, like being sideswiped by a Circle Line train. It was as if my brain spent twenty seconds on the ceiling and my stomach was still sitting on the duffed-up seat. My patience was being tried. What distance was this? Had I ever visited Ultima Thule? By astral projection? The Lois reminder had been thoroughly done, but what *was* all this?

Then I, limp next to my parental guide, reached the end of the line, which was ... not Ealing Broadway but – get this – "The Elephant Bar and Castle".

Like Ealing Broadway itself, this faux-station was open to the sky, but to a cloudless blue sky; and it also had a wide flight of steps leading out, not past pasty outlets but past donut booths and unEnglish shiny surfaces. The other passengers had alighted at West Action – this is becoming the report of a dutiful police constable – and we walked, I stunned, Fansion bovine, up the wide steps onto ... not the congested carriageway on whose far side The Stones used to play in 1963, but onto the forecourt of a motel-style hotel heavy with foliage and that particular plant aroma that could only mean California. I had then and still have no idea – you don't really think I would Google, do you? – what kind of plant caused the aroma. All I know is that it was strongest in the evening and was as intoxicating as the first cocktail.

— California!
— Indeed, sir. [*was he channelling Jeeves?*] La Jolla.
— But I've never been here.
— Two of your loved ones have ... This way.

As we walked past Reception, a bellboy intoned "Dr John! Good to see you again. It's been a while." He eyed me as if I was wearing an orange jumpsuit and carrying a broom.
— Good to see you again, Troy. We're off to the Elephant Bar.
— Enjoy!

The curving funnel that protruded above the perimeter foliage was a plastic trunk; and there was The Elephant Bar, throbbing with get-ready-to-party-even-if-it-kills-you music. At this point my main thought was: Will we have a drink? Then: This is just ridiculous; the name of the tube station is silly; this is all silly. I'm chained to Fansion. I want to go home. I hate American Bars ... and so *this* is when the actual punishment begins.

No, we would not be drinking. No need, as we were physically present but impossible to attend to. We just sat like two redundant oldies waiting for a taxi, beside a rubber plant, well away from the crowded bar.

A voice behind us...
— 'S-scuse thanks. S-sorry.

Usually I will not mark his stutters in this way; only so often. And yes, I knew who it was immediately, and things fell into place. The last time I'd seen Paul he was buying summery clothes for this trip, that he called a "brainstorming workshop on the sub-symbolic modelling of cognition". Or in his sillier moments: "Neural Nets for Ninnies."

And here he was, crashing through knots of young'uns in what looked like rugger kit. In fact, he was wearing a rugby shirt and shoplifting shorts. He left sniggers but also smiles in his wake. He then charged to the bar and we followed. I longed to tap him on the shoulder and give him a hug and suggest going on the mooch well away from my jailer, down to the restaurant-studded coast that I'd heard was just the ticket.

— LargeG&Tpluslimeplease.
This spat out at random to any bar staff that swam into view. Ordering drinks was a challenge, so he had to construct a one-word sayable sequence and say it like a mantra.

The G&T he drank greedily, then crashed on to the restaurant area where he had a cheeseburger, fries, and ice cream, and a half bottle of red, then back to the bar ...
— LargeG&Tpluslimeplease.
— How're we doing tonight, sir?
— [*long pause*] Keepsmilingthrough. [*huh?*]

This did not improve my mood at all. If I forgot this was my brother and what I knew of him (his brilliance, niceness, humour ... another of my triplets), I would be plainly seeing a loner who had chosen to spend his evenings like this rather than with a group of like-mindeds. Where were the others in this workshop? Why did he not go out with them? And I knew the answer. Chit-chat and anecdotage is the hardest thing for stutterers, especially with your tongue strung out with booze. You cannot relax; and after a day of what our Dad used to call "brainwork", you need to relax. This was *his* relaxing. Poor sod.

There was more LargeG&Tpluslimeplease, and more crashing around, leaving in its wake more sniggers, no smiles, and some grimaces. And then the DJ took up his station and the music changed from a background thudding to serious volume and intensive dancing in a kind of shallow pit beside the bar, like the pool in which you have to disinfect your tootsies on the way to the pool itself. Paul charged forth, full of what he would call goal direction and LargeG&Tpluslimeplease. Think Frank Bruno, shadow-boxing in triple time, constrained to punch with his shoulders not his fists. That was a dance called The Paul Barber. (As far removed from the Paul Jones as you can imagine.) On his face there was a look of excruciating pain, and around him were open mouths.

Most people would see a funny side to this. Many would want him to floor a beefy young American with one of his sudden sashays. But what it did for me was to flood me with love for my brother and a desperate desire to protect him. I'd never seen such loneliness. One thing he had to be protected from was the mischief of the DJ, who was choosing faster and faster records to stretch the limits of The Paul Barber. When the Martha and the Muffins number "Echo

Beach" came on, Paul tried to mark every beat in the spirit of St Vitus. In fact, he had a good sense of rhythm and did a good job, but it looked deranged. I glanced over at the bar to see if anybody was inclined to step in; but when I looked back, Shoulder Bruno had a dancing partner. In fact – apologies now for the crudity of this – he has three partners: a stocky Hispanic girl *and her breasts*. They seemed to be trying to escape from her blouse as she did a kind of pogo.

She was looking into his eyes, laughing happily and mirroring his deranged movements in a toned-down way. She was now leaning into his left ear and shouting words to which he grinned broadly and shook his head or grimaced at the start of a word of his own. They danced for four numbers then went to sit down after she'd bought them both cokes. Fansion and I followed in our usual creepy way, thankful she'd chosen a quiet spot.

— I'm Anita.

— Paul, from England.

— You, "Paul-from-England", are a phenomenal dancer. What are you doing here?

— Work. Bit of computer science, bit of cognitive psychology, lots of coffee drinking and trying to stop thinking about how much I'd rather be ...

— Sailing?

— ... at the beach.

— Unlike you, my dear, I've not been drinking, so take it straight when I say I think you're fantastic, everything about you. I've got a beautiful duplex overlooking the ocean and tomorrow morning you will be drinking your coffee looking out to sea. A sunny blue vista. We'll be going there soon in my bug convertible. I'll get you a black coffee first.

— B ...

Sorry, bad taste time again. This reminds me of the joke about the stuttering jeweller. A guy robs his till at gunpoint, and as he leaves with the money the jeweller says " ... C-c-c-c-c-c-c-come in."

Actually, Paul did look uncomfortable. It could not have been erotic anxiety, because he was no boy scout; but, reasonably enough, what do you make of a woman like that! His features settled as he seemed to decide it was best not to think about it. He had no credit cards or anything worth stealing so let's take her at face value. Actually, Anita's face was consoling: as open as a child's, with a chin nearly as prominent as Paul's own. She seemed innocent. They were two innocents; and we watched them drive away in her VW, more Noddy than Mr Goodbar.

Soon I was back on the Central Line, bracing myself for the side-swipe.

12: Football Focus to The King's Arse

It was back to Tottenham Court Road, then up the Edgware branch of the Northern Line and ... Hampstead. We walked past Louis Patisserie, a little piece of Hungary and heaven, to be trickled by in pursuit of my special torment. Then we rounded a few corners and came upon Paul and Anita, wandering. I wanted to stay well clear but Fansion hustled us along so we could eavesdrop. Paul was humming and Anita was saying:

— Tell you what, Paul, I would have thought a guy like your brother would have lived somewhere with more, uh, *edge* to it, or at least somewhere a bit chi-chi. I mean, Camden Town or Mayfair would have been no surprise, but this is kinda *suburban*.

— We like suburbia in our family. Quiet and spacious.

— Well I'll reserve judgement till I see inside.

The "reserve judgement" made my blood boil. We arrived on the front step, stopped and heard behind us a business-like clip-clop. Paul turned round, as I didn't need to, saying:

— Lois! Hi! Hey, this is nice. Nick held up, or is he already here?

She was not phased by this – typical of her – replying crisply:

— Nick? I've not seen him for months. I suppose he's in Newcastle. We split up and I'm with Leo now.

She produced her front door key and let them in; at which

point I must "bring you up to speed", as I never *ever* say.

At first, my lunches with Lois happened every couple of weeks, then nearly every week. My feelings didn't change, didn't intensify, and indeed there could be something school-mistressy about her that would be a turn off for anybody but me. She would correct my grammar and comment on my dimness in the areas of science and history – on just about everything that had a clear right and wrong answer. But she was perfection, with the perfection melting sideways after a couple of glasses of wine when her teasing of me involved a bit of chaste touching. Usually we met in good restaurants of a bijou persuasion. But one week we couldn't get a table in such an animal and found ourselves wandering south along Tottenham Court Road. "I'm starving" she said. (There was a wonderful ambiguity to the "starving".) "Let's go in here." "Here" was a big touristy pub specialising in pies. I had just been on a Dickens-reading jag and in my excitement sugges-ted we try to order brandy and hot water to go with our pies and mash. The barmaid did indeed heat a kettle and pour about half a pint into two triple Rémy Martins. That it was just coming up for Christmas did help things along. "You are the least Pickwickian man I have ever met" was the charac-teristic comment from her.

We drank – shoved onto the nursery slopes of drunkenness – but when the pies arrived we took one glance at them, turned to each other and, as if on the cue of a hidden dir-ector, kissed and kept on kissing for over five minutes. Towards the end, a tourist (Bristol?), probably there for the matinee in the Dominion, said jokingly "Don't let them poys get cawd." We ate them like the couple in *Tom Jones* and headed for home (mine).

Lois told Nick about this when calling off the wedding in a phone call I overheard. I wasn't happy about it, not because I wanted to keep it quiet but because I felt it was up to me to tell Nick. She wasn't having it.

— He said to tell you that you are a ... (followed by a rude word beginning with the letter "c"). There would be no Pete-voice to soften it this time. I wrote about ten letters to him, tearing up each of them. "There are no words" was one of the clichés of 2018. People too lazy to make a sentence to say how something bad had affected them would say this as a way of nodding to the unplumbable depths of their own sensitivity. (Yes, yes, as might be said in the *Daily Telegraph*.) In this case the words were there alright, but only accessible by somebody more serious than I was.

Like a ten-year-old, I thought how unfair it was that happiness never comes neat. Why couldn't I just enjoy my life with Lois without the Nick-taint. How can you be happy if you feel you've done wrong? *There!* Can I be that bad if I say this? "No, just a bit childish" comes the reply. Anyway, I think it's why drinkers drink: to take the taint away. It certainly went away over a bottle with her, before I returned to my abstemiousness.

Back to the present scene.

In we all trooped. I could tell – was this telling or memory? [*hardly matters*] – Paul's mood from the back. He was angry in his speciality way: like a bear that's just been sewn into the skin of a domestic cat. His famous (remember, remember) *menton volontaire* (wilful/strong chin) was even more *volontaire*. In fact, Anita's was too, though not in sympathy. It was more a matter of being desperate to make her mark on this gathering. Her eyes shone and she was

talking over people gushingly. When Lois called to Leo in
the kitchen, she seemed beside herself. It was lunchtime.

The Me had clearly not seen Paul for a while because he
greeted him before kissing Lois hello.
— And you must be Anita ...
— The very one. It's such a thrill for me to meet you, Leo.
And what a lovely home you have.
— Lager for me. [*Paul*]
— Drinks are on the way. Why don't you all sit down. You
seem to be milling.
— [*Paul, to Lois*] Nick started his new job then?
— I assume so. I've no idea.

Strained silence until The Me comes back. Sensing it, he
says:
— Don't get too excited, it's only my lentil soup and a pork
pie from that place in Holland Park.
— I'm not excited, mate. [*Paul*]
— What's up, er, *mate*?
— I can't keep up and don't think I want to keep up. The last
time I saw Lois she was engaged to be married to Nick. They
seemed happy and settled enough. And now she's living
with his best friend. Where does this leave Nick?
— In Newcastle [*Lois speaks*], probably going off to watch
Newcastle United with his latest bird.
— How do you know he's got a latest bird? You're just telling
yourself that to ease your guilt.
— What's [*The Me*] got into you, Paul?
— I'm sorry to have [*Lois*] fallen short of your stern moral
code, sir, but if I happen to prefer being with Leo than with
the guy you falsely call "his best friend", fact is: "Ain't
nobody's bizness if I do ..."

Anita suddenly bursts into song, with a good Sarah Vaughnish voice but in a kind of social orgasm ...

> I swear I won't call no copper
> If I gets beat up by my papa
> Ain't ...

— [*Paul, shouting*] Neet! Put a sock in it, for Christ's sake!

Anita now had tears in her eyes. Lois saw this and went into action.
— Well, Anita, if you're a fan of Lady Day I just *know* we're going to get along ... But hang on, Paul! *Football Focus!* It's been on for ten minutes.

She took him by the hand, led him to the sofa and turned on BBC1. I recall that the Nick-Paul-Lois axis was forged by football. But why she was an Arsenal fan I will never know.

What a girl Lois was. There were times that, years later, I wondered if there was something of the autist about her. I mean her silences, her sometimes robotic manner, her weird attention to detail, eccentric eating sequences (greens, then meat, then potatoes), her literalness of mind. But the opposite was true also. Look at the empathy and skill, dear reader/listener.

— Soccer. I mean footie. I must learn. You must help me, please.

Anita plonked herself down next to them, having failed to squeeze in between.

Meanwhile, The Me adopted a pigeon-toed walk and a stoop and terrible taste, saying:

— OK massas, ahl jess shuffle off to ma kitchen and fetch dem vittles.

They had the soup on their laps, and the pie etc. was put on a coffee table.

I was enjoying this. I mean enjoying *Football Focus*. Not because I like football (I don't; recall, recall) but because TV locates you in the past far better than walking the streets and looking in shop windows. It shows aspirations, not their outcomes ... *Ahhhh, Monsewer ees a pheelosopherr.*

When the programme finished, and Paul and Lois finished their Arsenal-based debate, The Me spoke up:
— What you working on now, Paul?
— Mainly psycholinguistics these days.
— More, please!
— Well, we started out with high hopes of mimicking speech production using a hybrid symbolic and sub-symbolic network ...
— This is, like, so beyond me. [*Anita*]
— A semantic bank would feed into a syntactic-phonemic bank and generate sentences from thoughts. Too bloody ambitious, too bloody naïve. I had fun doing something else, though ...
— More, more! [*The Me*]
— We got some slaves – aka undergraduate project students – to sift through texts and extract just the prosody (the rhythm and stress of the passages), while another slave-gang extracted the lexicon of other texts, then we blended them on this hybrid network. Say, for example, the prosody of a Churchill speech and the vocabulary of a Steptoe and Son episode. It was pretty funny, I can tell you; and so easy to do. We can use the technique for something more to the point, but for now it's just a toy.

At this point, who could not enjoy The Me's hopeless attempt to be casual, as he said:

— And I suppose you could do this for *poetry* too …

— Of course.

— Actually, I have to go to Oxford next week, to talk to Blackwells. [*Lois cringed at the obvious lie*] We could have a pub lunch and you can tell me more.

Anita was about to have another social orgasm …

— I know! You're planning a poetry performance. Invent a poet to blow apart the whole phony scheme. I had a poet boyfriend once and let me tell you he …

— Would you like to see the garden, uh … Neet? [*this was Lois*]

* * *

Doctor Barber's Crash Course on Poesie

At this juncture, as I turn on my laptop and upload Powerpoint, I tell the porters to lock the doors of the lecture theatre and lower the blinds. A bullhorn is at hand to emphasise certain points. Pin back those lugholes, ladies and gents.

A few years ago, in a review of a book on women artists by Germaine Greer, Anita Brookner described painting in this way: "a delightful prospect: the application of paint to canvas for the purpose of giving pleasure". [*puts bullhorn to lips*] Nothing could be less true than this. [*puts bullhorn down*]

Imagine this applied to poetry: the application of words to

a page with line-breaks, for the purpose of giving pleasure. To this a poet will say, "Well, what about *my* pleasure? What's in it for me? I'm not in the entertainment industry. I write for myself." In fact, *all* artists do it for themselves; they would do it marooned on a desert island. And, of course, it may not be "delightful" at all. Even to themselves. Which brings me immediately to the question of difficulty and "unintelligibility" in poetry. [*puts bullhorn to lips*] If poets write poems to get it right to their own ear, eye and sense rather than to delight readers, then they will be bound to be difficult. [*puts bullhorn down*] They have privileged access to what they mean, or, rather, to *why they write what they do*; and sharing this would make the poem a horrible mishmash of the authentic and the ingratiating. It would have no energy.

Next, the good modern poets – let's say Eliot, Pound, Ashbery, Stevens, Prynne, Raworth – [*pause as a number of people try and fail to leave because these poets are all men, and white*] are difficult each in their own particular way, because they are different personalities with different forms of life and reading habits trying to get different things right under their own ear, eye, and sense. [*puts bullhorn to lips*] It's not that there is this thing – "difficulty" – a kind of inner sanctum that they have tickets to. [*puts bullhorn down*]

Next, those I call the Cavalier Counterfeits believe in the inner sanctum theory. The crucial step is their pretending to have tickets to it by simply *willing difficulty*. There are lots of ways of doing this. They might, say, do versions of Ashbery, Prynne or Raworth that mean damn-all, though sounding kind of right. Or they may write banal scenarios, epiphanies, or anecdotes that end with a couple of meaningless yet would-be resonant lines.

Sorry, "mean damn-all" and "meaningless" are wrong. They may well mean something in the sense of there being a crackable code beneath the word-salad: maybe the poem is "about" watching the racing at Kempton Park on the TV. No, I mean these counterfeit poems have no ideas in them, which includes no aesthetic projects or worldly concerns. [*shows first Powerpoint slide*] Nietzsche wrote this as a young man and would-be poet:

> A poem which is empty of ideas and overladen with phrases and metaphors is like a rosy apple in the core of which a maggot lies hid ... In the writing of any work one must pay the greatest attention to the ideas themselves. One can forgive any fault of style, but not a fault of thought.

To take issue with Nietzsche, here: ideas and "thought" are not the same thing. See the Ashbery poem "Ode to Bill" on your handout. Ideas should be there, but "thought" suggests some prosy propositions that can be winkled out. Which is not to say [*the lecturer wipes his brow at this point*] that a poem does not need some thought run over it, as it were. See directly below the Ashbery poem on the handout the quote from Raworth: "I write down fragments passing through my mind that interest me enough *after thought has played with them* for me to imagine I might like to read them." The Counterfeits simply eject phrases and sentences in the hope that *somebody else* might wish to read them. They themselves have no interest in these fragments.

That's all the lecturer has time for. Depart!

* * *

Now, in a more conversational tone, having left the hall and relaxed in the empty student bar ...

The conceptual artists and their hopeless dogshit are beacons of brilliant honesty comparing to the Cavalier Counterfeits, of which there are many. I DO NOT have it in for poetry, by the way. I love it. And that's why I'm going on like this.

In passing, the Counterfeits inadvertently gave birth to their shadow-selves: the Tacky Transparencies, who simply express themselves (often their pain) in a kind of distressed prose; and nowadays at speed with a rocky soundtrack, shouting to give it – ahem – "energy".

Hard fun over, I can feel the sourness rising, so I'll stop right now. Just to say that this is what I feel *now* (the "laptop" was a giveaway) but it was also what I felt then though in a cloudy, emotion-heavy way. I felt indeed that my next move must be towards something poetic – not simply sitting down to write poems, I'd tried that and failed and failed – but some move into the poetry world consistent with the "Leo Barber-artist" project.

At this time I was reading even more poetry than I usually did whilst still, in a kind of bovine way, doing things that sort-of counted as conceptual art ... and all the while appearing on TV as a talking head or studio guest, as a cheerleader for the avant-anything, who was secretly more excited by the new Raymond Briggs than by the latest wunderkind of "found-sculpture". These "art" things were stealings – imitations. I'll mention just two of them.

I love Roy Fisher's poetry. Indeed, in some ways he is my ideal of what a poet should be: a chameleon, for one thing (one will do). I had been reading his masterpiece, a long poem in sections called *A Furnace*. In "The Return" section we have these lines:

> Nature
> is depicted by
> the vanishing of a gentleman
> in black, and in portraiture,
> being maybe a Doctor John
> Dee, or Donne, of Hofmannsthal's
> Lord Chandos,
> he having lately walked
> through a door in the air

This was enough for me. You've no idea how easy it is, if you have standby money and people like Unilever and IBM falling over themselves to sponsor you, to recruit a team of boffins and sharp enthusiasts to follow your bovine path and reproduce this image. You simply wait for a cloudy night, go to the top of a high building and project a gaunt hippyish geezer in fancy dress walking out from and back into the sky; and then film it.

"There always was a frankly poetic element in Barber's work. This is its coming to a glorious fruition" wrote some useful idiot in the *Sunday Times*. I did acknowledge Fisher, and I'm delighted to say he was both amused and disgusted.

Second: brazen stealing. People would tend to imagine that I spent my evenings among the torments and ecstasies of creation. But (1) I'm not particularly creative (this must have emerged by now) and (2) I watched comedy on TV in the evenings whilst Lois was doing her Labour Party work. *Not the Nine O'Clock News* was hit and miss, but one thing on it was perfect: Rowan Atkinson wandering along, catching sight of a camera, waving to it goofily, then walking slap-bang into a lamp post or tree. All I had to do was pick up the phone to one of my favoured boffins – Paul helped me find them – and suggest making an automaton that repetitively (or "recursively", in their lingo) did just this, picking itself up each time – to the point of auto-destruction. I suggested it be made of wood and could combust at the end.

"Neither afraid to reference popular culture, nor indeed to risk the Camus-esque or Beckettian cliché in his quest for a visualisation of human stoicism, absurdity and futility ..." Oh, forget it. And I forget where this appeared. *Spectator? New Statesman?*

Let's get back to the jolly football foursome.

By this time, Paul had had enough to eat and drink and was probably looking forward to a walk on the Heath, while Anita was giving up on social orgasming that kept being nipped in the bud (uncomfortable image, missus). They prepared to leave, and the four of them drifted to the front door. Said The Me:

— See you next week in Oxford then. Pub lunch, somewhere central?

— Righto. I know just the place. Does a good chilli. The King's A-a-a-a ... The King's A-a-a-a ...

— The King's Arse. Yes, of course.

This seems cruel but Paul liked it. It was such a relief from our mother's idea that a single Paul-stutter was the end of the world as we know it.

— ... Arms ... The King's Arms. We've been there before. Wednesday at one?

— Excellent. I look forward to it. Lovely to meet you, Anita.

Next time we can all have a football-free dinner.

— Oh, I love football. Can't get my head around cricket though ...

As for Fansion and I, it was back to Hampstead tube, down the Northern to extreme predictability. I knew we would be leaping west to Oxford next, and we couldn't get there before them. Couldn't we maybe have a spot of lunch, be expansive, reflective, chew the fat? But everything was lean and shrouded in Fansion's silences and ironic smiles. We changed at Camden Town to the Morden Branch, off at Tottenham Court Road, then west to a station called ... not Oxford Circus but – you're there already – "Oxford".

The "Oxford" tube looked like a Parisian Metro station, with deep blue and bright white tiling. The narrow exit led up to book-lined caverns, then a door, which turned out to have bookshelves on its other side, which led to something that was easily recognizable as the lower level of a bookshop. All the books I could see were on philosophy or psychology, so there was nothing to laugh at at all.

How did Paul, as down to earth and private as a vole, put up with this? To explain: one overheard conversation was between two beardless boys who dressed like their fathers and who were trying outdo each other in condemnations of the stupidity of a fellow boy, with lots of stage dolt-speak.

— And then he said "Whadya mean the argument is, uh, self-, uh, defeatin'?" An admissions error, surely.

— Modus tollendo tollens. Mince-for-brains, or what?

Yes, it was Blackwell's bookshop, so we were very near The King's Arms; and that "spot of lunch" notion came round again. It would have been nice if one of the busy-busy types

on the tills hailed Fansion, but it didn't happen.
— Aren't you hungry, Dr Fansion?
— Never. Your hunger will go in a couple of minutes.

There was Paul, sitting before a half-finished pint and chatting to some folks on the next table. The Me was at the bar ordering two bowls of chilli and two pints. Shall I tell you that they would later hold their forks in their right hands and that the bar was crowded? I was, at this juncture, and as the Leo-saga sort of changes gear, getting a bit fed up.

The next-table people left and we took their places. After a bit of family chit-chat and some polished lying from The Me about how much he liked Anita and how lucky Paul was – this could be managed only by saying "Anita" while thinking of her breasts, I'm ashamed to say – the Me said:
— Actually, it was your language production model or network or whatever you call it I wanted to talk to you about.
— Go on.
— I've been planning a sort of intervention into the world of poetry for a while now.
— God help us! [*laughing*]
— My idea was to generate poems by using the prosody – metre, if you like – of one poet and blending it with the lexicon of another.
— It can be done, if you buy me another pint. No tutorials to give this afternoon.

Then with his third pint before him, Paul said:
— But promise me one thing: if I help you with this, keep it quiet. I don't want to get the reputation of being one of these fancy fannies who actually *wants* to do this kind of thing.
— Agreed. In fact, the whole idea – the whole idea of the scam, if you like – is that I publish the poems that result

and then reveal that they were done by a computer program.

— It's not a program! It's *sub*-symbolic. It'll take too long to explain.

— I mean "generated mechanically" then.

— OK, but bear in mind that because it's sub-symbolic, because the transitions between words are done probabilistically, by doing statistics, the syntax of the sentences produced will be loose; it'll be wayward.

Oh yes, dear reader/listener, can you hear the smacking of the Open University pedagogic drama?

— So much the better; but explain.

That smacking again approaches ...

— There's no program of rules that says, for example, "a verb phrase begins with a verb and it governs a noun-phrase further down the tree". Instead, the network has been trained to expect after words like *kick* to have a word like *the* or *a* or *his,* and then, after one of these, a word like *ball* or *bucket* or, indeed, *esteem*. There are no semantic rules, either, so only statistics makes *ball* more likely than *esteem*.

I'm ashamed – again – to admit that The Me excreted a superior little smirk at this point and said:

— I can't say that worries me. Anyway, maybe there are no syntactic rules in our heads either. Maybe it's all just a matter our being very good at statistics.

Paul was a very placid man; but bulls too are placid most of the time. He looked as if he was getting up to leave at this point. Maybe only his half-finished pint kept him.

— Don't try thinking, Leo. You think like a child. Just shut up from this point on otherwise I certainly will not help you. I make it a condition of helping you that when we leave you go straight to Blackwells and buy one of the little introductions to Chomsky – the John Lyons one or the Judith Greene one.

— Agreed, sorry.

— And given the lack of inherent syntax there will be no "end of sentence". So you'll have to put those in yourself.

— It'll be fun. Like putting in line-breaks.

Silence as they looked at each other like two men who'd just had a pointless fight or discovered they were in love with the same woman. Then Paul:

— Actually, there is something you can do in return. Anita has written a children's book including her own illustrations.

— Happy to look at it, of course. What's it called?

— No idea. Not really my scene.

— Is it called *Maisy and the Enormous Pie* or *Charlie Follicle Finds a Fart*?

— It's bound to be one of them.

Laughter, and then a reminder from Paul to go to the bookshop.

I'll tell you how things turned out as Fansion and I travelled back to Lesser London ...

Yes, this was what I had in mind. Take two poets I like but who are completely different from each other, take the prosody of a poem by one and the lexicon of the other, and when the printouts arrive from Paul's lab – which they did, with surprising speed and bulk – allow "thought to play with them" as little as possible, get them typed up and put together a book. It would be essential to submit it not to one of the major poetry presses like Carcanet or Bloodaxe but to a house – Weidenfeld or Allen Lane, say – which generally does not publish verse but is definitely impressed by my dogshit celebrity. Best not to involve an agent, who may be a bit of a boy scout poetry buff ... *What is a buff, by the way?*

Here's an example: the prosody of Jeremy Prynne and the lexicon of Hugo Williams. Others I used were the prosody of Frank O'Hara and the lexicon of Geoffrey Hill. (Larfs aplenty here, me hearties.)

Here's my attempt at writing the metre of a little eleven-line poem by Prynne. (I was always hopeless at doing this. For homework once we had to write some trochee lines. I was stumped, so Mum did: *Gaily the troubadour strummed his guitar*. Got 9/10; and it's not all trochees, is it?)

/ = long, stressed
x = the opposite

//x x/ /x, ///
/x /x /x /x x/x
/x /x x/ //x/x, /x. x
/xx /xx xx, /x
x// x/x x// x
/x x /xx, /x /x , /x
// /xx/ /xx/. /xx
/xx /x x// /xx, x
/x /xx x/xx, /x
/xx. /xx xx/ /x/,
x/x /x, x/ x/ x/.

And here is a snatch of Hugo Williams' lexicon:

Illness, National Health, cubicle, nervous, penis, Burgundy, hairpin, toilet, crawlers, Champagne, jellied eels, Big Top, woman, lubricant, Newcastle, unspecified, mental, bathroom, rubber, aprons, cosmetics, tarpaulin, alarm clock, reptilian, lousy, compilation, employed, bottom, road map, mildewed, sheets, trouble, folded, blind, party, hide, pounding, pregnant, coffee, lips, tell-tale, remember, father, mother, yellow, Lucky Jim.

And this is what came through one fine morning, tucked within an endless roll of computer paper. I gave it a title.

Steam Girls at Night

Fall slowly full of darkness, world is rain
somehow ordered, folded, trouble-flutter of home and
desk. Mildewed first time airline to shoe tie, take
place now it's late, can't hang
up darling and drifts through the pregnant dance,
toilet and Newcastle, Georgie pounding, watched you
crawl to the working alarm clock. You excite
the hardly-there road map and the blind-in-bed, I
sweep the remembering Jim of Bulk Haulage, over
an Axminster. You steam girls parade round,
are yellow champagne, as night pulls down her pants.

I give this one as an example only because of its cheekiness. Generally this blend reliably generated poems of obvious and heavy *avant* intentions. They rolled off by the yard, and many of them would go into my first collection, *Nude with Violin*.

To interviewers I made up some rich abstractions about why it was called this, but actually the source was a Sunday lunchtime radio drama from the '50s starring Jack Warner (as Dad) called *Meet the Huggetts*. When it finished, the announcer would say that the actress who played Mum (Kathleen Harrison) was "appearing in *Nude with Violin* at the Globe Theatre, London". My next collection would be called *The Eagle House Four*. No, not a reference to Schopenhauer's "fourfold root" – How did I keep a straight face telling Melvyn this? – but to a Shadows-style rock band that played at our school socials.

So yes, I did get a book published, and no I didn't stick to my guns about not using an agent. One thing I certainly did not want to do was to *submit*; and let the ambiguity hang. I would never dream of submitting work to magazines under my own name and certainly would never stuff sheets into a padded envelope and send it to God Knows Whose slush pile. No, once I'd found a literary agent who was "with the program", who was intelligent and unashamed to use the leverage of the name Leo Barber in all its gorgeous sales potential, it became another of my famous doddles. She – her name was Lydia Lockette (no, really) – agreed that sending the work to specialist houses was not on. I never told her, of course, where they came from, and she seemed to know by smell they were not the simple product of a pen-holding me. Penguin took them, as many years later they would publish poor S.P. Morrissey's novel. I didn't design the cover but gave the job to a friend of mine who needed a leg up.

I had a lot of fun doing this; but it was hard work, as I didn't trust anybody else, certainly not some Oxbridge clever clogs, to do the lexicon gleaning and the metrical feeting for me. Actually, it was the first time I'd laboured over *any-*

thing; and felt childishly proud to reply "Yup", as if in the process of unloading a wagon, whenever Lois poked her head round the studio door with a "Still at it, darling?"

There was also the necessary process of thought while playing with them. (You can probably see some cheesy thought at work in the "Steam Girls" one.) Sometimes this was just a matter of tidying up and sometimes it was something that felt like composition. Who am I to say how counterfeit it was?

Part of the fun came from seeing what happened if I threw, say, Wallace Stevens' lexicon into the oxbow lakes of John Ashbery's syntax. In fact, thinking of these two ... just as Prynne's prosody would survive as his own through any lexicon you could throw at it, so Stevens' lexicon was recognisably his own through any prosody impositions. As for Ashbery, something else happened. He is the poet of slyly assembled shaggy-dog sentences, and these did not survive the approximate, statistical, probabilistic, stochastic – shoot me in the head now, please – networks of my brother. To meander you need a rock-hard syntax; at which point I see a long hook coming at me from stage right with the word "Bore!" hanging from it.

I think I'll leave the poetry business there for now and return to it later. Meanwhile, let's just bear in mind The Me and Fansion travelling back from "Oxford" and abandon the – a word I learned from Paul – *punctate* mode for the time being (though Fansion did once use it). Actually, they're travelling to Charing Cross; but don't worry about that for now.

13: Mwy Bruvvah!!!!

Happiness writes white, so they say. Well, my happiness with Lois would speak white noise if I gave it half a chance. I mean, if I tried to describe our happiness to somebody, my fevered thoughts would overlap so completely that it would just be a matter of blather-static where the odd phrase like "so lucky", "different each day", "give thanks" might be made out. One or two things can be said though. One of them – sorry, and don't panic – is about sex. I'm only saying it because a later event needs its smackerel of context.

We were determined that married sex – yes, we were married now – would not be something you did before you went to sleep if you both happened to be in the mood. We had plenty of rooms, so we set aside a room for it. Suppressing a blush, I admit there were also elements of role play. No, I was never a centurion and she was never Miss Muppet but we put some imagination into it. We did this, I should say, not because sex needed spicing up but as the overflow from the spice we already had.

No, far from the centurion scenario, some form of Terry and June was more likely, with the idea being that a potential viewer could not see the action coming. Actually, talking of Terry Scott, one evening we were watching a variety show on TV where Scott was reprising his schoolboy act of a big chubby man in short trousers and school regalia plus the song "My Brother", pronounced *Mwy Bruvvah* (*locked granny in the loo ... caterpillar stew ... mwy bruvvah ...* etc.), when she turned to me with a misty-moisty look I knew so well, prior to opening negotiations about me in school uniform and her as a teacher of the old school in tweeds, twinset, corset, and a cane on the desk. We reasoned that the top half of the uniform would be easy (given my petite frame, admitted to at the start) but the short trousers could be a challenge as, generally, twelve-year-olds don't wear short trahziz these days. But she *insisted* on them. Did we do it? Not telling you.

I now darken things a wee bit. All this trouble having been gone to, I – is this the word? – "reasoned" that we could film the performances, enjoying them in some late aftermath. Her first response – I had chosen my moment propitiously – was a drawled "Well, why not." But when I got the builders in – she being away at a Labour Party Conference – to put in a one-way mirror between our special room and the dressing room next door, and had some smirking mates set up a video recorder there, she was not only unimpressed but turned on me with "Leo, this is you at your absolute worse. It's a bloody pathology." I simply adopted my pigeon-toed walk and stoop and replied in a Birmingham accent, "Oi now when oi'm not wanteed", before shuffling off.

Yes, the Labour Party. She'd decided to carry on working part-time, with the rest of her working day being dedicated to the "Frognal and Fitzjohns" ward. I was all for it, as I am an instinctive socialist on the simple grounds that it's the moral option (I'll leave it at that). I even helped with leafleting and envelope-stuffing when her pregnancy slowed her down (not to mention slowing down our special-room use), but never did canvassing. I was happy for our sitting room to be used for ward meetings. How many times did I walk past as an old geezer started up, "When I saw George Lansbury address a packed hall in 1938 ..."? But Labour activities caused our first serious argument. In those days wards had fund-raising parties – in fact, Labour Party parties. Anybody could buy a ticket, no need to be a LP member, and then they paid for drinks. Lois thought we should throw open our house for one. I said I would rather cut my throat. "Your so-called socialism is skin deep ... must maintain your precious bourgeois privacy ... don't want the great unwashed brushing past your bookshelves ... they might nick one of your pencils, take photos ..." That's what I heard, more or less. I pointed out that it wasn't the Tough Eggs (thanks again, Mr Wodehouse) from Camden Town I was worried about, or even the Good Egg social workers who would shiver in horror at our comparative luxury, or even the ten or twelve bearded men any of whom could have been the young Jeremy Corbyn, it was the influx itself. Actually, it wasn't that so much as the assumption that I was *expected* to do it, that it was the *right* thing to do, that not to do it would be an admission that ... I give up. As I try to say this, I'm becalmed.

It escalated: I was "a straw man, a lip-service merchant"; she was "a Lady Muck, a Mrs Jellyby". It descended till it reminded me of an argument between two kids I'd overheard in an Infant School playground, where the plumper of the two was winning the argument till the other said "Fatty!" and stomped off in triumph. We called each other "fatty" until, thinking better of it, we stomped up to the special room.

She regarded my artish forays and poetic experiments in an amused, maternal way, but did perk up when reviews of

Nude with Violin started to come in. The ones in the major poetry magazines tended to be cautious-sniffy. In the *PN Review*, somebody I had never heard of said, "Nobody could be less a man of mystery than Leo Barber, nobody is less likely to be working away in cool seclusion" before assuming that it was metaphysically impossible to publish a collection without a good track record in magazines that are only read by people with poems printed in them. "Some left-field innovative moves, but not a single metaphor or simile ... There is a kind of surface brilliance and sheen-of-the-new laid over something that may be no more than modernism-by-numbers." I was almost ready to say, "Fair cop, guv." The ones in the Saturday *Guardian* and the Sunday papers were, however, another story. They could not contain themselves: "exciting" ... "a revelation" ... "holds promise of returning an energy to the English language" ... "fizzing with invention" ... "the courage that Barber has shown in his art, conceptual or otherwise, is here filtered through a fine linguistic gauze to emerge as something with a 'terrible beauty'" and "these poems are not only threaded with serious intelligence but they demand it from the reader". Lois liked this. She loved my being praised, even when bollocks was flying through the air like hailstones; and I loved it when she was impressed.

Actually, my thoughts were more on the news that Lois was going to have twins, and I was pouring more creative energy into choosing names than on anything else. I'd said Lancelot as a possible middle name for a boy; and she took me literally when it was time to register (hence Lance) – and so I paid little attention when Penguin told me they were entering me for The McVitie's Prize for Best Debut Collection. (Jokes about taking the biscuit we can take as read.)

I'd heard of it and always ignored it, especially as it seemed to be won each year by a *sly writer of prose*. But yes, winning this would be the ticket. There were other prizes too from the biscuit tsars (for Best Collection, and Best Single Poem) and all of the contenders would read a poem at a shindig in the Queen Elizabeth Hall, making fifteen readers in all. The winner would be announced at the end, and each of the three would make a speech.

I said earlier that Fansion and I were heading for Charing Cross, and indeed Charing Cross is a plausible station for the South Bank; so here I am with my companion of gravitas walking across the Hungerford Bridge to the South Bank complex early one April evening. It could not be mistaken for the same walk taken in 2018, as there were no beggars. And when you got to the other bank it wasn't filled with street food, performers, gambolling youths, and, above all, there were no rough sleepers. About the people, one thing could be said with certainty: none of them gave a toss about The McVitie's Prize except those on their way to the QEH who had poetic skin in the game.

There were three judges: a poet I had never heard of, an academic I had never heard of, and Joan Bakewell who had interviewed me a couple of times on one of these late-night lineupy programmes some years before. I liked her and her twinkly eyes a lot.

When we got to the venue and sat to one side, there was a tension you could cut like cake. This was because it's more usual for award ceremonies to be just that. It was a bit much to expect these sensitive souls to give a reading and then tell them that – sorry – you've not won. What's more, all fifteen poets were sitting in a line on the stage like targets in a funfair. And what's *even* more than that, I had no idea that my torment would be written on the body of The Me so plainly. He grimaced, he fidgeted, he kept checking his watch and taking scraps of paper out of the pockets of his black mohair suit (worn with an open-necked white shirt and black Cuban-heel boots, as you may recall, if you were there).

I'll explain. The unexamined plan was, in the event of my winning, to blow the gaff, lift the lid, and generally uncork Pandora. My first words were going to be, "I'm afraid you have just awarded the prize to somebody who has never written a poem in his life." I would then, not mentioning Paul, go on to explain what had been done. Paul's role would be played by a "tame boffin" (nice name for a soft-rock band, The Tame Boffins). Then – God help me – I was going to say something along the following lines: "The lessons in all this for modern poetry are plain to see. It's become too easy to persuade yourself that the emperor is wearing clothes when these clothes are something you've clothed him with yourself." (Limp, or not?) "I suggest you give the prize to one of my colleagues on the shortlist." (Thinking: even if he is a Tacky Transparency.) That's enough, I think.

The reason why The Me looked so grim? He didn't *want* to win, because he didn't want to say any of this and reveal himself as the opposite of Leo Barber (more of which later). And just before he'd taken his seat in the shooting gallery, Joan had patted him on the shoulder and said "Be of good cheer!" She may have said this because he looked down in the dumps; but *maybe not*.

We watched the readings; and yes, The Me did his stuff with grim passion – the p-word not yet a cliché in those days. Then, when all of the readings were done, Joan came on stage to announce the winners. When she came to *Nude with Violin*, she said, "All three judges agreed that this was a remarkable achievement. We differed among ourselves as to what exactly was remarkable about it [*audience laughter*] but its brilliance and originality shone through. Speaking for myself, I found that each reading of many of these poems – not all, I would say – revealed new treasures and new challenges. The prize goes then to Leo Barber."

It is possible for young children to laugh and cry at the same time. This was an example of something similar. First, The Me looked horrified, then horrified and ecstatic, then ecstatic and confused, then triumphant. No, of course he wasn't going to go through with the plan. The main reason was that it would translate out as a public "Joan, you are naïve and dim, too easily duped by celebrity." For some media people I would have been happy to do this, but in the present case no, no, *no*.

There were also two Bakewell-unrelated reasons for holding back. First, this would not have been a case of The Me being a provocateur or a turner-over of stones to reveal ugliness (as for Jimmy Paxton). It would have been a man approaching middle age being a sour clever-dick. The third reason came to him as he was idling through the early printings of the book. *He liked reading the poems*. Yes, he remembered the occasions when his thought had played with them, but he found images came to mind. He found ideas came to mind too as he read them with an attention *that gave no toss about whether there was a thinking creator there or not*. They were linguistic objects that could nourish the imagination, if you happened to have one, or rather the right kind of one. Also, they were not simple products of chance, because one poet's prosody and another's choice of words was not a matter of chance. The Me – The Me and I – had never bothered about all that postmodern or post-structuralist or last-post stuff about the death of the author (and didn't like what was on offer), but I was happy to line up with it on a temporary basis.

The Me would not have owned up to a fourth reason then, but I will now: Leo liked winning, and Leo rather liked the idea of spreading his wings into the world of poetry. It married nicely with the art projects and made the dogshit smell less bad.

In his thank you speech, The Me was humility itself, and he could begin with a truth:

> I'm afraid I've not prepared an acceptance speech simply because I never expected to win. [*a lie hot on the heels*] But let me just say this: when you strike out in the dark, as I did with these poems, the best you can hope for is not to strike a sleeping monster who will gobble you up for being such a presumptuous fool. Well ... [*at this point The Me was thinking of a wonderfully over-the-top award acceptance speech that Olivier had made in the USA*] not only have I not been gobbled up but I have been received into the poetic fold with such GENEROSITY, with such overwhelming GENEROSITY that I simply don't know how to thank you. No, I contradict myself. Thank you, Joan, thank you to ... [*the only names that came to mind were Bill and Ben*] ... to Joan's two marvellous co-panellists. Sorry, the nerves are getting to me. Shall I seek counselling? [*audience laughter and applause*]

I didn't stay for whatever kind of shindig occurred after all this, because sustaining the pose of a poet and being a hovering mute as the Sensitives gossiped about the poetry scene would be beyond me. I went straight back to Lois to enjoy a bottle of Pol Roger – in our special room. If I recall, that evening I was a Liverpool docker; she was a scouse scrubber with backcombed hair and laddered tights that she was trying to repair with nail varnish at the start ..."Whah yew playin' aah gerrl?" The champagne? I think we'd stolen it.

Actually, that was the last champagne we had for a fair few months, as some days after this Lois had it confirmed that she was pregnant. I know I've mentioned this before and may be confusing you with the order of play, but please bear with me. What floats above any of the events and any order of them was my happiness. Contentment, as in the French word for happy, is better. I don't really do happiness in the yippee-bang-on sense because there's always some tension over the next step, but yes, all this throat-clearing aside, it was a happy time: the poetry punt was coming off, I was going to be a dad, and Lois and I were perfection.

Bear this in mind as Fansion and I walked back to Charing Cross tube, then took the Edgware branch of the Northern Line to the station gripping the top of Haverstock Hill (otherwise known as Hampstead). By this time I was wishing for something a bit farther afield – I did once visit China – and I was wishing too that what did come next would not in fact come next. A glimpse of Paul, from behind, thumping along the pavement to *chez nous*, confirmed it was. Yes, it was a few weeks on from the QEH event ... for the third time, please "bear with me" on this. (A "book of words", "box of tricks" expression; I daren't even think about "methinks".)

Shortly after the QEH evening, I got a call from Paul. I knew it was him before a syllable was said because there was silence on the line, meaning that he was struggling to get a sentence off the ground. This usually happened when there was urgency. Eventually:

— ... It's Paul. Can I have a word?

— Fire away.

— I mean, can I come round to see you to have a word? I'll be in London next Tuesday visiting UCL and need to ask you something.

— Tuesday seems OK, yup.

— Will Lois be there?

— What's it all about, Paul?

— ... It's ... it's ... well, delicate.

— You mean "well delicate" in the sense of "these two guys is well gay"?

— It's a very *personal,* um, issue.

— Oh, alright. Lois is having lunch with somebody, so why not come about one.

And here he was. The Me opened the door with a look of brotherly concern, and we ducked in behind. It was unknown – it was impossible – for Paul to refuse food and drink, so when he did The Me's concern was taking up residence in his face.

— What's up, mate? And sit down for goodness sake.

[*at this point Paul made a hideous attempt at a smile, a hideous lunge towards shared humour*]

— ... I ... I'm in love with a lady.

To explain: this was a family joke. The four of us had been watching Parkinson's chat show one evening when David Niven was a guest delivering his streamlined anecdotes. Parkinson was setting him up for a yarn that involved Niven climbing into a girl's bedroom. He said, "You see, Michael [*draws on his cigarette*], I was in love with a lady ..."

From that point on, if male lust was on display – a wildlife programme showing an elephant on musth charging at a female with a yard-long erection, a mate loading his pockets with *Durex* for an evening out, or tamer cases with Mum and Dad present – we would say, in synch: *He's in love with a lady.*

— Explain!
— Not a word to Neet, right?
— Right.
— I happened to meet somebody in Wadham a couple of weeks ago with whom I hit it off.
— "With whom I hit it off"? Please, get on with it.
— I was interviewing her for a place on the PPP course. She goes to a school in Highgate. Very bright girl.
— Glad of that. Don't say you made her an offer conditional on her going to bed with you?
— That had better be a joke, Leo.
— Yes, "What kind of admissions tutor do you take me for?"
— I'm not the admissions tutor. Just interviewing. We give them scores out of ten.
— Get to the point.
— Can I bring her here?
— What's wrong with a hotel, your rooms at Wadham ...?
— Our age difference argues against an hotel and she would be recognisable at Wadham. Actually, to be honest, because this place is so handy we thought we could manage it during the school lunchtime, especially if she has a couple of free periods after 2.00PM.

It was not just for the obvious reasons that this made me

want to throw up. Waugh has a great speech in one of his novels where a woman turns on her Catholic and divorced husband – I probably have this wrong – for suggesting that it would be absolutely fine in the sight of the Pope or God or both if they popped off to bed together because they were not technically divorced in the sight of ... that kind of thing. It was the *coldness* of it all, the feeble, frigid thought-out-ness, plus the prissy little "argues against" and "recognisable" and the "*an* hotel"; not to mention the grim joke of our being *handy*. But a strong idea came into my head, which I'll get to soon; so I thought I'd act on that.

— OK, then.

— Really!

— Yes, really ... but it must be a one-off.

— [*pause*] If you say so.

Yes they could come here, and they could use the special room; and what's more they could, without knowing it, use the video equipment behind the one-way mirror.

I chose a day when Maya would be changing the beds in the afternoon and when I might plausibly be pottering around for a few minutes after she arrived (to turn the recorder on). And of course we had to choose a day when Lois would be away.

I had no intention of watching the damned recording, at least only to check it had recorded. I had no immediate intention of doing anything with the recording either, so why did this idea come into my head and why did I go along with it?

First and almost foremost, up to this point I'd thought of Paul as a good guy who put the ratty me to shame. But in the words of the only poem I know by heart:

> For sweetest things turn sourest by their deeds;
> Lilies that fester smell far worse than weeds.

Then, still on the thinking-through-emotion tack: he had come along to stain my married home with his ... only seedy bloggers pile negatives (a phrase that would make a nice embroidered sampler) ... plans. And then the cold strategic thought that sat beside this, that grounded it almost: this tape could be a weapon. I might need his help again, and I might have to employ a little *leverage*. I hated myself for even thinking this, but acted on it anyway.

— Actually, Sherry would like to meet you when she comes.

— What's Sherry short for?

— Scheherazade.

I'd wanted to smack him, but at this point The Me contented himself with doing a deranged Frankie Valli, screaming *Sherry, Sherry baybeee!!!!*

at top volume right in his face.

— Steady on, mate.

— I'll steady on, old matey. But if she is sherry, who is *sherrier* and indeed *sherriest*? [*this was a steal from an obscure Ashbery poem*]

— Eh?

Fansion and I left at this point.

Now for some mature reflection. Lois and I had no secrets from each other; and it was vile to have to keep this to myself. (The logistics of their meet-up will have to wait.) It was like going round with a disgusting taste in your mouth.

Oxford interviews are at Christmas; Christmas was coming; and I love Christmas; and this was taking the shine off. But

I was determined not to let it sink deeper than the shine. I threw myself heart and soul into the Christmas tree, the decorations, and into anything else that came to mind. "What's got into you?" Lois said as I suggested yet again that we watch a Christmas film in the evening. This was in the video era, so it was not the doddle it is nowadays. *It's a Wonderful Life* (both crying like babies at the end, especially me), *Miracle on 34th Street*, and all the others.

As will be obvious by now, I'm blessed with good luck, and it was good luck that we'd watched *Miracle*, an' oi'll tell ee for woi. Shortly after my McVitie's triumph, the *Guardian* asked a number of prominent "modernist" (ha!) poets to write a Christmas poem in order to pose the musical question: "Has modernism lost contact with the homely virtues?"

I didn't want to ask Paul for help, and hit upon the idea of ventriloquizing a fictional character, keeping the reference sufficiently obscure for the necessary degree of "difficulty"; so ...

There's a scene in *Miracle* (fabulous film) where Kris Kringle, the twinkling old geezer who either thinks he is or *is* the real Santa Claus, has been sectioned in Bellevue hospital, laid low by the thought that his lady protector has abandoned him, and is sitting in a towelling robe staring into space. The next day I also happened to watch a programme about humpback whales. All I did was, in an anything-goes spirit, speak in the voice of Kris in that moment, plus added whales. *Smaart!* as they say in Manchestoh.

This poem was well thought of (but only Derek Malcolm cracked the reference).

Bellevue

Boiling alone in the snow of this
terry-towelling robe, all tests failed by design

I gave them a life philosophy they called
"disposable, desultory verbal doodling"

– the icing above the central constriction:
"What's 4 plus 7?" I answer "Exhausting Restriction."

My Goddess failed me so I'm failing away.
She didn't believe who I was: "Kindly,"

she said, "would make a good grandpa," she said.
In thought I'm a humpback off the Irish coast

crashing and blowing in December, my turquoise fins
the vestigial wings of an Angel Fish. You see

I can't breathe in this sea of faith, though I hear
faery remedies for my sins just beneath. Later

will be the usual conjuring tricks with the fates
and bonhomie feasts. I've made myself an island

closing my eyes against harpoons. But if she just
dipped her toes in one cold wavelet I might sense

her friendly spores or her innocence. Then
I could go home, heading due north. What

could be easier to believe in than reindeers
pulling a festive whale through the night sky.

14: Between the Ceiling and the Cupboard-Top

The "mature reflection" continues with thoughts of Scheherazade Burstyn-Coyne. I'd seen her locking up her bike by our front gate. I saw her hat, one of those girls'-school hats that looks like a top slice of Saturn. I wasn't having Paul answering my door, so I did. She said, in a flustered way, "Oh hello, I'm Sherry ... Paul must have mentioned ..." Then she collected herself and fumbled in her bag for a copy of *Nude with Violin*, handing it to me, plus a biro. "I wonder if you'd do me the honour, err, *Leo*," she said.

I resisted so many temptations at this point. Why not write *For Sherry, hoping that my brother passes the entrance exam, Leo*. Or why not ...

Actually what I would write now is: *For Sherry, yes, I suppose you have pretty eyes, but each of them is for the main chance*. No, bitchy only. I could have been charm itself, but nonetheless carefully written: *For Sherry, who is so difficult to admire. Yours ever, Leo*. You can tell, dear listener/reader, that this is still under my skin.

Then I remembered that one-way mirrors don't work unless the room being videoed is in good light, with the observing room being in darkness. I had to think fast. This was fast but daft. After I'd told them to "help yourselves to drinks", I added, as they were thanking me, "Oh, by the way, this may seem a bit weird, but the wiring in this place is ancient so we had to put the burglar alarm on a slave circuit near the room you'll be using. It will only work if you keep the ceiling light on. Don't worry, I don't see the need to train a searchlight on you." Giggle-giggle from our Sher.

I left for a brisk walk on the heath followed by lunch at The Spaniards. I remember sitting in the most distant and darkest oak-panelled saloon I could find, over a steak pie and a pint of orange juice and soda, thinking of A.E. Housman. I knew little about him and had only dipped into his poems, but I'm sure I'd read somewhere that when he lived in London – if he did, if it was him at all – he would sometimes lunch at The Spaniards. He would have a pint of bitter with the food, and the hops in the beer, being soporific, would encourage the wooziness that aids poetic composition. He would walk back over the heath to an iambic rhythm bringing phrases to mind. Something about this – something like innocence and self sufficiency and maybe sexlessness – cheered me up at this point. But it also tee'd me up for seeing Sherry cycling back to school with a lopsided grin. "Leo! Hi there!"

I knew I couldn't face Paul, and just hoped to God that he'd remembered to leave before Maya came to do an afternoon's cleaning. It didn't matter if he saw her; but it bloody mattered if I saw him.

We never used the special room again. Don't panic. All I mean is that we abandoned this room and used another. I suggested to Lois that we use it as the nursery because we could keep an eye on them through the one-way without disturbing their play. (By this time we knew it would be twins, not yet knowing whether they'd be identical or fraternal.)

We now shoot back to Fansion and I, who had left Frognal after The Me's Sherry-baby performance. It was down the Northern to Leicester Square on the Kennington branch, then westward on the Piccadilly. After Barons Court we alighted at "Hammerhome" – no, it doesn't get any better, does it?

Why "Hammerhome"? I hadn't the foggiest. But we waited in the cold and the fog for a bus; yes, a *bus*. As we stood shoulder to shoulder like, uh, like, um, a possibly-dead person and his spirit guide (possibly), I ventured:
— Do you mind my asking, why a bus?
— I was going to tell you, Mr Barber, but essentially time is marching on, by which I mean that this must be brought to fruition all within an Earth day. Given this, we need to make some rather substantial leaps in time – some number of years. If we did this on the Underground it would be deeply unpleasant, I can assure you. What we'll do is repair to somewhere that is essentially wasteland, a kind of buffer zone, in which we'll be protected against the worst of the spatio-temporal-psychic shake-up.

My mind turned to the Chernobyl exclusion zone – this disaster had recently happened; so we are talking both present time and the revisited time, if you gets me drift – but you don't get to Russia by bus (another suggestion-phrase for a sampler).

— Ah, here we are.
We climbed onto the number 33 and headed west. I know my London bus routes and was hoping it would be going past The Bull's Head at Barnes, as if that mattered. No, we didn't. We changed somewhere along the route onto the 371 and crossed the river. Better than The Bull's Head (though without the jazz), we passed the Dysart at Petersham. If I

recall, this featured in L.P. Hartley's *The Hireling*. Sorry, I'm wittering again. I tend to witter when something unpleasant I don't really understand is coming up.

Past Ham and on towards Kingston, when Fansion pressed the button for the bus to let us off at the next stop. Once again, the question is: why? There was a roundabout, a William Hill bookie, a convenience store, houses, a bit of grass and some benches, and that was it. We sat on a bench. Fansion said this:

— You see, this is neither London nor Greater London. Nothing wrong with that, of course; and it's safe for you.

— How many years do we "leap"?

— About eight or nine, ten maybe; in these cases one cannot be too precise. It'll help if you close your eyes, Mr Barber.

I did not take his advice because vision is what I'm all about. No, there was nothing wrong with the place in terms of what was there, only in terms of what was not: people-things (I don't count betting shops). No pubs, no coffee bars, no kids playing, no couples, just houses and the road before them. Buses came and went in blurred red lines, like melted sealing wax, Sky dishes went up and hedges came down to create car ports, darkness alternated with light with the nullity of the piece that won the Turner prize. (Jealous? Moi?) I lost my sense of time. Just as hours are compressed to minutes in the dream of an anaesthetised patient, so years were compressed to chunks of minutes, not, I think, by the dream-trick but by taking away my sense of passing time.

There was change, but nothing changed, like minor ripples on something that was essentially nothing. Then the feeling of despair, the feeling that hell is the *absence* of other people and their gossiping, flawed, striving lives.

Yeah, but what if you were like sitting beside a beautiful deserted loch with the sun shining?

With nature, there is something else there; you aren't really alone. Built areas like this take that something away ...

Yeah, but what ...

Shut UP!

As I was saying, even Paul-Sherry was better than this *absence*. Of course, war and torture *aren't* better than it, but these are also a kind of human absence. Actually, I can't really speak this out, *tell ee the troof*. Another Roy Fisher passage might help again: from *A Furnace*, from the "Introit" section:

>   – and that body of air
> caught between the ceiling
> and the cupboard-top, that's like
> nothing that ever was.

We like things that are like things that were or are something. I think I'll give up at this point, though not before saying: I looked at this stretch of road and realised why we make things – art, stories, poetry, music. Without them, it's just a place to live and a road to get us to work and to supermarkets.

I stood up and waddled about, feeling giddy and queasy. Fansion told me to be careful as I swayed past a middle-aged woman on another bench reading *The Daily Mail*. I felt as if I could easily fall into her. How many times (I then thought) could I get away with falling into people without their thinking it was intentional? I remembered my Dad, who was scared of his Dad, telling me about the time he walked past his father three times, dropping a glass of water each time. I laughed at the idea of falling into people as a way of expanding one's social circle. Laughed and thought: Yes, we need humour as well as art to fill the void I was failing to describe.

I came to on the number 33 as we approached Hammersmith – sorry, "Hammerhome" – on the way back. Fansion spoke to me like a dentist supervising an extraction with gas.

Then it was back to Frognal by the same route. By this time, clever old Fansion had acquired a key, so he let us in and led me to the expanded kitchen, now with French windows leading on to a garden strewn with child-friendly objects. It was clearly the aftermath of a weekend lunch; and it was what looked like high summer.

Let me run down the personnel.

First, there was he who Lois and I called "Mr Punch" – the offspring of Paul and Anita, born a few months after the twins and in reality called George. We called him Mr Punch because he had not only inherited his parents' *menton volontaire* but sported too an aquiline nose, added to which he sounded like a baby klaxon when excited, which was often. He had Paul's body and Anita's mind.

Paul was there, rather more brisk than the old Paul, and more confident and with a horrible hairstyle he had acquired in the '80s, one that really only suited the excellent Jonathan Ross – shortish sides and a high, gelled quiff like cheap plastic. (I had noted the birth of this monstrosity on my bus journey as well as the tacky suitings that went with it.) Anita too had hair accommodations that also involved some sweeping back and side wings. She'd also gained in confidence, and no mistake; as we shall see.

Both Lois and The Me had put on a bit of weight and clearly bothered less about clothes. In her it was a relaxing into maturity; in The Me it seemed to mean his relaxing the reins. In some eyes – to my eyes now – The Me was diminished. We'll return to this shortly.

Then there were my beautiful children – Lance (I explained the name earlier) and Belle. Beautiful because they looked liked Lois, but beautiful too in their characters. (Yes, yes, I know ... please make allowances.) Belle was observant-shrewd-serene. Lance was loud-impulsive-sensitive. Both were mischievous-marvellous-hilarious. (Lay down your weary adjectives, lay down.)

Before I describe the scene – a scene in both senses – let me expand on the "diminished". In the years since the Paul-Sherry episode I had rather given up on conceptual art, installations, performances, and the usual dogshit menagerie. It wasn't just that everybody was doing it, I'd just had enough. That ladder could be thrown away. However, nothing had really come along to take its place. Against the grain, I'd got Paul to churn out more stuff for a second collection, and had added some of my ventriloquizing ones to it – about Tony Hancock preparing to broadcast his pathetic sitcom for ITV after dismissing Galton and Simpson; Jean Simmons as Diane Tremayne in *Angel Face* under a motor car, quietly re-engineering the reverse gear so it would kill her father and stepmother: no, not bunnies known for their happy dispositions – but the reviews ranged from the indulgent to the querulous to the non-existent. Happy as Lois and the children made me – there is a dangling modifier coming up, if that's what it is – I needed a brilliant public life for the happiness I was designed for.

Paul and the twins came in from the garden carrying a biology textbook. Paul speaks:
— Well, that's photosynthesis and the eye sorted.
— Did you thank Uncle Paul? [*Lois*]
— Thank you, Uncle Paul! [*the twins singing together to the tune of "Thank You for the Music"*]
Then Anita (*the new Anita*):
— It's so neat, isn't it, that Paul can be such a *support* for you now we live in town?

Yes, they lived in London, in a fine house by the river in Chiswick. Paul had been headhunted to be the Director of the Leverhulme Centre for The Brain Sciences in Bloomsbury (jointly funded by UCL). The job went with a Professorship at UCL, though he could hang on to his Wadham Fellowship. He was a *mover*, as they call it in sciencey circles. But this did not help his troubled speech. I writhed through his inaugural lecture, which took place at a time when he was experimenting with little phrases like "you know", "as it were", "as a matter of fact", before word-hurdles; and I coped by imagining other phrases he could have used – "heavens to mercy", "shitting hell".

— I have to admit to missing Oxford [*Anita is banging on*]: the feasts, the most general of general conversation, the beautiful architecture. But then I think my husband's favourite architecture is an open-plan office with banks of computers. Admit it, darling.

— I'm a hell of a lot busier.

— And yet you still find time to help your nephew and niece with their biology homework.

— [*Lance, loud and clear*] My Daddy helps us with our English homework. And Mummy does the maths, don't you Mummy?

— My Daddy [*this is Mr Punch with the baby klaxon in his throat*] made me an electric car last week.

— My Daddy can draw pictures and he can draw cartoons of famous people. [*Lance*]

— And ... [*Belle*]

— Can we keep it down now, kids. [*Lois*]

— And our Daddy can write poems, whole *books* of poems. [*Belle*]

— Yeah, but [*Mr Punch*] my Mum says they're stupid and don't make no sense.

— What does she know. [*Lance*] My Daddy can do lots of things. He once invented somebody who helped the country, he appears on TV, he is in galleries, he writes in the papers.

— My Daddy understands all about the brain.

— SO DOES MY DADDY! DON'T YOU, DADDY? [*Lance*]

The Me was the only one amused by this. In fact, he seemed to be reconstituting. Sitting next to Lance, he gave him a strong hug.

— Of course I do, Lancey.

— Yeah, yeah, and my Mummy and Daddy says he's just a jack of all trains and a master of, uh ...

— It's "trades", you idiot. [*Belle*] You're stupid. And you say things like "don't make no sense".

Belle had been sitting on a stool until a blow from Mr Punch knocked her off it. She banged her head on the floor and we took her to casualty (she was fine; and the varmints, as we called them, enjoyed the adventure) as the guests took themselves back to Chiswick.

As for that "reconstituting" look, The Me was indeed reconstituting; I was reconstituting because I now had a project. It came suddenly with the thought that the twins would never again have to scrape the barrel for, or to gloss or spin, the achievements of their Daddy. Daddy was going to publish a heavy scientific tome with a university press; though note I said "publish" not "write" – Paul could do that – and note too that "scientific" is not quite right because it will be aimed at The Great Naïves. As for the deeper springs of all this, you're as good a judge as I am.

Coddling my plan, turning it over and over like a precious coin, holding it up to the light and having a secret laugh at it, I waited a few days and then contacted Paul. I had just been put "on line" – against my will – and so I composed a careful (whatever is the opposite of "fired off") email to him, which went like this.

> Hi Paul,
>
> Good to see y'all two Saturdays ago. Some good things do end in tears (that's the tears that rhymes with ears not with hairs). Anyway, the varmints had a lot to tell their friends about the visit to the Royal Free. Lance did not need amplification, of course. Belle has perfected the head-cocked "suffering" pose.
>
> Actually, I'm writing about something else. You may think I've gone mad, but even if you do, something good could still come of it. (The opposite of the "good ... tears" business.)

In the first place, I've recently been going through a bit of a dry spell on the creative front – why does that never seem to happen to you? – and it got me thinking about where all this stuff comes from. Or rather, how the life one leads gives rise to new ideas, or in my case to very few of them. I don't like psychologising as most of it seems to be post hoc guff; but I'm attracted to brain-based work. Of course, for all I know you may think ideas about how novel ideas arise in the brain is all a lot of toss compared to vision, attention, language, memory, and all the rest of it. But ...

[*takes deep breath*]

what I had in mind was a collaboration. I work in what they now call "the creative industries" and you are Mr Brain. I was thinking of a book – full of hard science but with the common touch – that we could co-author on the neuropsychology (or do they now call it neuroscience?) of creativity. Make a bitta dough, my boy.

Am I bonkers? Say it ain't so, Jo, or rather, Paul.

Love,

Leo

I heard back in a day ...

leo:

not toss at all!!!!!
can you come along to the centre around coffee time next thursday?

cheers

p

All this is to set up my next jaunt with Fansion. Going up in the lift at Russell Square, I felt I was nearly home to my present day: no smokers, lots of foreign faces, more people struggling for dirtier niches, youth that had rattled itself loose from the fashion concerns that measured out my young life. There were fashions alright, but nothing was at stake.

Round a couple of corners and there was the glittering carbuncle of glass, steel and Portland stone squeezed between two reticent old buildings. And there, wandering in, wearing a suit and tie, top button undone and the tie black, was The Me. As anticipated in Anita's little speech, the place was open plan. It reminded me of Orson Welles' film of *The Trial*. No privacy in which to scratch your balls or yank up your tights. And there was The Me thinking the thoughts I was thinking now, fenced off from future knowledge (lucky sod), waving through the glass wall of Paul's office.

Once inside the office – all four of us – Paul adjusted the horrible and vertical Venetian blinds and settled behind his desk like a king. Having rung for coffee, he said:
— No, not remotely toss. The issue of how ideas – "representations" more generally – come into consciousness is the great ignored issue in theories of prefrontal function. One only sees a version of it in John Morton's model of lexical access; and that's not frontal. Nobody thinks about it ...
— It's not popped into their consciousnesses. [*The Me as clever-dick, of course*]

Yes, dear listener/reader, here we are back with these Open

University dialogues. I can't remember *exactly* what Paul said in these scenes I saw, but you can bet your life it was less stilted and machine-generated than my version. I'll do what I can, avoiding the corny "taking-a-sip-of-coffee-he-mused" stuff.

— Apart from work on the left orbito-frontal region as a kind of pre-conceptual intuition-centre, we've been obsessed with the frontal brain as the place where a controlling homunculus sits and enables self-control, planning, set-shifting, and all the rest of it, with the more philosophically-minded thinking about the implications of this top-down, monitoring executive for self-awareness. But of course, the sane, mature, adult, wakeful mind is not ONLY something that is "in control", it's something to which relevant, or not very relevant but novel and *interesting,* thoughts occur.

Paul said this with perfect fluency and with the kind of excitement normally associated with his brother. The Me seemed to be restraining himself from letting loose an all-American *Whoooooooo!!!!* Paul continued:
— I don't know how much detail you want at this stage, but ...
— Go on. I'm all ears.
— The best general theory of frontal functioning is Tim Shallice's Supervisory Attentional System (or SAS) theory.
— The three letters that send a chill down the spine of the enemy ...

The Me's comment was touching on the speech that had just been made by Michael Portillo, referring to the Special Air Service (SAS); the one that began his transformation from political contender to zany in bright-red trousers on a station platform. Paul ignored this overfamiliar gag-lette and busied himself with his computer until a figure with six rectangles appeared on the screen above his head. Inside the top one was Supervisory Attentional System, with a thick, black, downward arrow coming from it. Contention Scheduling was a box on the right. Perceptual System was a box on the far left. Never mind about the others for now, or for ever. Inside the middle box, by the way, were ovals called schema control units. In fact, the kind of stuff I had spent my life avoiding.

— Don't bother about the details and the jargon, but think about this. Most of the things we do and think about are routine, so they don't require us to pay attention to them. Think of driving a car – I mean the actions you take, changing gear, braking, etc. Or making a cup of tea. But sometimes there's unpredictability – you see a friend and pull over, or the kettle doesn't come on. Or you have something novel to do, like finding your way to the railway station in a strange city. Or there's something completely new to master, like a new boardgame. Or you have to abandon one routine and switch to another, what we call "set shifting"; you might be told by your boss, for example, to sort the goods in the stockroom by price rather than by type. All these things require a top-down supervisory system to take charge. Needless to say, critics say this is no more than a lot of stimulus-response chains with an homunculus on top ...

The Me was looking serious and was fiddling with his tie as if about to impersonate Oliver Hardy. He spoke:
— I was thinking more along the lines of the SAS being another word for the self.

No, this is *not* a case of *l'esprit de l'escalier*. I'm not a mere art-fart, as may have emerged. Sorry.

— Well, exactly. In fact, a friend sent me a draft of a piece he was writing on the SAS and theory-of-mind development in which he says something like "the SAS (i.e. me ...)". But it's a *necessary* kind of theory despite this, and there's a lot more to it than I'm saying. The only problem is I need – we need – to set up something that's its symmetrical opposite.

— You mean, the SAS needs to be turned off.

— EXACTLY! [*see above comment on* l'esprit de l'escalier] Representations bubble up *unsupervised* from our knowledge and memory stores and from emotional centres that might bump up against one another to create bottom-up novelty; not a system that *copes* with novelty. Computationally, my first thought was a connectionist network without a teaching signal.

— Like these neural nets you used for the poetry?

— Kind of. Not quite. Now, I'm not dumb enough to equate a teaching signal and the SAS ...

— Me neither ...

— But it's a good first step to see what happens when we boost bottom-up deliverance and get rid of the teaching signal of your bog-standard network. I'm not talking here about something as basic as Hebbian learning ...

— Nay nay, thrice nay.

— You'd better be taking this seriously, Leo ...

— I am! It's just that I'm excited. This is how I get.

Yes that was how he got, and I still get, and the conversation continued till lunchtime. Which could have been a celebratory lunch. But Paul was holding back because Neet-not-so-petite had told him to cut back on the beer and the pies and the chips. I felt sorry for him, for this and for what was coming. Over ham salads and small glasses of Frascati, we decided to sell the idea to Oxford University Press. I would come up with a catchy title and Paul would be first author. I slipped in the fact that my autobiographical musings, along with some judicious tips for increasing one's creativity, would also be in there somewhere. I don't think he heard, because he was watching a cottage pie and chips waft past.

15: "The law of chaos is the law of ideas"

Fansion and I didn't hover over the lunch, and it was back to the chain gang of rattling trains for me. Anyway, what I need now is to give you some idea about how the book came into being.

I was amazed by Paul's speed. Partly this was due to his access to the kind of IT that speeds everything up. But it was really down to the man himself. You see, he was more than a boffin; in fact, he was more of an artist than I ever was. Seized by a kind of madness that made him generate ideas like crazy in the form of yards of ragged text, which I had to comb through and prune, and a gallery of "black box" and neural-network figures, it wasn't difficult to grasp the *general* idea behind the forest of detail at the time, but to reproduce it now ... uff; the struggle begins.

Having invited you to pin back your lugholes, I must warn you that this will be far more challenging than my poetry lecture. Any road up, this is what Paul's contribution was (two-thirds to three-quarters of the book was the plan).

First, he described the SAS theory and the evidence for it and gave a critique. Much pruning and combing needed here.

But then, to my surprise, he had a chapter called *A Big Fat Caveat*. This warned that it would be "naïve" to think that creativity would be unleashed simply by knocking out or turning down the SAS. If we had no SAS, or a reduced one, we would be trapped in blind impulse, stimulus-driven, slaves to habit, while living in a continuous present. Creativity would be "out of the question". *However*, the SAS relies on "a veritable plethora" (Big Fat Cliché) of bottom-up inputs that are "grist to the mill" (another Big Fat Cliché) of creativity. These are used "in the service of self-control". What we must do is to retain the bottom-up boys while *not* using them in the service of self-control but in the service of "creative solutions and imaginings" ... I'm no psychologist, but this looked slippery to me, so I ignored it, as did the dimmer reviewers.

Then he sketched the outline of his "Selector Theory" in which "representations" bubble up till they crest a threshold and The Selector selects between them based on certain wired-in criteria. Note that, in contrast to the SAS, The Selector does not intervene and boss about: it's the Judgement of Paris.

Then the difficult stuff – his "hybrid" computational model of his theory, taking up most of the space. "Hybrid" because half of it was symbolic (having a program – lines of instructions in a computer language). This was what he and his chums called GOFAI: good old-fashioned AI. The rest was connectionist. No symbols here, just nodes with levels of activation, perhaps in banks, and connections between them varying in strength with the learning "experience". You can label these nodes as meaning "green" or "bum-fluff" or anything you like, but they're only numbers, and all that happens is that lots of algebra gets done very quickly and in parallel.

Usually, these networks learn by feedback based on the

discrepancy between what the network ought to output and what it actually does. Paul got rid of these as there is no "ought" in the system. In a really simple case, three banks of units could interact without supervision – colours, events, animals. The output could be a red elephant having tea. But if there was a bank of emotion units, and if this was set to "negative", the output might be a black snake in the bed. This was easy for Paul. More tricky was how you give "semantic content" to our interpretations of what the nodes meant (e.g. 0.09 activation might be "at breakfast"). This was the symbolic half of the model. At the lowest level you had what is called "predicate calculus", consisting of individual things without properties (e.g. x and y, and z) – "arguments" is the term for these – and predicates. F could be "is female"; G could be "kisses frogs"; H could be "is a frog". In addition, there were the connectives like v meaning *or*, & meaning *and*, $\rightarrow$ meaning *implies*, ~ meaning *not*. Some people call this a language of thought (or LOT).

The next level up was syntax with hardwired structures for noun-phrase, verb-phrase, clause, adjectival phrase, and so on. Under certain constraints, random number generators combined arguments, predicates and connectives, and when a critical mass of these was achieved they were mapped onto syntax. It was possible – God knows how – for, say, *Fx & Gx* to map to a clause/sentence giving "it's a female frog-kisser". Maybe then, with K being "frightened" and H being "is a dog" (Ky & Hy), you combine the two to get the sentence: "If it's a female frog-kisser it frightens a dog."

I'm lost
take me home
please

make me a cup of cocoa
&
turn
on the telly
I told you I'd spent me life
avoiding
this kind of stuff

At this point, trying to revive myself, I'll tell you what my contribution was to all this. Inside the "black box" that was supposed to select between these outputs (The Selector, recall, and recall it was also the name of a band making a comeback at that time) I put a photo of Pauline Black (lead singer) to sweeten the pill, as it were.

I'm embarrassed, not by what I've just said, nor by the fact that I have no real clue about these models and how the simulations worked or failed to work. I'm embarrassed by how banal this is. I mean the basic idea. I mean, of course, creativity is not just selecting among what pops up. Come *on!* Isn't it more like hunting?

But what Paul did was impressive, right enough. He was brilliant at mapping elements of the model to brain loci and processes, even if it was speculation. I got him to expand this stuff so we could happily say the book was about the brain, not about his modelling spasms.

Are you wondering at this point, "What have I let myself in for?" You may also wonder whether all this is a bit old-fashioned. Where are the pretty pictures of brains in red, yellow and blue? Where is the term *neuroscience* and the intransitive use of the verb *light up*? The fact is: Paul was happily behind the curve. He was, of course, involved in neuro-imaging, but he thought he was on firmer territory when he studied stroke patients and animal models. He was not on firmer territory constructing models like the one I've failed to describe; but he was happier. Why? He thought there was fool's gold among the real stuff in neuro-imaging and could foresee the future when any fool without the teeniest shard of biology education could yack on about the hypothalamus and about what "apparently" lights up when we think about bum fluff. He was his brother's brother, a kind of reactionary who still used the term "physiological psychology" and cringed at the word "neuroscience".

In fact, as I write this, I have a sour taste knowing what my plans were and how they would come off; and not at all looking forward to the next scene between Paul and me that Fansion was – I was sure – taking me to. Patience, please, before I finish my description of the book. I can go on, I don't have to go on. I'll go on – and on and on.

I did a lot of work on Paul's text, as I said, and did this while writing my own bit. I decided to be the soft brioche around the meat of Paul's matter. At the beginning I wrote a lot of guff about Keats' idea of negative capability, interpreting him to mean "tune down your SAS, relax, and drift downstream" (and a great idea for a new kind of vacuum cleaner will bubble up). Then there was a lot of autobiographical stuff (fiction, really) about how ideas come to me – *larf!* – when I had, as I put it, "switched off the planning, error-correcting, self-conscious aspect of my Self". And then there was invented reportage about what "other artists" had said to me about the creative process. These were people who were safely dead or had otherwise passed beyond attention. Yes, there was a lot of "taking-a-sip-of-coffee-he-mused" stuff here.

Then, at the end of the book – the only part most buyers of

the book would read – I had a chapter called Five Exercises to Tune down your SAS and Release the Creative in You. To give me my due, and to explain this spike of the dog turd, I had read bits of Shallice's book and learned that there were five kinds of situations in which the SAS comes into play.

(1) planning/decision-making
(2) troubleshooting
(3) novel/ill-learned action sequences
(4) dangerous or technically difficult actions
(5) overcoming strong habitual response tendencies or temptation

Here then were my five exercises. First you must set aside a morning or an afternoon to do at least two of the following:

(1) Sit in a chair, close your eyes and imagine that you are at a point in your past when nothing had to be done, when you just had to assimilate events, though there is really no "had to". Some point in childhood is ideal. For example, when you were watching the school football/netball team play while drinking a bottle of pop. If you find your mind drifting to the present and tasks before you, *gently* return it to this primal scene. The mind is not like a monkey in a tree. You must not try to master it; just shift *gently* back to the netball, darlings.

(2) In that half day, nothing even the titchiest bit difficult must be attempted or thought about. Do not evoke trouble that you have to shoot. Don't, for instance, shop in that branch of Marks & Spencer where the bossy woman on the basket checkout expects you to pack your own bag and says "Just stand to one side and I'll pass to you." She's not worth it, doll. Leave it.

(3) If there is novelty on the horizon, run away from it. Don't open any post, watch TV, try a new fruit-tea flavour, pick up a book (unless you've already read it), hold a conversation with anybody who is not a totally predictable bore.

(4) Making a cup of tea is fine, so long as you have all the materials easily to hand. But threading a needle? Reaching for a CD on a high shelf? Ironing your wife's best knickers? Oh no, dear, no dear, no. Back off, playmates! You know it makes sense.

(5) Indulge your habits to their farthest reaches. I struggled here. I suggested developing routines over the weeks. Going to the papershop for your *Daily Mail* and saying exactly the same thing to the Patels, something that could invite no response by virtue of its being either boring or silly or both. One suggestion was: "They say Catherine the Great changed her lover as often as she changed her nightdress. Cheers!" Try to say it in three syllables wearing the same clothes and looking up at the Panadol.

I shamelessly claimed that doing this would "sweat out" novelties from the dormant creative mind. I invented testimonials from "a friend in advertising", "a mate who's a set designer", "one of my brother's fellow scientists". I claimed to follow this regime myself. And yes, it meant steering well clear of Paul's Big Fat Caveat.

What we had produced then was prime, *premiere cuvée* dogshit. The so-called theory of creativity was – to reiterate – banal and its presentation unintelligible to most, and probably, in its details, full of gaps and errors (unless my brother was a genius), and there was the Big Fat Caveat an' all, while my brioche bookend was ... Got the idea?

In passing, I'll tell you why I am over-exercising the term *dogshit*. In two words – Howlin' Wolf (real name Chester Burnett). In the late '60s, Howlin' Wolf's record company decided that a cool way to make some more money out of the man would be to have him record an album and then add "psychedelic" context – Hendrixy guitars, Beatle-ish electronics, that kind of thing. They played the result to him and asked him what he thought. "It's dogshit" he said. As I read the report in *Melody Maker,* whenever it was, this stamped something into me. Those are the only words needed, no point in reflecting on why. And Chester Burnett was the perfect man to say them. I saw him perform at Hammersmith in one of those blues packages around this period. He was huge, and would bring his huge self to the very lip of the stage staring down the audience – that's how to do it, Johnny Lydon – playing the majestically slashing chords of "Down in the Bottom", not needing the rhythm section behind him. Not only was this the kind of electric R&B that makes you feel life is exciting and anything could happen, it chased away teenage social politics, troubles with a looming mother, and all the little crusts of itchy nonsense, like a leaf-blower.

Well, all that sounds fine and dandy, now don't it just. But it's "the symmetrical opposite" (ones of Paul's favourite phrases) of my own dear self. I constructed the leaves and never get round to blowing them away. Not that you could call this a leaf, this present project and the Paul plan; more like a concrete bollard about to be dropped onto a table set for afternoon tea.

* * *

The title I'd thought up for the book was *The Law of Chaos and Ideas: Neuropsychology of The Creative Mind*. Huh? I read then and read now a Wallace Stevens poem every night shortly before going to sleep, and in *Extracts from Addresses to the Academy of Fine Ideas* I saw the line, "The law of chaos is the law of ideas." Chaos because that's almost what the removal of SAS would seem to encourage – actually it *doesn't* but we'll let that pass – and ideas because that's what we're after. Just to keep Paul happy, I avoided the word "neuroscience".

The combination of "Paul" and "happy" ... well, let us see.

Meanwhile, back at the flange: as Fansion and I went down the Northern Line I was in receipt of a significant lung-lunge and head rearrangement. Oh dear, oh very dear ... off at "You Stun" station and across Euston Road walking east; and there was The Me. I really can't recall where I'd come from, and why I was walking and not being driven, but I'm pretty sure I was en route to Gray's Inn Road and a materials shop to buy watercolour paper and pastels. We moved up behind him and heard a loud "Leo!" Just behind us was Paul. The Me simply froze and fixed a grin, but I know he was, in one of our dad's army phrases, shitting rivets. Why?

A couple of days ago I had emailed Paul my "first draft" of the book. There was a single author, Leo Barber, and the book was dedicated "To my brilliant brother Paul from whom I have learned so much." Paul's meat-of-the-matter was presented as *my own*.

Now, I have to own up. No, not in the groovy George Melly sense with which we began, but really owning up to my deserving the c-word of the Pete-and-Dud dialogue. How can I sustain my beloved lightness while I say that my plan was to steal the book from Paul because his Scheherazade-self bloody well deserved it and because ...? We've been through this before. And what if Paul said he would go public about this and at least tell Oxford University Press? Well, did I not have a videotape of him and Scheherazade Double-Barrel that would certainly interest Anita and open the prospect of darling Mr Punch growing up in San Diego?

Actually, as it turned out, Paul didn't seem that angry:
— We need to talk, mate.

They ducked into a big pub of the Departure Lounge variety, which I'd always thought was the model for The Midnight Bell in that wonderful Patrick Hamilton novel.

The Me went to get a couple of pints and Paul settled at a table. After a big swallow each, Paul extended his hand and The Me shrank out of the way, nearly spilling his pint. I had been expecting a punch. In fact, Paul was going to shake The Me by the hand.
— You've saved my life.
— Whaat?
— I was trying to figure out how to tell you that I wanted out. It's really your kind of thing, this book, not mine. Soooo relieved you spotted that.
— Why? I mean how?
— Where do I begin? The central idea is bollocks, and my Big Fat Caveat is a stupid evasion. I enjoyed designing the models; but that's my problem. Anyway, when you run the networks they get stuck in local minima and output bugger-all of interest. And as for the symbolic model, well, naïve doesn't even get close. As if you could just map a primitive LOT onto syntax in that simple way! Did Chomsky die in vain!

— I didn't know he was dead.

— He's not. Lighten up, for God's sake. You look like you've seen a ghost.

The Me began to relax but did not trust himself to speak.

— And the other thing is [*Paul*]: my experience of creativity is not like turning off a supervisor: it's like *turning it on*. Bashing your head against the facts until there's a chink of light.

— Well put.

— You can have it for your next book.

— *Causing a Chink: The Neurotrash Diaries*. Penguin will take it.

— Get another pint in. [*Paul had already finished his*] Oh, and can you leave off the dedication?

— Can't I just say "For Paul"?

— That's OK.

You intended to do a bad thing and then found you didn't need to, but "The waste remains, the waste remains and kills" as Mr Empson has it. He's right, as we shall see. And kills.

Delivery of the final version of the book was marked by a boozy lunch in Soho that the OUP guy said he would sleep off on the train back to Oxford. I recall feeling sick afterwards, for reasons not only linked to lunchtime drinking ... nicely put, eh? Actually, Fansion did make me revisit the lunch but I really can't be bothered to describe it.

* * *

A few weeks after publication, and with what I am sure was a touch of glee, Paul forwarded me an email that had been doing the rounds of the London cognitive science community. It was one that the American philosopher Jerry Fodor had copied to a colleague at Birkbeck, his reply to the *London Review of Books* after the editor had send him "my" book to review. This is it ...

dear mary kay,

thanks for sending that book by leo barber as a possible review-victim.

I followed the author's advice and tuned down my sas so the creative decision to review it or not would come to mind. I lay down in a darkened room and began telling my prayer beads in an habitual fashion. the bottom-up creative deliverance appeared. it was that this is either a spoof or it was written in crayon by a maniac.

seriously, my advice is to get the waste bin to review it.

best,

jaf

Yes, Paul had said it was "really your kind of thing". I tried to calm myself by doing some watercolours of our back garden. It didn't work. Hell!

And then the reviews came in from the Sunday papers and magazines like *The Spectator* and *New Statesman*. "If ever there was a dark horse it was Leo Barber ... such bold erudition combined with a mind-boggling grasp of detail ... An edifice of sophisticated neuro-speculation and provocation ... The central section of the book is a kind of existence-proof of creativity itself ... How does he do it? ... Barber-as-artist has been dormant for a while, and now we know why – a triumph! ... flashes of Barberian wit ... a neuro-computational Keats is what we are treated to". That kind of thing. There were, of course, sceptical voices, and there was a typically brilliant parody of it by Craig Brown in *Private Eye*, but more typical was the review by some "existential therapist" I'd never heard of in *The Mail on Sunday,* referring to Five Exercises to Tune down your SAS and Release the Creative in You. Doing these exercises, she said, "was like opening a door onto a garden. I nearly wrote 'secret garden' but it was a garden in which we could *all* play, our goal-obsessed, controlling selves set aside like obsolete tools."

And soon I received a call from my agent saying that a television production company had been in touch about making a programme for Channel 4 under the working title of "Leo Barber meets the creative brain." I thought it best not to think about it too deeply and said immediately to go ahead. I did though make a number of stipulations, the main one being that there would be no cameras inside our house and that we should set up an "office-study" in a TV studio as if it were a piece of fiction – which it was.

They filmed me walking to The Leverhulme Centre and filmed somebody who looked a bit like Paul from behind handing me a copy of Shallice's *From Neuropsychology to Mental Structure.* They filmed me reading the book in my pretend study with a pencil in my mouth, whipping out the pencil to make furious notes using a desk easel, then staring up into infinity like the brothers Goss (of Bros) in their heyday. They missed a trick by not playing the boys' "When Will I be Famous?" at such points, which were frequent.

I got them to cover my "studio" in whiteboards so I could, in my continual fits of inspiration, scribble the book's network figures onto them. By the end it looked like one of the duller Pollocks. In the voiceover I said things like, "I decided to liberate the network from the teaching signal" and "I was *pretty sure* by this point that unless I added a further layer of hidden units the net would be sure to get bogged down in local minima."

By the way, a few years later the scribbling-bollocks-on-the-wall move was copied by poor Paul McKenna in a programme where he pretended to predict the winning number of the National Lottery. They filmed him in his "flat" – *a flat with blackboards on the walls*. He found that if he was to do this here predicting thingy he had to engage in "deep mathematics". My followers come in many forms.

Obviously, Paul didn't want anything to do with this, but the production company got hold of the emails of some of his post-docs and persuaded them – not much persuasion was needed – to appear on the programme and explain brain stuff to the gentle-but-aching-for-enlightenment probing by me. It was rather like a show trial. After these interviews, which were supposed to capture my process of discovery, I would jump on a bus – a bus! – and rush into my "studio" to wipe some of the networks off the board and draw a schematic brain, with different coloured lines linking brain regions in different ways, each colour representing a different facet of nothing at all.

When it was my birthday, *The Guardian* described me as "artist-provocateur, poet, and neuroscientist" and I was *not embarrassed*.

No, I was not embarrassed. Didn't have time to be because everything was moving so fast. So fast, in fact, that it barely registered that Lois was standing for the Council. She got in, and the sight of all those congratulatory kisses from men younger and more, uh, how to put it, engaged with "social reality" than me, just about blew my matchstick edifice down. In fact, we were beginning to take different paths at this time. Things were still good, and the varmints were a dream, but when we had dinner together there was something like a formality between us, put there, I think, by her, to protect her new inner life.

She appreciated my dismissive jokes about the programme, and one Friday night we sat down to watch it.

We usually chatted during programmes, but this time she was silent, watching the screen with an expression it was impossible to read. At the ad-break she rushed into the kitchen to make tea, responding to my questions with "Let's discuss it when it's over."

"When it's over" felt like a horrible phrase at the time.

16: This Damned Moonlight

"That was disgusting, Leo. Do you ever stop to ask why you do this? I shouldn't have watched it. As an expert, do you know if it's possible to stimulate my cranium electrically to wipe the memory? Seriously, I wish I could." This was what Lois said, and the aftermath of her saying it was indeed perpetual, frozen seriousness. We did all the usual things together and enjoyed them but the lightness and humour had vanished from her.

That's enough background before we return to the Fansion-and-The-Me current ...

After the Soho lunch with the OUP guy, it was up to Oxford Circus and westward on the Central. After St Paul's there was not Bank but – go on, guess – *"Banco de España."* No mucking about with custom-built Heath Robinsonia this time: it was simply the station itself in high summer and high tourism, dotted with lovely Spanish women and stocky Spanish men. We were swept along and up to the pavement where, across the wide boulevard of the Paseo del Prado, was the post office (Real Casa de Correos). It seemed, now I see (what tense here, Moriarty?) it again, like the Spanish white cliffs of Dover, splendid and white and symbolic. No, not that: when I'd returned in 2017 it flew a huge banner in English saying "Refugees Welcome." No-no, nothing like

the white cliffs at all. Changed me mind. I must STOP WIT-
TERING and get down to the darker purpose.

After the TV programme, I had been doing all I could to get
myself right with my wife. I would have shaved my hair off,
taken up badminton, learned to play the harp, if I thought it
would warm her towards me. Holidays, treats, anything you
like, was my strategy. Some years before she'd wanted us to
visit Madrid, but I'd backed off. No big reason, just that in
my youth I used to nip across there for a few days, staying
at the Mexico and haunting El Prado, sketching Goyas
mainly. I felt Madrid belonged to me. Well, enough of that
now. Of course we'll go, and hotel luxuriously this time. The
twins stayed with my Mum (Dad had died two years earlier)
and off we went, happy-ish.

Fansion and I shouldered through the crowds towards
Atocha and El Prado in the scorching heat. Eventually,
across from the main entrance to the Prado, we turned into
a square sloping down to the Paseo and up to a restaurant
terrace where Lois and The Me were taking a seat for lunch,
having struggled to win through to a table with a parasol.
We did our usual hovering act on a nearby table without
one. I burned up and Fansion was a block of grey ice. Clearly
they were just breaking a long silence, and I knew that they
had just crossed the Calle Atocha from the Reina Sofia gallery, which houses, as you may know, a wonderful modern
collection in a strange granite pile like an isolation hospital
or barracks, fronted by two transparent lifts. Though a
Prado man at heart, I loved the place. The Me was probing:
— So ... *Guernica* was all it's cracked up to be ... for you?
— And more. It's the most potent art I've ever seen. And it's
enormous. But you were impatient.
— Not really.

— You kept complaining about the Japanese schoolchildren and cracking little half-jokes.

They ordered lunch: a substantial one for Lois (prawns to start, and then those foetal lamb cutlets, about ten per serving, plus chips and a Russian salad). Where did she put it all? And how could she drink the better part of a bottle of Ribera at lunch?

Stop wittering! It doesn't matter what The Me ordered. It didn't matter to him.

Her appetite and moodiness stirred something up in The Me and he threw marital politics to the wind and said what he thought:
— You know, I've never been convinced by Picasso. I think potency is *all* he's about – the potency of his ego, not the potency of his emotion at German bombing. You know, being forced [*why did you say that, you idiot!*] to stand before it made me see how much Wally Fawkes took from him. You know, the jazz clarinetist who drew the Trog cartoons, and the Flook ones too, I think.
[*Trog did the George Melly drawing I keep harking back to*]
Also, it reminds me of the 1950s curtain and furniture fabrics my aunts and uncles used to call "contemporary" ... angular, black-and-white, with *built-in obsolescence*. For me ...
— For you, for you ...
— For me it's not emotion but a strong *design* programme. If I am to be forced [*shut up, you moron!*] to look at a painter who's more of a designer, then I'm sorry, I'll take Burne-Jones over him any day.

The wine and water had appeared and so had a rather dangerous smile on the face of Lois.

— Nobody forced you to look at them. I could have gone – would have preferred to have gone – by myself. I would rather go by myself than with someone who *forces* himself for reasons best known to himself to say these stupid things. You are just WRONG. Of course it's a powerful reaction to the horror of a new kind of war, where civilians are butchered from a great height. If you were a philistine there would be some excuse, but you're a trained artist.

— Maybe I ...

— And a trained careerist who talks this shit as a cover for his career as a pretend conceptual artist. Excuse me while I laugh.

— That's very nice. Thanks. That just happens to be my artistic preference.

— It's nothing to do with art. I mean with the graphic arts. Look at the poetry. You win a major poetry prize with stuff generated by computers, passing it off as your own work. I was pleased at first, because I thought you would own up in the end *à la* Jimmy Paxton and shine a light into dark corners. But of course you didn't ...

— Eat your prawns ...

— [*whilst eating*] Of course you didn't because it was more logs on the career fire. Burn up, chaps. Tell you what: if you had your time over today and did a Jimmy Paxton you *wouldn't* expose the project at a big rally. You would stay in character and stand as an MP. You'd start a new political party. As long as your face is on the posters, Leo.

The Me was looking away across to the Prado as from a quicksand base to Eldorado. They were silent as Lois tucked into her *chuletas* and the wine, until The Me said:

— That was hurtful, Lois. You surely can't mean it.

— I meant every word, and I haven't even started on your creative brain book. Same goes. It would have been fantastic if you had collected all these kudos and then turned round and said, "I don't know a sodding thing about the brain. I know that the front and back ends of the book are bollocks. I used to read bits out to my wife to make her laugh. My brother did the clever stuff. I'm no more a neuroscientist than Alan "Fluff" Freeman, master DJ."

The Me forced a laugh.

— OK. [*Lois*] What's the difference between white and grey matter?

Now The Me was running for the shelter of the facetious.
— The colour?
— What is the difference, come on?
— Now there you have me … Reminds me of the joke about this Wildeian guy who said, "You know, life is like a bowl of fruit minus the strawberries." "Why?" someone challenged. "Well," he replied, "*there you have me.*"
— Oh, for God's sake.

The Me abandoned this route, saying:
— Paul wanted nothing to do with either project. I couldn't abandon him.
— You would abandon *anybody* in the service of glory.

Fansion could see I was suffering from the sun. I hope this was why he fast-forwarded things with his modem so we were "now" walking behind them to their splendid hotel. The Me looked depressed from the back and probably looked suicidal from the front; and there were signs of concern from Lois. She kept looking towards him and armed him up the steps.

No. The Me was not depressed. He had had another of his famous *ideas*. It was ultimately a plan for Lois but the initial hard work would involve a bit of fantasy. He could see Lois was softening and hoped she would take the bait. We doubled our steps and slid into the palatial suite behind them.

The Me threw himself onto the bed, saying he needed a siesta. She said more brightly, as her old self:
— Do you want only a nap or a *refreshing nap?* ("Refreshing nap" was our code for afternoon lovemaking.)
— A NAP. Why not go for a walk or something.
— I doant vant you to be alone ...
— Off you pop.

Lois busied herself at the desk then turned to him.
— It may seem cruel, but I'm only reminding you of what you already know. The Leo I love is better than that. There are lots of ways of owning up – some very subtle ones. I can help you ... Darling?

The Me fussed with himself in bed then sat up straight to say:
— I suppose you have me bang to rights, darling. It's alright, though. For months now I've been thinking much the same thing, whilst being a bit kinder to myself. After all, wasn't the Jimmy Paxton project about a real danger in the world – nationalism? I'm not just mucking about and reaping the glory. Look, unlike Picasso I'm not faced with a real horror to spur me into art.

Yes, this is cumbersome. The Me said something like this. This will do. It's not the main deal anyway.

— But what I want to do now is to produce art – and I'm not going to call it conceptual – that raises awareness of a horror, just as *Guernica* did. It's a private kind of horror, a sort of hidden, everyday horror. It's local and domestic. I read recently [*this was a lie*] about a study of suicide in women. Of course, women kill themselves for all kinds of reasons, but one of the most common is that they're victims of a hideously controlling husband. A husband who gaslights them – remember, we read the Patrick Hamilton play? – and who undermines their confidence.

— I could tell you some stories.

— Quite. And the fact of this control only emerges in their suicide notes.

— No social support.

— Exactly. My idea was this: I would ask women, just free-range women who I happen to know, to use their imaginations about what this would be like – women who I was pretty sure had good marriages – to write at least six suicide notes in the voices of such women. Women's handwriting is very distinctive.

— Rounded, loopy. I know. Guilty as charged.

— And no man could do this, no matter how imaginative and no matter how loopy a writer ...

— And then what?

— I would cut up the notes into sort-of shards, but wide enough to retain strong phrases, and arrange them. Not the Burroughs-Gysin cut-up business as there would be no continuous sentences. It would be punctate [*Paul's word again, very handy*] in the way that pangs of pain are punctate. [*I found that embarrassing*] I would also cut up stock photos of women's faces and arrange them as in the text, not so as to produce a composite face. [*for one thing, The Me didn't want Lois to think he had nicked ideas from Marcus Harvey, who did the Myra Hindley painting from kids' handprints around this time*]

— Interesting.

— Yes, as an *idea,* but I really don't know yet how to make the face shards and the text shards relate to each other.

— Who have you asked to write notes?

— [*The Me had to be careful here*] I asked Piotr's wife, though it would be in Polish. I'm planning to ask Anita ...

— I bet she'll jump at it!

— Um, it's awkward because I don't want to offend the husbands, and they've got to be mates of mine, or people who owe me one. Gary's wife, Paula? Mayra of Mayra and Mick?

— Tread carefully in both cases, I'd say. Tell you what, though ...

— What? [*The Me's excitement was obvious*]

— I could give it a go. You have your nap. I have a pad somewhere.

It was as simple as that.

— You can use real names ..."Leo", "the twins", and so forth ... to help you focus. They'll be cut out, of course. But I don't want them to smack of the generic. And boy does that smack. [*a laugh that was distinctly sinister*] I'll make myself a cup of decaf. Want a tea?

It was as simple as that, though I knew that poisoning Lois and putting one of her notes beside the body would not be simple.

Yes, you did register this right. Not easy to admire, am I? There has to be some kind of explanation at this point, so here goes ...

I don't mind people seeing through me. It's not difficult. I don't mind people doing this and judging me. But for *Lois* to do this, for the woman I love above all – let's hedge on the twins, if you don't mind – to do this ... I don't know what word to use. A joint life becomes impossible then. Every day I would witness the erosion of the love that keeps me going and of the story I need to tell about myself. *I could not hide away with her.* However I put this it comes out as *conceptual.* It's not conceptual: it's an unmediated feeling in a third of a second.

"Why not divorce her?" you might say. Don't be ridiculous. Lois was a beautiful, intelligent, sensual woman in fresh middle age. Do you really think I could bear the thought of somebody else having her! I love her totally. And this means that she must be totally mine. I use the present tense. I still love her. I feel pathetic. Can one be thoroughly ruthlessly bad and pathetic at the same time? Here comes the Paul-phrase "existence proof" again. Is it again? I'm losing track. A reviewer used it.

Fansion and I cleared off around this time. It says something about me that uppermost in my mind as I left was not the substance of all this but a shudder at the thought of being back on the Central Line and leaving the glory of Madrid behind.

It's background time before the scene that, above all ("above all" I keep being drawn to this pompous bloody tick of a phrase), I really do not want to revisit. I don't want to tell you the background either, because up to now all I seem to have been guilty of is ambition and vanity. No, I'm something of a snake, at all at all.

I had to find a poison that was fast-acting and painless. What ol' clever dick did was to go alone – Lois politicking – to one of Paul and Anita's dull get-togethers where I knew there would be some medics I got along with. I took Christina Bowles to one side and told her about the secret life Lois had writing murder mysteries and how she was hampered by not knowing the name of a fast-acting ... are you with me? "I was helping her out as she wanted to keep her secret," I said. It was *tam-something-or-other*. I then needed to buy some from the internet. Paul helped here, though I told him I wanted to buy painkillers for my knees (at that time a minor issue). However, Christina did warn me that the taste was "extraordinarily bitter". No sweat, guv. I would devise a context in which pink gins would be consumed with their bitter ingredient, Angostura bitters.

Did you notice The Me saying "remember we read the Hamilton play"? Yes, Lois and I would sometimes read plays together in the evenings. It was fun – and funny too because of her inability to do accents. Imagine Blanche Dubois as a Cheshire lady. I suggested a 1930s evening with me dressing as Noel Coward. We'd read *Private Lives*, eat what I thought of as 1930s food – Omelette Arnold Bennett, perhaps – and drink 1930s drinks. Pink gin, some of which would contain a wee splash of *tam-something-or-other*.

From that moment on, my web tangled me up in myself. She must not speak to Anita about this, I told Lois. "Actually, I don't think I'll ask Anita. She's such a blabbermouth and I really want to hide this under a bushel for now. So better keep schtum about the whole project. Thanks." I had to get my skates on, whatever.

But what's far more awkward is the issue of plausibility – the plausibility of my motive. It looks pretty damned implausible, dunnit just? If this were a motivation given after the fact, especially in an episode of *Midsomer Murders*, it would seem OK. Yes, it *would* sound better post hoc. But that's not the issue, is it? The big clunking fact is this: I have come across as – I have presented myself as – not a serious person. I mean, I seem like somebody who plays rather than takes action, not the kind of person who would cold-bloodedly do anything big, let alone something that's – spit it out – evil. Yes, I'd intended to blackmail Paul, but nothing was done. Maybe around then I crossed the river into a more serious land. Or was it when I stole the substance of that silly-arsed book? It's nakedly absurd that I would decide to kill my wife who I loved "to the moon and back" (to quote a phrase Belle taught me). Oh, this is too much, sorry.

Just one last thing. Lois and I were together all the time. I mooched around at home when not eating out with friends or going to receptions and the like, and her political meetings, canvassing and so forth, left her very free. We lived and played together. Imagine looking up from your plate, from your pillow, across the room on a sleepy Sunday and knowing that this other person is not on your side. She does not approve of you, and yet you worship her. "Imagine!" – as Frank O'Hara ends *Autobiographia Literaria*.

* * *

We were back on the Central after our Spanish jaunt and then back onto the Northern. If you want to know how, why not consult a tube map. Sorry again. It feels as if I'm speeding towards a cliff edge with dogs snapping at my heels. Fansion got his key out and let us into the Frognal house. I could hear early Duke Ellington playing "Drop Me off in Harlem". I think the twins were having a sleepover somewhere, and recall that the Omelette Arnold Bennett was not a success –

tasty enough, but sloppy. It was The Mc's first attempt at one; and I don't like poaching. We arrived halfway through the meal. Lois clearly resented The Me's attempts to control her wine drinking at dinner because "We need to save ourselves for the pink gins." "Why?" The Me would make feeble little remarks like "Eggs are appropriate," as Coward used to say; "he often enjoyed 'something eggy on a plate'".

However, when Lois and The Me got stuck into the play reading, things improved. The project was easier too because, with her head in the text, Lois could hardly notice that there were *two* bottles of Angostura bitters. They agreed to read the thing until they'd had enough.

The Me gave it all he'd got, doing a Coward for Elyot and an Olivier for Victor, though the Olivier was mediated through Richard III. She was the identical Cheshire lady for both Amanda and Sibyl. (Recall that Elyot and Amanda are divorced though still in love and that they meet again by chance when they are each with different partners.)

Ol' clever dick had decided that most of the gin swilling would be done before they started reading, in case they wound up the reading too soon, and while they were listening to music and, when the spirit took them, dancing.

I want to lay off physical description. The time has passed for that … My smoking jacket and slicked hair. ("Makes you look ratty." "Thanks, darling.") I want to avoid it because Lois looked devastating. No flapper could compare. Her little black dress and string of costume pearls. Her gayness lit up The Ratty One's weird restraint.

The reading started well enough. They laughed at stage directions such as Elyot having to wear a "comfortable" dressing gown. Most of the early speeches were only one line long, so the staccato was fodder for corpsing.

The whole play is *"unbelievable, a sort of dream,"* to quote Elyot. Remind you of anything, stranger?

Most of Act One was fine. It was fine until Elyot and Amanda gave way to their love. He declares his love plainly and she pretends not to have heard him. There was a tension in The Me's throat around this point, and he had ceased the Coward impersonation.

ELYOT: You love me, too, don't you? There's no doubt about it anywhere, is there?

AMANDA: No, no doubt anywhere.

ELYOT: You're looking very lovely, you know [*The Me gazed across at Lois at this point, held it too long, forced his eyes back to the page, and read*] ... in this damned moonlight [*then it cracked and gushed forth*] ... in this DAMNED stupid, pointless, shitting, bloody moonlight. Why moonlight? What's the point, for God's sake, when it's too late! It's too late, Lois. Why did I DO that?

At this point I thanked God that I was experiencing this from the outside rather than the inside, as The Me went into a foetal position, biting down on the knuckles of his fisted hand as if he were an animal in a trap gnawing through a trapped limb.

When Lois rushed over and held him, and he grasped her tightly, we could see that blood was flowing freely. His face was running with tears.

— Darling, darling … What's happened? I've never seen you like this. You're scaring me. Speak! Tell me what's going on.
— [*it wasn't hard to find an excuse*] What you said in Madrid. It's true. Every word. Everything is for myself. What a waste of a life. The life of a phony; and it feels too late to change now. I'm fixed like this. I infect you and the twins in this way.

Lois didn't reply and led him into the kitchen to wash his hand, then went to find a bandage. The Me sat in the middle of a sofa staring at the "special" bottle of bitters. When Lois came back he croaked that please could he be left alone and that he'd be up to bed "in good time" (whatever that meant). Lois departed. Yes, she was shaken, but seeing her now, today, in cold blood, it was clear she knew she wasn't being given the full story.

We watched The Me as he slowly roused himself, fetched the poisoned bottle and sat holding it, initially in despair and then in a matter-of-fact way as if he was about to enjoy a nightcap after a hard day at the office. Eventually he put it back. If I recall correctly, I thought of drinking it as a clean escape, and then remembered the plot of *Romeo and Juliet*. I mean, for all I know she might have been pouring pink-uns into plant pots and saving herself for brandy later, as she sometimes did. He made himself comfortable on the sofa … "Composed himself for slumber" was the phrase The Me and his wife used to share.

Thank God I won't have to describe the morning scene, the cold corpse of my wife, the laying of the note beside their bed, the disposal of evidence of the night before, the arranging of the spare room as if he had slept in it. I will, though, show you the note I'd chosen, that Fansion and I examined.

Darling Belle and Lance

In the morning you will have no mother and your father will have no wife. But then he never needed a wife, only attractive company, a sounding board and a slave to the reality he'd constructed for me. He tells me my political work is self-indulgent, and that I'm lucky to share his brilliance and wealth. He's an insinuating, creepy, controlling bore. Fundamentally a bore. A bore because his only life is a domestic life in which he can yak on and ignore everything beyond his front gate. His "work" outside the family is a joke, and for this he punishes me. My darlings, I'm so so sorry, so sorry. But if I had carried on you would have been dragged down into this hell with me.

Mummy

Not a bad effort, rather unfocused, touching truth here and there, but the vocabulary is ridiculous: even Belle would struggle with "insinuating". It would have to do, I thought, as I rehearsed various speeches for the police.

17: Aftermath – The Tracks

Neither do I have to describe how I broke the news to the twins. Lance was beside himself. Belle went white. All she said was, "We don't want another Mummy." She'd seen what happened with her friends. I could easily promise that. I knew there would be nobody after Lois. (There wasn't; though bear in mind how this began, with Princess Margaret.)

The only thing that brought them any comfort was Lois' obituary in *The Guardian,* not a full-scale one of the kind reserved for the truly famous, like dead members of The Stargazers or The Fraser Hayes Four, but in an adjunct called Other Lives, for the merely worthy. I'd had no idea what a big figure "Councillor Barber" was on the local scene. Her "great beauty" was referred to, as was her leadership of successful campaigns – for a local police liaison officer, and against the closures of an infant school and a library, etc. etc. Had she told me about all this? No idea. Probably couldn't get a word in edgeways.

I would have been happy around this point never to set eyes on The Me again. I was feeling tired. Maybe The Me was rubbing off on me, and all I could comfort myself with was the thought that there would not be much more of this. I knew, from the rather modest cat-gut bungee twang I received on the Central Line after we'd changed at Holborn, heading west, that the next episode of this sorry tale would not be very long after the death. We alighted at a station called – I can't contain my hilarity – "Quin Sway" (maybe – of course not! – a reference to the novelist Ann Quin, who once remained mute throughout an address she gave [not] at the ICA, nihilism holding *sway*). We walked up Queensway towards Whiteleys shopping complex/cinema as a droopy The Me emerged; and I know he'd been to see a film there.

There is a kind of pornography of misery that I'm trying to avoid, and in any case, well, just use your imagination. I was never big on the cinema but I did start going to films alone in the afternoons. It was a comfort.

The Me crossed the road and dawdled into a pub on the corner, and as we followed we heard him order his usual pint of orange juice and soda before settling in a corner and opening *The London Review of Books*. He'd put on weight and exactly the opposite kind of weight you put on when you get married: the kind you put on when you regret killing your wife. Oh, an example of a "leading question" is: "Have you stopped torturing your children?" I'll shut up.

We sat nearby until all three of us heard:
— Leo! Is it? Well, I'm buggered.

The voice boomed, a sour-clotted-cream voice, the voice of a fatty. And there was the fatty emerging bar-left. Not only fat but tall, late middle age, wearing a kind of shell suit.
— Don't you recognise me? I haven't changed a bit. I wear the fat-suit as a disguise.
— No, really, I've no idea. [*people did sometimes pretend to know him, and The Me looked concerned*]
— What you drinking? I'll TELL you what you're drinking ... large G&T, Brian, and another pint for me. Cheers.

The guy turned towards the bar revealing a pigtail collecting the side strands of his lank hair, and a look passed across The Me's face that said: I do NOT know this man. The Me folded his *LRB* and rose. At which the pigtail spoke quite sharply:

— It's Nick. Nick! Nick Morris.

The Me struggled to believe it. Could skinny sardonic Nick have become this generic bloke-in-a-pub, this tacky-lone-some lump? It was only possible when the constant smile fell from his chops, as it did giving his full name. Yes, it was him.

— Sorry ... Nick. God, Nick, how long's it been?
— A good few days.
— Sit down and tell me about yourself. Are you, uh, well?

Nick did not give his full attention to The Me because he was monitoring the bar for fellow flies.

— Never better. Under Doctor Beer. Oi, Garry ... who's the twat who said The Arse would get three points from Newcastle? [*plus more football white noise*]
— Talking of Newcastle, what happened to the job you started up there?
— Long story, mate. Let's just say I got a bit more out of them than they got out of me. Fact is [*he said this as if it was at last slowly dawning on him*], it's not what you know it's *who* you know.
— You jacked it in?
— I had an epic fanny [*The Me looked blank*] ... An epi-phany. Why work for The Man? Did a bit of roadying. Christ, I could tell you some tales. Then bummed around Europe and the States. Did a bit of this, a bit of that, and now I'm retired. I live round the corner.

— Good area!

— [*Nick's smile fell again*] Gaff's a bit on the small side, mind. How are you doing, as if I didn't know?

— So you heard about Lois?

— Lois who?

Nick was clearly not pretending. He was at a loss.

— *Lois,* your ex, and my ex-wife.

— Nope, drawn a blank. Are you divorced then?

— She's dead. She k-killed h-herself, Nick.

— I say, steady on old chap. Have you caught your brother's stammer. How is B-B-B-Big P-P-Paul du-du-du – help me out – du-doing?

And this was the guy who used to routinely thump anybody who took the mick out of Paul's speech, who nastily lost a fight in the gym in this cause against the hardest nut in the school. *This* was Nick. The Me's face hardened and he pushed his drink away.

— Are you married?

— [*Nick turned to a couple on the next table and sang partly to them as well as to The Me*]

> The girl that I'll marry
> Will have to be
> A nympho who owns
> A distillery

Yes, Nick was a generic bloke-in-a-pub now, but he was also – well, probably – a woman hater. The sort of guy whose bonhomie suddenly cracks and he says something like: "Tell you what, though, mate, all these lesbians need is a good dickin'." At this point The Me decided he'd better act his way out ...

— Well, you certainly seem on good form. Look, why don't

we meet up for lunch or a proper drink? The appalling thing is, I have nip down to Richmond in an hour to view a house. [*true, but the appointment was for the next day*] Here's my contact details. [*The Me gave him a card with false contact details for occasions exactly like this one*]

— Richmond's full of ponces. Fur coat and no drawers.

— It may get even fuller now.

They stood up, and Nick hugged The Me. It was not one of those theatrical hugs. It was the real thing. And from my angle (not from The Me's) I could see tears in Nick's eyes ... He said:

— Take care, mate. You take care now.

Had he really forgotten who Lois was? Paul invited me once to a talk on Wittgenstein at the Leverhulme given by the philosopher Jim Hopkins. Very good too. At one point Jim showed a drawing of a cooking pot with steam coming out of it. Wittgenstein had pointed out the absurdity of asking if there was *really* water in the pot – I think the point was about conscious states – and this stayed behind with me. Had he *really* forgotten her? What goddamned point am I making? Somebody could make a point of it, but not me and not today. Sorry.

Something about this meeting jolted me out of my blues – was there really something-water in my boiling pot? Do I ever shut UP? – and I became excited about a possible move west. Richmond was not really in London, and I loved so-called Turner's View and wanted it to be my view whilst not loving the phrase Turner's View. The move nearly broke the bank and the twins were not on board; but I had to have a change of scene.

* * *

Instead of retracing our steps to "Quin Sway", we went to the nearby Bayswater station in order, I assume, to join my beloved District Line; and I also assumed this was to go to Richmond, at the end of the line.

When we settled in and found somebody to be (what amounted to) a governess for the twins, I immediately felt at a loose end. I mooched about the place getting my bearings, trying out restaurants and cinemas; and one day I asked Piotr to drive me downriver (or is it *up*river? – in Twickenham, any road up) to Eel Pie Island, to try my hand at nostalgia. (Think back to my Rolling Stones lecture.)

Sorry, as a slight echo of the Stones reference – Jagger in Richmond. I'd assumed Mick had moved away from there after the divorce from Jerry, but no. He'd bought a penthouse flat at the end of the terrace next to mine that he reached by a transparent lift (à la Reina Sofia) on the gable end. We'd never met and so I was constantly on the lookout for him, till one morning I went to buy a paper and there he was, in velvet slippers. "Hi Mick" I said. He gave me a very hard look, followed by that big grin:
— Jimmy! Jimmy Porter.
— Paxton, Mick.
— [*in stage-Cockney*]: Well, stroll on and love a duck. Pop rahnd for a cuppa sugar if you runs aht. Be lucky, me ol' cock sparrer!

He left after giving me a light punch in the belly and that was the last I ever saw of him.

Anyway ...

I had never seen the island in daylight – and it *did* disappoint. The old island was a rickety dream, but this place was as safe as mutton, or milk, or mango ice-cream. The bridge across was now a sturdy metal corporate job. And once there you were transported into something like a set for a pre-schoolers' TV programme ... a nest of harmless eccentrics and retired hippies. As you wandered along the lane, you expected *Bill and Ben* or *The Woodentops* to scamper out from behind a garden shed.

As I knew, the hotel where the gigs used to be had burned down long ago. In fact, according to the guy in the Eel Pie Island Museum (on the mainland), the owner had burned it down for the insurance. This museum was, by the way, a scruffy gem containing a copy of Melly's *Owning Up* in a glass case, of which you've heard too much already.

When I got back I felt the kind of itch I hardly ever felt when needing to start a painting. The need was to write something down. I find writing prose is like digging a trench, so I took my stabilisers off and wrote a poem about the island. Yer tiz (in the voice of the island):

Eel Pie Island

Come across my bridge, fast-back.
Now isn't a little hippie fancy better
than speechless fury? Why wield

your peashooter against those waiting
in line for *An Evening with Toby Young*?
Why not try tiring of writhing-seething?

You have created Speechless Fury as
a stabled rocker in the Lord Sutch mould

but really he's the straddling core

of failed retrievals, parti-coloured
righteousness and horns-down ad-hom.
Look at this lazy green river and imagine

the worn smooth rocks in your own.
Wander my lanes pearled with eccentricity.
Here is the private mood of my air far from

your brains-out subjunctive. The not-
existing hotel would never have
resounded to your 3-bar blues (so greasy).

I myself have managed to cool my heart
by burning it down for profit.
Thus cooled I can frame these thoughts.

No more could you frame yours from
their cataract-wreckage than backcomb
the not-existing hair on your crown.
The past mood is indicative, take attitudes
to that. It's so very much easier.

You may ask "Toby Young"? Can't staynd 'im – simple as
that. By the way, I *do* have plenty of hair on my crown.
Poetic licence, matey.

It channelled a kind of anger in what I thought was a successful way. It had a bit of oompff and a nice sprinkling of
difficulty. I was happy with it and immediately sent it off to
the *LRB*, who immediately rejected it, causing me to read it
over for the third time. Well, it's too solipsistic and falls
apart before the eyes of any reader who has not recently vis-

ited the place. It's crabbed; and its "difficulty" does not invite thought … So I turned my mind back to furniture and fixtures.

But all was not a poetic washout. Around this time some idiot academic had said on the *Today* programme that one of the many problems with modernist poetics was that it lacked humour. (Had he never read Peter Manson?) … So the call went out from *The Observer*'s literary editor to modernist poets she'd heard of – note that the *Eel Pie Island* poem is about as modernist as "Mother bloody Dale" (Brendan Behan, circa the early '60s) – to write a funny poem. I had no intention of trying my hand till a musician friend told me he'd been asked to write a song for a wedding that must be called "For Those That [*sic*] Truly Know". This came to mind one night before going to sleep:

Wedding Song

Why does the sailor follow a star?
(Thanks, by the way, for reading thus far.)
Why do young Yankees go on with the show?
For those that truly know.

Rivers and rivulets only flow
Mountains can only wave hello
Odysseus will only bend his bow
For those that truly know.

Flowers are fruity like ice on a stick
Boundaries are bounding around dear Chiswick
Newlyweds scamper across summer snow
For those that truly know

Frankie and Johnny, thee I anoint.
(Chuffed you're still reading up to this point.)
Love is their beverage now they are joint.
They're those they truly know

Rivers and rivulets only flow
Mountains can only wave hello
Odysseus will only bend his bow
For those that truly know.

It was a hit. It warmed people towards me, and I certainly needed to be warmed towards because I was out in the cold after Lois' "suicide". I warmed towards myself as well. I think this was all mixed up with living out of the mainstream in a decorative place. Let's not dwell on cause, shall we? Why start now? Whatever ... I reflected on what actually gave me pleasure these days, and the whimper came: *Father Ted*, *Friday Night Dinner*, and a few sitcoms that weren't as good as these. Yes, I had gone soft, or admitted to a softness there all along.

I asked my agent to put me in touch with Graham Linehan and Robert Popper, because I had an *idea*, something else that had been sparked by the *Today* programme. They would have preferred to do a sitcom based on *The Sea, The Sea* with Bill Nighy as the Charles Arrowby character, but I talked them round by way of all the famous faces I could recruit as guest stars.

I'll come back to this after we rejoin Fansion and me.

* * *

I knew quite a number of years would be skipped as we

trundled west on the District because, just past Ravenscourt Park, I felt as if I had been swung round by my lungs. We took a cab from outside Richmond station ("Where to, Dr Fansion?") which took us up Hill Rise, where we crawled in traffic behind Anita, a rushing, flushed, waddling Anita. The cab let us out and we sat on a bench on the Turner's View terrace and waited for her to get to The Me's front door. Of course, we trickled in behind her (dolled up to the nines she was).

The Me was clearly not expecting her and not pleased about it, but he was as pleasant as ever. He took her to the large sitting room on the first floor where a play was being broadcast on Radio 4 Extra and he had been taking tea. He spoke, gesturing to a chair:

— So, this is a nice surprise. Everything alright?

— Yes! Everything is at last alright, now I'm alone with you. I don't think I've ever been alone with you in a room before. [*The Me had strenuously avoided it*]

— I don't understand.

— Yes, you do. The way you look at my body [*indeed, The Me did study her breasts, falsely thinking she was too bound up in herself to notice*], the way you avoid my gaze afraid you'll give yourself away. We both know. I'm here for you now. I'm yours at last.

— You've got it all wrong, Anita. [*The Me was schoolmasterly and horror-struck and praying she wouldn't say "Don't fight it"*]

— Let's stop messing about, shall we. Come!

At this point she flung off her jacket and unbuttoned her blouse. Then for reasons that abide in The Me's beloved realm of sitcoms, The Me said:

— Bra?

— There! I knew you'd perk up.

Yes, they were indeed magnificent, far too big for the body, but in *themselves* ... let's just say that the rest of her, limbs and head, were merely slave-systems or vassal states, there to service these two fine objects. The Me was a curious man so he walked across and lifted them gently, one in each hand as if it were a guess-the-weight competition, before being shocked by himself and sitting down like a caught-out schoolboy.

— Do you mind if I sketch them ... I mean, sketch you like that?
— You WHAT! Let's go upstairs. Chop-chop as you British say.
— No.
— Why not?
— You're my brother's wife, I have ceased to be interested since Lois died, and, well, I just don't want to.
— Then why did you touch me!
— It was wrong of me. Look, get dressed. Like a drink of something? Your usual?

She dressed at once and left, poker faced, without a word or a backward glance. Fansion and I left too. Back on the District, changing at Hammersmith, then onto the Piccadilly, and one stop to Barons Court with a small cat-gut episode en route.

Barons Court. It was early morning and misty as we walked through a graveyard towards the hospital. It was a Dickensian scene, but there was nothing remotely Dickensian on offer. This was what had happened ... No, Anita did not accept a drink and had nothing to drink until she drank the best part of a bottle of bleach at home, expecting soon to be dead. No death, but unimaginable earthly pain was what followed. She was picked up in a local park and was now in intensive care.

Fansion and I were walking in behind Paul and The Me. Paul had begged me to come, for moral support, and I was planning to hang back at the door to her room. There was no need. Anita was asked to vet the visitors and she vetoed me – of course. But Fansion and I went in behind Paul, making this a new experience.

Anita was sitting high up in bed, her thick hair pulled back and piled atop her head. She didn't look vulnerable or in pain: just very angry. She was like an angry Queen, and with a dignity that scared the life out of me. Speech was impossible but she had a slate she could scribble on in felt-tip. Between the breasts, which The Me had been assessing just a few hours before, was an oxygen tube.

I could get Dickensian-sentimental now and sketch scenes with Paul and George (I can hardly call him Mister Punch now), but it's better just to give the bare facts. It would have taken months, if not years, to reconstruct the innards she had burned out with bleach; and Anita knew this. She lay still, resigned and said/wrote that she regretted the attempt. Of course, The Me – I won't call myself "I" – was worried about what she would say; but why would she confess to Paul? She didn't confess, but when she was moved out of intensive care and into a normal room she pulled the tube out from between her breasts and ceased breathing for long enough to cause profound brain damage. Life support was turned off two weeks later.

In intensive care I had kept tugging at Fansion's sleeve for us to leave, but we stayed till Paul left – probably part of my punishment. It was only a short journey for us now: back to Hammersmith, then one stop east to ... "East Kensington".

Again, a cab – "Alright, John?" (the Richmond cabbies had been more respectful) – and quite a long ride this time. We turned into a small warren of new brick and neglected greenery, the architectural equivalent of the no-man's-land we'd encountered on the road to Kingston. The name above the door was *Elmside Lodge*, and it housed my mother, a "home" she'd insisted on as a couple of her friends were there. It's a bit late in the day to tell you about my struggles to persuade her to end her days at a place in Kew, far nicer and near me. Stubbornness (or dementia) won the battle. Fansion knew the combination for the door, of course.

Nobody was about except a lost-looking The Me. We followed him along some beige corridors till he knocked on a door. She answered it, supported by a zimmer, and carrying the TV remote, holding it up, saying, "There are some messages for me" and then:
— Your Dad will be here in a bit.

Mum had, like Nick, become a generic. A generic shrunken, malodorous, ignored old lady in a "home" circa 2018. Close up, her face had nests of tiny blackheads, her skin was grey, her hearing aids had been lost long ago, and the lenses of her spectacles were encrusted with grime. Her clothes were cleanish but rumpled and most of them belonged to other people. (At Christmas they had wrapped up a bottle of *Brut-for-Men* as her present.)
— How are you, Mum?
— Never better. When's Lance coming?
— Soon, Mum.
— Belle?

— Very soon.

— Don't see much of Lois these days. Where's she got to?

— She's fine, Mum.

The room stank of urine. If you bent down to pick something off the floor the fumes were ... I could go on. I nagged and nagged them about all these "issues" but they fielded them off with routine excuses. I was always on the point of saying "You're *professionals*, for God's sake. It's your job to keep her clean/find hearing aids/prevent her room from stinking like a lion's cage/etc. etc." But the worry was that if I kicked up a fuss they would take it out on her. I was considering getting a granny flat built in my place, but as I said, the move had nearly broken the bank. And of course I had other things to think about. I always had other things to think about.

— I've bought you some chocolate biscuits, Mum. Are these the ones you like?

Silence.

— Mum?

I wanted to interject: *Are you mad on them?*

— Your Lois has been in to see me.

— Oh yes.

— Brought me that lovely photograph of the toddlers.

— You mean the twins.

— I know, the *twins*. I'm not blinking stupid.

The Me could usually conjure up something to say – this is where you came in – but now, with his mother, not. The silence seemed to last about half an hour as The Me helped himself to a biscuit or two. He sat and watched as she turned the TV off and on and switched channels whilst looking just above the set to the photo of the twins on the wall. William Rees Mogg came on, then Boris Johnson, then Liam Fox.

— Shitbags!

— Mum? Are you OK? I thought you were all for Brexit.

She hugged herself tightly and said with passion:

— Stay together. Don't leave. Be nice to each other, as that silly sod David Niven used to say. Those so-called carers. Don't start me off. Stay together, that's what I say.

— You've changed your tune.

— I never see that American girl these days. Anita.

— No, you wouldn't.

— Christ, she could chat on, and all about herself.

— I agree.

— Somebody told me she died of sugar diabetes. What you doing this afternoon? Going out somewhere?

— I've got to go for a wig fitting ...

Wig fitting? Now's the time to explain about my sitcom. I never used to listen to the *Today* programme when Lois was alive because there was always too much going on. But after she died, I failed to escape "Thought for The Day" as I waited for the headlines ... and here was Anne Atkins. She was somebody who knew she was a bad cop, a poisonous, authoritarian, bigoted numbskull, but she had lost the toss and had to play the good cop today. She talked about the joy that music or poetry brought to her family, or about flowers in the Spring, or the gift of life that God has given us, but something about the delivery gave the game away. I think it's called "double bind", where you say sweet things through gritted teeth as your knuckles whiten. So I looked her up on the internet and here was a magnificent trove of

Daily Mail ordure: anti-gay, anti-women Bishops, in favour of free speech for the likes of David Irving ("entitled to his point of view"), blaming the dispossessed for their own misfortunes. It was as if somebody had opened her skull from the back as she was buying a lolly for a disabled (white, middle-class, Christian) little girl.

I learned that she was married to a vicar, and that her elderly father lived with them (used to be head of the King's School, Cambridge), and that there were problems with her children, some of which she blamed on cannabis (as a stick with which to beat Nick Clegg). I thought of doing some background research and even reading one or two of her novels; but this would not really be about the woman herself. And anyway she might sue, so ...

The general idea was to set it in her family. Her vicar husband was, in the sitcom, the most mincingly gay creature you could imagine, making Alan Carr look like William Ewart Gladstone. He had a black "personal assistant" who was similarly overt. Her father was basically non-verbal, but he was wheeled on in his chair to give advice at certain points so that the Anne Atkins character could interpret his gurgles any way she wished. Each week something would go wrong and she would cope with it with saccharine serenity; but then it would suddenly crack. She would eff-and-blind with the worst words Channel 4 would let us get away with. She would smash furniture, put faeces in the food, and poke children in the eye.

She was called Beth Boston and the programme was called *Thank the Lord*. It wasn't anti-Christianity (on which I'm rather keen) but anti a certain kind of chintzy middle-England village green religiosity that masked ... I think you have the idea. Each episode ended with a prayer in which she respectfully asked God to punish her enemies: that some-body's child would be stillborn because she'd blasphemed; that weighing things up and taking a broad general view of things, Len McCluskey should be blinded.

Each week, Beth would be played by somebody different. Joanna Lumley in the first episode, moving on to Paul Whitehouse, Lenny Henry, Siouxsie Sioux, Mark E. Smith (just before he popped his clogs: he had to be paid in cash), Germaine Greer, Brenda "What? Another One?" from Bris-tol, Tricky, and, next time, Leo Barber.

The Beths all wore a Beth-wig, which was an enormous three-dimensional cartoon of AA's hairdo, with a wave at the front that dwarfs could surf down. There was only the one wig, which had to be adjusted for each bonce.

I didn't have it in me to construct the plots but I helped with dialogue and had vague ideas for situations: Beth's attempt to make anal sex a crime, for instance ... It ended with her husband coming to her bedroom at the end of the final prayer and then a high-pitched "OW!!!" just before the credits.

It made me happy, and I found I got on with actors ... Now, back to Mum.
— A wig fitting!
— For my TV show.
— "For my TV show." Why don't you lead a normal life? You've got a lovely wife. Just make yourself comfortable. Pass! [*she pointed to the biscuits*]

She ate two at once and vomited a little biscuit phlegm down her front.
— Bowls, in kitchenette!

The Me went to fetch one of the grey cardboard-maché bowls on the shelf beside the kettle (that didn't work) and the rotten fruit. The Me gave her the bowl, which she cradled like a child.

As he stood up to leave, one of the "carers" came in without knocking and dumped a plate of food and a cup of weak tea beside her. Looking at Mum, he said:
— Bit sickly again today, Ada. Here's your lunch. Lasagne today.
— Don't like pasto.
— Course you do. Pull the cord if you've got any issues. [*the unreachable cord that only worked one time in four*] Then, to The Me:
— She's a sweetheart, isn't she, Leo? A real character. Lovely lady. Catch you later.

The Me kissed his Mum and said, "You're the best Mum in the world," and left.

He got outside but had forgotten to phone Piotr first to come round in the Mercedes. I know that that day he'd gone to the Polish jazz café (very good) near Hammersmith for lunch, so The Me settled down to wait on a bench. I sat beside him as Fansion said:
— I'll see you later, Leo. [*Leo!*] Shan't be a tick.

But as I looked round to The Me, he'd vanished, and I was on my tod. That tune through the window. Was it Russ Conway playing "China Tea"? Hardly matters.

It's a lonely business, this.

THE RETURN

Well, stranger, these were the words of Leo Barber.
Thousands and thousands of words flung from the prison of
    his mind.
Strange it was to witness him alone in silence, stock still, as
I, with a copy of the *Evening Standard* and its unsurprising news
Of himself, walked again into the confines of these sad, sad halls;
Mother lives, but son fails to, stark message of the headline
Leo B Dies On District Line. This I spread before him.
Yes indeed, 'tis I, John Fansion, speaking now fresh from my
    silence.

Thousands and hundreds of years have I served as such a guide –
Guide through the death dreams of people varied and confused.
Do not think "Leo B" provides me with novelty!
Not uncommon are others with such multicoloured traits
In colours cancelling mutually. Sometimes
Their colours are as *lights* mutually mixed
Causing thus a shining white; but some, like he,
Are painters too, their colours are pigments, *paints*
Thick-layered, painted canvasses turned black.
As we've seen, sin-black: murder, blackmail,
death-causing contempt.

Punishment? That's not my job. And yet return he must with me
From Greater London to the world after his death, witness the
    wash
Of his wake and the facts churned up by it upon the bank.
Underground adventures? Material bodies quite ignored by folks?
No, not that. No more. Spirits we'll be, though audible and
Visible each-to-each. No doubt hard to comprehend this
Paradox. But I, a mere factotum, cannot help you out.
Paradox number two comes now: When we descend into your
    world
Ambiguously, percepts enjoyed by us will be from no single
Point of view. Apprehending the whole at once is what we'll do.
Finally, my "box of tricks" I'll set aside. Simply I'll tell my
    sensibilities:
"Take us now to X." There is no way that they can
Disobey.

Knowing him as I do, knowing the uppermost in his
Mental life, straight we went to the obituaries in the press.
Nicer news, perhaps? Nice enough to make him smile.
Unlike material smiles. Imagine charcoal strokes on gauze
Gauze crinkling in a breeze. Comments to me oftener than not
Concerned the photographs. He sucked the sweet, sweet
Juices from expressions like "an indefinable, fathomless talent"
"Will o' the wisp" "ever-youthful engagement".
Later, though, he pondered in a sadder mode on:
"Touching the hilarious, his over-reaching opus supposedly
About creation and the brain. Sitcoms were more his *métier*."
"Rumours abounded post the suicide of his wife.
Since then he darkened, later to emerge with the crazy gang

Tastelessness of *Thank the Lord*. He'd found his level finally."

Often he questioned me, not about the overarching point of this
Rather *apropos* upcoming steps. It's such a bore, you know,
To know so much. Honestly, I said, please let me lead you
By the hand, and when you've seen and heard your fill
You can say "Cease!" "Along the lines of Goethe's *Faust,* you
    mean?"
"I've no idea," I said. (My knowledge is of who really *did* do
    what to
whom and where, and when.)

This section's called Return. Return wc do to the
Queen Elizabeth Hall, scene of the living man's poetic *gloire*
    – recall.
Now we are here to "Celebrate the Life of Leo Barber".
Gauzily he seemed to fidget at the thought. "Who paid for this?"
He asked me, confident I'd know. "Fran" I said, confident that no
Surprises would spring from this.

Passing over silently the poets who'd brought poems
Entitled "Leo", likewise the Jeremy Dellers, the L.A. video from
Damien Hirst ("That smirk, that belch-like smirk," my client
    said), we'll
Concentrate our minds upon provocateurs present that day
Supposedly his heirs. Quite truly his heirs. Long ago the Jimmy
Paxton stone broke the surface of the lake. Rippling still.

Godlike, Sacha Baron-Cohen took the stage, good at the put-on.
Modestly he praised the bravery of our man, tipping his fig-

urative hat to his "balls". Leo joyfully tuned in to this.
The "Ripples" I referred to several lines above, ripples there were
In the hall at the announced name of Chris Morris.
Why such sounds? Previously Morris had addressed an
Interviewer with these stinging words: "Barber was a conman
Exactly in this sense: Jimmy Paxton's certainly no artwork
Any more than Harold Wilson was one such. Paxton was a
Magnificent move for his career."

Godlike Morris, good at satire, lingering still
In the iron sky of your present time, quicksilver with
Hyacinthine curls bedecked, took to the stage smiling.
Addressed the gathering (shocked to silence) with these
World-stunning words: "Why heap more praise on Leopold?
Look what already he has taken from you! Rather I
Presently shall treat you to refreshing revelations."
With an angry glance at smatterings of hecklers he
Continued in this well-sharpened vein:

"Yes indeed, Jimmy Paxton was constructed by a man
With the name of Leo Barber. Who, though, now I ask,
Made up the substance Leo Barber? Sagacious Leo
Was himself invented. Invented by an artist whom you shortly
Will have sight of – Karly "Flogger" Hoskins.
Middlesbrough is where he hails from, Bright Hour Art
Collective is his base. Master of prosthetics and voice-
Novelty. *He* made Leo Barber – disposed of now, finally.
All being well we'll see him here." Behind the head
Of godlike Morris crackling appeared, then a faint head image
On a giant screen together with the words "Howay, man!"

Much-gifted Morris then addressed the image as it leapt
Boldly into sudden sharpness. Habitants of the hall relaxed
Precisely as Patrick Marber, good at playwriting and sidekick
    satire,
Was to be seen in string vest and flat cap sitting in a hovel chair.
Morris then addressed him thus: "Are you there, Flog?"
Marber spoke as K "F" H: "Why-aye, Canny Lad.
Gettin' propa hungry while hangin' on for yous. Time for us
    dinners.
Need to gahn up the chippie."
Ripples in the hall broke as waves, waves of delight.
Urgently then did Morris address him with these well-chosen
Sentences. "Please could you tell us why you came to feel
That it was time to pull the plug on project Leo?
Perhaps you ran out of money. You don't seem flush." This
Injunction to reply was not disobeyed by Flogger:
"Over the years, Canny Lad, I, Flogger, found Leo-speech
harder to imitate. You hear my speaking style!
I divven find it easy to say: "*Ultimately*
One must distinguish taste from mere preference ..."
Laughter from the hall plentiful here as Morris,
Manifesting fine editing skills aplenty, had spliced Leo's real voice
Onto the soundtrack. Oh my word, there was more of this,
More than I care to document, till finally he addressed Hoskins
With this air-slicing question: "But what about the body
Clearly dead at West Kensington?"

Bonhomie of roughneck gone. Sparking through the joints
Of this Middlesbrough male: a crackling of real fire, as he spoke

Quite without comprehensibility. Rapid like automatic firing
Were the spat words, was the white noise of his anger.
Only these words could be gleaned: *gan, dee, nee, divven, howay,
Man,* and *Canny Lad.* Finally leaping by him camerawards
Almighty smashing ensued; and godlike Morris waved
Himself away.

Notwithstanding his gauzy aspect, reading Leo
Failed to be difficult at this point. Frontal attacks, spears of
    spleen
Must surely be preferable to the status of a butt, albeit am-
Biguously. All of this encourages brief reflection upon the
Freshly dead man. Normal human feelings are not, or no
Longer are, mine to enjoy, but nonetheless I felt
Positively towards this man, knowing full well the denouement
Waiting to be endured. Always I return to the stolid thought:
What is to blame? The actions of the man freely taken or
Predisposing conditions in his colours only a god could withstand.
Very few are godlike. That is the sadness.

Spinners of fate float above us now twisting their locks; below us
Much-enduring Paul trudges full of purpose up Hill Rise wistfully
Regarding drinkers in The Victoria Inn. Clear to see that beer lies,
Together with so many things, in the hinterlands of his mind.
I shall tell you now Anita's death was not that which curdled
Brother-love, but rather certain conversations had by him:
    Lois, not-
Withstanding Leo's words to her, informed Anita of the suicide
"Artwork" and this found its way to the memory banks of Paul

Spreading a sceptical stain from lobe left-temporal and
    beyond, once
"Suicide" was dubbed the cause of death. Similarly, his friend
Christina Bowles, good at medicine, mentioned before
Lois' death the wife's assays of crime fiction, also her putative
Poisoning plot. Never would this be a hobby of hers, Paul knew.
Now, with Leo gone, dead on the tube, harmlessly alone,
What was to impede the inquisitive from their run of free rein?

Splendid was the aspect of Leo's well-built house in afternoon sun.
"These words that have escaped the barriers of your teeth" –
Thus Paul addressed custodial Micky *blocking* his entry to the
    hall –
"Guaranteeing your dismissal following our next family meeting.
Go away and shut up!" (A twinkling echo of the silly
Secretary of Defence towards the Russians.) Words causing
    the man
To shrink away.

Sauntering with demeanour of ownership into the hall
Paul skipped up the wide well-built stairs directly into Leo's
    study-studio.
Everyone was cognisant of Leo's meticulous and ordered way of
Plotting out his life: everything was filed in regimented
    frame-works,
Paper trails snaked about his chic cabinets; Paul hesitated not
    a jot.

Resourcefulness was not required to find a file marked LOIS-
    EXIT

Containing five "suicide notes" in the hand of his sister-in-law.
Inhibiting the raging bull within, fighting back tears, Paul
Telephoned the police who came with haste and took the scripts
Safely away; also every computer they could find. One
Such machine had a lucid tale to tell: ordered from a shady
California lab – specialty poison, the first syllable of which
Was *phan* not *tam.*

None resisted the conclusion that Leo had
Committed murder. All were sad that his failing heart made
    possible
Leo's neat flight from justice.

Attention fell at once on Paul. Journalists
Gathered in dawn choruses outside his Chiswick home.
Georgie was scared, his father furious; but something must be
    done.
Finally he thought he would succumb to the *Observer* magazine,
Slaking their thirst for photographs, he fed them also fresh meat
Dripping with the metaphoric blood of his dead brother.
Yes indeed, this man had killed his wife, but to add to this
First: His winning poems had their birth in Paul's own lab.
As for "his" preposterous book on the creative mind, the
Story almost tells itself. The title of the piece:
"Leo Barber: Counterfeit Creator, Real Murderer."

Watching my client during this, I
Thought I saw his gauzy face relaxing somewhat
Almost as if posthumous fate was taking something off his chest.
Then, when we came to view the Primetime

Exposé inspired, post this, on BBC One, he addressed me
Thus: "I wonder what the viewing figures are – or should that
    be 'were'?"

So he spoke, and we settled down to watch a score-settling orgy
A filmic despoiling of his grave, soundtracked by soft guffaws
From the man himself. Some though there were for the defence.
Collaborator and one-time lover, Fran, was such a one.
Addressing the camera with the following intelligent and
Sharpened words, as well as with a gaze reviewers likened to
That of Cruella de Ville, she opined in the following way:
"Intellectually, the poor guy was all over the place.
Artistically, there was only minor talent, if talent at all.
And yet he was a *genius* in one domain: Oh, he could mould
The fly-by-night stuff of mob stupidity like no one I can think of.
If you like, or if you don't, think of it as sculpting with shit.
Individuals are rational (Kahneman and Co. are wrong) but
    groups
Imitate and imitate, draining themselves of sense. Look
    around you."
"What about his murdering his wife?" speaks the interviewer.
"Well, hardly would

I defend him there! Would you like me to say
'Minor thing, that?' *Huh*? Lois, from my slight knowledge,
Was a prig. She backed him into a corner. He was fighting for
Dear life. Cornered, he went for her throat. Sad enough."

It then turned out, displayed to him, that a new verb had
Emerged: to *leobarber* – meaning to try to pass oneself off

As X and fail. "I thought I was impressing her in the bar but
She could see I was leobarbering for all I was worth" – that
Kind of thing. Around this time my client seemed to think
Precisely that the worst had been and gone. Resignation
Of a kind sat upon him and I could see that he felt strong
Enough to address me with these fully-welcome words:
"Can we see how the twins are getting on?"

Change upon change there had been, and now they lived in
Islington, Arundel Square, in a large house much distressed by
Building work. There we went one Sunday. Three people
Sitting round a long pine table with toasted cheese and Guinness:
Lance, Belle, and, sketching Belle, a slightly-built, fair young man
Speaking now and then in a low, reedy, implicit voice.
Leo was his name and – correct – Leo his father, Leo as
Jimmy Paxton. "We'll need," he said, "a ramp for the downstairs
      loo for her."

Pennies had yet to drop, and now we heard
My client's final joke: "'Her' better not be Anne Atkins."
I will tell you, "her" was Mrs Ada Barber of Elmside.
Godlike, warm-hearted Belle, good at drama, favoured
The idea of making a home-within-their-home for granny.
What's more, godlike, resourceful Lance brought it to
Fruition, arranging builders, live-in care and all the rest.
Meanwhile I can almost hear you asking, stranger, how
This young man, Leo Bailey, son of Jacqui, came to be there.
Simplicity itself: After the Underground demise, Leo wrote
Straight to the twins sharing now the fate with him of the
Father-free. They met him, liked both him

And his dear mother, invited him to live with them in Islington,
Handy for Central Saint Martins (he being a tutor there).

Resourceful Lance replied to
Leo Bailey thus: "Don't fret, it's all in hand. And by the way
How did you two get on at Elmside today?" "Wonderfully!"
Was the happy word from the younger Leo B; while Leo B
The ghost-elder was gauze upon a becalmed ocean.
(I had expected a cleaving of him by the cutwater
Of this intelligence.) L Bailey and Belle then laughed
before the explanation came:

"I said to her, 'Hello, I'm Leo,' to which
She made reply: 'No need to tell me the name of my own
Blinking son. I'm not completely doolally, you know.'
Amazingly, she thinks I'm your dad, convinced
Of the fact." Immediately Belle addressed them thus:
"You must not tell her dad is dead. She'll think
That you are. And *then* she'll be properly upset."
"No fear of my doing that,"
The younger Leo spoke in reply while
Adding this question, with loosened tongue and
Softening mind, given that he was unused to the
Beerdark beer before him:

"Tell me this – how is it that the news
The world received of your father killing your mother
Has *added* to your happiness? Or seems to have. I had
Assumed you were relieved of the thought that she
Abandoned you. I know there's plentiful cheek

In what I say." Lance, good at straight talking,
Responded to him with these hard-truth words:
"No problem, Lee. I speak for Belle too when
I say the hardest thing for us to understand,
As well as to bear within our minds, was the thought
That he was so significant to our mother as to stimulate
Her towards that act. How could a man like that
Weigh heavily on a godlike woman such as her.
He was a little man."
Adding to the case, Belle allowed these words to
Escape the barrier of her teeth: "Just a little man
Jumping up and down saying *Look at me*."

At this point Leo Barber, my client, could not
Be ignored. Bodied forth he was by the wind
Of his misery, speaking thus in a new-to-me
Rasping metallic voice. "Make this end now!
Please take me away." And indeed I did,
Stripping him of his earthly colours down
To the quivering green flame of his soul.

SHAM UMBRELLAS

Scene One

Leo Barber's wife and sister-in-law are in Greater London. They are sitting outside a café north of Oxford Street near the Bond Street Underground Station in a pedestrian walkway with many restaurants and pubs.

ANITA: Tell you the truth, Lo, I don't mind being dead. It's not too bad. I mean, you can drink coffee and eat – though I don't know about you, but I never feel horny.

LOIS: It's not normal drinking and eating though, is it?

ANITA: Yeah, you drink the coffee and have some taste of it and then it doesn't go any further down, like one of those Babyccinos ... like candy floss. You get the taste of food but never feel satisfied, or properly hungry either. Guys look cool, but you don't want to jump their bones. And of course you never have to go to the john.

LOIS: Dead but half-alive above the waist just about sums it up.

ANITA: And it should be boring but it's kinda not?

LOIS: A paradoxical state, right enough.

ANITA: I mean, is this being dead at all. I'm still moving around, talking.

LOIS: [*with some irritation*] You still have your compact body and feisty personality. Both intact, Neet.

ANITA: [*she senses the aggression and almost returns it*] OK, you're a kinda veteran of all this by now. What's the point of it then? I always seem to have to drag things out of you.

LOIS: We're here because we have a role to play.

ANITA: But you and me don't have a role. Johnny Fansion has a role – a Greater London tour guide. But when's ours going to end, or start? Huh?

LOIS: [*winding her up*] Who knows? He's been at it for well over two-and-a-half thousand years.

ANITA: Such a stuffed shirt. Hard work, I find him.

LOIS: He's old school. I like him. The fact is, Neet, our role is to witness the final end of Leo Barber.

ANITA: Leo! He's an asshole. He's the reason we're here and not on earth ...

LOIS: On earth doing what? Going to the loo ...?

ANITA: I mean, what's the big deal about Leo Barber? "King Leo" as Paul used to call him.

LOIS: It's *his* death-dream we're in. That's why.

ANITA: Death-dream/schmeth-dream. It's a load of bol-locks. What about *my* goddamn death dream! What about yours?

LOIS: I don't know. A lot of it is difficult to understand.

ANITA: And there's just so much around here I don't understand. Hardly any of it makes sense to me.

LOIS: Me too. But when you were properly alive, on Earth, you didn't seem that bothered about all the stuff you didn't understand, like … oh … pretty much all of science. You weren't at all worried, or you kept it very quiet if you were, about the things that the human race doesn't understand, like how conscious states relate to the physical states of the brain.

ANITA: It's not that, clever clogs. It's more like a story that makes no sense. The characters do things for no reason and events just pop up and … pop down. Pop away.

There is shared laughter.

LOIS: I know what you mean. Sorry. Anyway, I have some good news for you. What we're here to witness will happen very shortly, round the corner in the Wigmore Hall.

ANITA: You mean like the *Andy* Wigmore Hall?

Only Lois laughs this time.

LOIS: You're priceless, Neet. Why are you talking about that rat-faced greaser?

ANITA: Who is Andy Wigmore anyway?

LOIS: Aaron Banks' number one hanger-on. One of the "bad boys of Brexit". Visible on the end of the line-up, smiling that lovely smile of his in Trump's lift.

ANITA: Oh, it makes sense now. Paul and Leo were laughing about the idea of a Festival of Brexit. They were saying it could be held in "The Andy Wigmore Hall". All male, playing British Bulldog and drinking beer till they threw up over themselves, sticking pins in wax models of, uh, that kind of thing.

LOIS: Now I see. No, it's the Wigmore Hall alright. Just think of it as the Wigmore Hall, but Greater London style.

Scene Two

The Wigmore Hall. The women are handed programmes as they enter. A number of people are already there, attending to the empty stage. As in the Wigmore Hall on Earth, there is, along the cupola at the back of the stage, an allegorical painting called The Soul of Music.

ANITA: Hey, that's a cool picture.

LOIS: Yes, it's almost relevant, though I don't quite understand how ... so here we go again. Let me tell you what will happen. You'll see rows of green flames slowly emerging from the door on your right (stage left, if you like) and then vanishing into the door on your left. These are people's souls, stripped of all the traits, mental and physical, they had on earth. Going into the door on the left means that the souls are being reborn with different characteristics, or "colours" as John calls them. The characteristics are flashed over the *Soul of Music* painting in black-and-white.

ANITA: Lo, I've reached maximum bollocks. You can't see a soul. It's not a thing. This really is crazy. And reincarnation! Jeez – it's for the birds.

LOIS: You aren't literally seeing a soul. You see something that *represents* one.

ANITA: Like, I guess, when you see something on Earth you're only seeing a representation of ...

LOIS: Liquidity, solidity and so forth?

ANITA: Exactly! But am I going too deep for you?

LOIS: No, not too deep, too bollocks. Have a look at the programme. We can see when the soul that Leo has is coming up.

ANITA: Oh that's sweet, each person has said a little something as a farewell to who they were. Listen: "I usually did the right thing, but never well enough." Actually, come to think of it, that's not sweet at all. This one's nice: "I'm happy to say goodbye for good to this role. Good luck to Rose and the kids."

LOIS: Look at Leo's.

ANITA: Yuk! Pretentious as ever.

LOIS: Go on, read it.

ANITA:

> The slopping of the sea grew still one night.
> At breakfast jelly yellow streaked the deck
> And made one of think of chop-house chocolate
> And sham umbrellas

Huh?

LOIS: It was one of Leo's favourite poems. If people asked him about poetry he would pretend to have a terrible lisp and say that *Sea Surface Full of Clouds* was his favourite poem – this poem.

ANITA: Kinda typical of him, though, to choose this rather than say something straight off the shoulder.

LOIS: Aren't you allowed to be typical when it's your very last chance to be typical? Isn't that alright by you? As a visual artist, Leo liked visual poems, which this is; he also loved food, certainly lambchops and dark chocolate. I think it's fabulous.

ANITA: Who's it by?

LOIS: Wallace Stevens.

ANITA: No way!

LOIS: What's so surprising?

ANITA: I'm amazed she found time to write high-fallutin' poetry as well as being the Duchess of Windsor and, like, fighting with your horrible Royal Family an' all. [*she is completely in earnest*]

LOIS: [*stunned silence, then a short burst of horse-laugh*] Wallace *Stevens*, dear, not *Wallis Simpson*.

ANITA: OK, so I wasn't an English-major. Hey, look at that!

At this moment a row of green flames, each about six-feet high, emerges from the door at stage left and makes a slow, wavering transit to the door at stage right. They move in a downstage arc. As a flame reaches the farthest downstage point, the whole row pauses for a minute or so as a string of astrological information is beamed onto the painting upstage.

The flames vary in size, in consistency of the flame, as well as in depth and brightness of the colour green.

Then as the first flame comes downstage and the astrological information is displayed ...

ANITA: What the hell is this goddamned ...

LOIS: ... bollocks?

ANITA: Exactly! Astrology. Everybody knows it's all a load of you-know-what. [*reading out ...*] Sun-Aries; Ascendant-Aquarius; Moon-Scorpio; Conjunction between Venus and Mars; Square of Mars and Mercury; Venus in Gemini ... Oh, for God's sake.

LOIS: So, would you prefer to see miles and miles of DNA code, O Stern Rationalist?

ANITA: I don't want to see anything. It's offensive. It's amateur hour.

LOIS: What's being done is to tell you the characters the soul will have when it reaches Earth.

ANITA: [*with heavy irony*] Oh, now it all makes sense, Inspector. You're winding me up, aren't you?

LOIS: No, really. This is it. Small-scale, homely, village hall am dram. I like it.

ANITA: Apart from anything else, what about free will?

LOIS: Nothing. Being disposed a certain way doesn't stop us being free to act.

The pair are silent for a while, then ...

LOIS: Hey, that's the one that Leo had, just coming to the front now.

ANITA: It looks kinda different. Cleaner, its green's more bright. It's less ragged than some of the others.

LOIS: [*laughing wryly, but in earnest*] I'm tempted to say it looks hardly used. A soul not famous for being brought into play.

ANITA: Some truth in that, Lo. Of all the assholes I've known, he was the most superficial. It was all surface for him ... surface, appearance, style, pleasing to the eye, and no more. Talk about "sea surface".

LOIS: Tell you what: he would agree with you. He and I have had that conversation. He was first and foremost an artist, though maybe not a very talented one. Art was what made his life what it was. For him, art just *was* surface. He would say: "You wouldn't put down the *Mona Lisa* for being all surface. It *is* all surface. You see a beautiful body, but who cares about the pancreas or the cochlea? Art *is* appearance. Plays are pretend. Where there is truth, it resides in the surface. It's put there. If the truth is not in the surface, and you have to dig for it from clues, then the artist has failed. She's just produced a crime scene."

ANITA: Do *you* buy that?

LOIS: Only up to a point. But yes, he enjoyed the surface of life and tried to make good surfaces for people – when he wasn't winding them up and glorifying himself. We interact with people's surfaces, after all. Look ... Here's what his soul is bound for next.

ANITA: Sun-Taurus; Ascendant-Scorpio; Mercury-Taurus, Venus-Capricorn ...

LOIS: Bit heavy this. All those Earth Signs and Scorpio. No Leo at all. Little fire and lots of planets in opposition. Good luck with that, sir. One of his hippy-scientist friends told him he had as much Leo in his chart as it is *astronomically* possible to have.

ANITA: You amaze me.

LOIS: And you me, my dear.

ANITA: Two things. You seem to actually believe in all that

bullshit; at least you know a lot about it. But mainly that you defend him. You take his side. You're *on* his side. This is the man who murdered you simply because his ego was too big and fragile to cope with anybody else touching you and because ... I mean, too fragile to withstand a few home truths from your lips.

LOIS: I still love him. Always will.

ANITA:

    I swear I won't call no copper.

LOIS: [*her head in her hands now*] Oh God!

ANITA:

    If I gets beat up by my papa
    Ain't nobody's bizness if I do

LOIS: I'm just wondering what happens to people if you smack them round the chops after death. Now listen to me: If Leo had ever hit me, I would have left him immediately, taking the twins. I don't know whether you have the imagination to understand this, but for him to hit me would have been worse than his killing me. Yes, he did murder me, because he was incapable of digging deep enough to withstand my knowledge of him. He also had a shallow, childish idea of love, which is total possession. But that's not his fault.

ANITA: So none of it is anybody's fault. Blame the stars.

LOIS: One of the tramps in *Waiting for Godot* says at one point: "I'm tiring of this *motif*."

ANITA: We both are, Lo.

LOIS: It just remains for me to wish you better luck next time.

Also available from grand**IOTA**

Production of this book has been made possible with the help of the following individuals and organisations who subscribed in advance:

Thomas Bahr
Judith Baumel
Chris Beckett
Karen von Bismarck
Andrew Brewerton
Ian Brinton
Jasper Brinton
Peter Brown
John Cayley
Charles Capro
Martha Cooley
Claire Crowther
Ian Davidson
Stuart Dischell
Lila Dlaboha
Sharon Dunn
Rachel DuPlessis
Ginger Eager
Martin Edmunds
Charles Fernyhough
Allen Fisher/Spanner
John Fulton
Todd Gitlin
Andrew Grainger
Robert Gray
Paul Green
Penny Grossi
Charles Hadfield
John Hall
William F Hayes
Randolph Healy
Halyna Hryn
Peter Hughes
Dan Hunter

Diane Jones
Gene Kwak
Steve Lake
Lawrence Lee
Julia Lieblich
Richard Makin
Michael Mann
Megan Marshall
Jeffrey Masse
Lourdes Massing
Mark Mendoza
Thomas O'Grady
Toby Olson
Mark Pawlak
Sean Pemberton
Nicholas Ribush
David Rose
Lawrence Rosenwald
Lou Rowan
Dave Russell
Peter Sarno
Bob Scanlan
Lloyd Schwartz
Steven Seidenberg
Alan Singer
Katherine Snodgrass
Valerie Soar
Lloyd Swanton
Eileen Tabios
Troppe Note Publishing
visual associations
AJ Wells
Yara Arts Group
Andrew Zurcher

www.grandiota.co.uk

Lightning Source UK Ltd.
Milton Keynes UK
UKHW041126070721
386773UK00001B/85